Gasparilla Gold

Judge Wilhelmina Carson Series

Gasparilla Gold

M. Diane Vogt

Mystery and Suspense Press
San Jose New York Lincoln Shanghai

Gasparilla Gold

Mystery and Suspense Press
an imprint of iUniverse, Inc.

For information address:
iUniverse, Inc.
5220 S. 16th St., Suite 200
Lincoln, NE 68512
www.iuniverse.com

ISBN: 0-595-21271-9

Printed in the United States of America

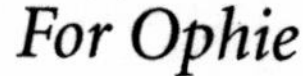

For Ophie

Acknowledgements

GASPARILLA GOLD would not have been written without the enthusiastic support and advice of my reading group: Michelle Bearden, Kate Caldwell, Betty Cohen, Laura Howard, Allison Jennewein, Deborah Jordan, Rochelle Reback, Robin Rosenberg, Wendy Cousins Savage, and Amy Sharitt Leobold. As always, my great friend and business partner, Lori-Ann Rickard, provided the cheering section every author needs, along with the all important critical eye. My assistant, Linda Lee, and the folks at Breakthrough Promotions provide the support and publicity work so essential to this business.

Members of the Florida Chapter of Mystery Writers of America, and other mystery writers listened to my rants, offered editorial service and web design, and support mystery writers in Florida and everywhere. Booksellers who support the small presses and new writers can't be appreciated enough. Through all of your efforts, Wilhelmina Carson has found a home.

Readers, family, friends, neighbors and co-workers who enjoy Willa's adventures have encouraged Willa to keep going.

Perhaps most importantly, to Robert, my partner in everything.

Thank you all.

Saturday evening.

The cleaning crew had been working on the streets in Ybor City since the parade ended. Miguel, a young city sanitation worker turned the corner at Seventh Avenue and Sixteenth Street, pushing a large trash can on wheels toward the dumpster. His supervisor had told him to hurry up. They had a lot of work to do before the businesses opened tomorrow.

Who would believe people could be such pigs, Miguel thought. In his country, maybe, but not in Florida, "land of flowers." In his country, people weren't tidy like they were here. He'd noticed it himself, everywhere. Tampa was a clean place. Nice. Miguel wanted to stay here, with his father's family. He liked Tampa.

The heavy can was piled with garbage, high over Miguel's head. He couldn't see the ground. Miguel's left hand braced the garbage, towering twice as high as the five-foot can should hold.

Miguel was preoccupied with his thoughts, not watching where he was going. He wasn't in any mood for delay. He had been picking up beer cans, beads, condoms, half-eaten candy and almost every other type of human detritus possible from the old urine stench found around every corner for the past few hours. He was cold and tired. He wanted to finish his work and go home.

Suddenly, the wheels of the can struck something on the inside of the sidewalk and rolled toward the building on the right. Miguel cursed himself for not paying attention and impatiently pushed the heavy trash can, trying to roll over the problem in the sidewalk. He was on his way to the large dumpster in back of Maria's restaurant so that he could dump the can and start again. Miguel had to have this stretch of Ybor cleaned up and he didn't have time to fool around. This was his first week on the job and he was on probation. He couldn't make his supervisor mad. He needed this job if he was to stay in this country. Miguel put both hands on the middle of the plastic can and pushed harder.

The trash can wouldn't budge. Worse, now both front rollers seemed to be stuck by a block of some kind. Miguel wanted to make as few of these trips to the dumpster as possible. He wanted to finish quickly to make his supervisor proud, so he'd piled the can too full. Miguel couldn't see over the top of the can to go around the blockage. He shoved the can with all of his strength. Instead of rolling over the block, the can turned over and spilled its contents all over the sidewalk.

Shouting a loud stream of startled Spanish curses, Miguel jumped back to avoid having every foul liquid available at the parade splashed all over his clothes. Then, he righted the can and went around to the front of the mess. With the shovel that hung on the side, Miguel began to shovel garbage back into the trash can.

His shovel hit something solid, still covered with the garbage he had spilled. Miguel didn't know what he'd hit. Continuing to curse, he bent down at the waist, trying to see what was causing him so much trouble. In the vague light from the street lamps around the corner, the big lump looked like a pile of garbage. But he was beginning to think it was some drunken pirate who had passed out and hadn't awakened.

Miguel had run across two other drunken revelers on this stretch of Seventh Avenue tonight and he was annoyed that another one was causing him so much trouble. "Americanos!" he spat.

He reached into his pocket for his flashlight, put his gloves back on and swept the garbage off the pirate with his other hand, pushing aside the gooey mess. When he saw the man's pirate costume, Miguel became even more impatient. These Americans seemed to have nothing better to do than to party themselves into a stupor while hard-working Latinos cleaned up after them, he thought.

"Wake up, senior. Wake up," Miguel said, shaking the man as roughly as he could, given the disparity in their sizes. The drunk didn't stir. Miguel almost left him there then, to sleep it off, but something about the pirate

didn't look right. Miguel continued to shake the pirate, imploring him to wake up and move along. Soon, the supervisor came around the corner.

"Miguel, where the hell are you? We need that can, now!" The supervisor shouted in Spanish. He was walking quickly and stopped just before he tripped over the mess on the sidewalk.

"He won't wake up," Miguel said.

"The hell he won't," the supervisor responded. The supervisor had cleaned up after sixteen parades and he knew how to deal with these pirates. He pushed the pirate hard with his boot. The pirate's head lolled around loosely, revealing the depression in his skull where it had been resting on the heavy piece of concrete jutting up out of the sidewalk.

"Miguel, this man is dead!" the supervisor shouted. "Who is this?"

When the police officers got to the scene, they checked for identification on the body and found none. They interviewed Miguel and the supervisor. There had been a lot of revelry that night, but these workers hadn't been part of it. No one recognized the dead man.

Chapter *One*

A week earlier…

Surprises are like electricity. They can be life enhancing, but just as often, disruptive. Sometimes, even fatal. Regardless, surprises are unavoidable. I've learned to view unexpected events with a heavy helping of scepticism while awaiting the perpetually uncertain outcome.

My name is Willa Carson. I've lived thirty-nine years, practiced law and I'm now a United States District Court judge. I know things are often not what they seem, and I don't like being out of control. Gasparilla month was one unpleasant event after another, beginning Friday night before the Parade of Pirates with the biggest shock I'd had in years. A surprise that hit me hard and promised to affect my life forever. The surprises that followed piled on top of one another too quickly for me to keep ahead of them. Which is no excuse. But it does help to understand how I was feeling and why I was so slow on the uptake.

Just as I drifted into an uneasy sleep Saturday morning, my alarm ocean began its violent roaring, jarring me back into events I'd been trying to escape. Opening one bleary eye, I saw it was only six o'clock. I craved eight hours of uninterrupted sleep, but knew it was impossible.

The Gasparilla Parade of Pirates, Tampa's much smaller version of Mardi Gras, was about to begin. Despite the busy day ahead, I'd spent a short and mostly sleepless Friday night, tossing about on our king-sized bed, looking at the clock every hour, trying to keep from waking my husband, George. Our two dogs, both 90-pound Labradors, jumped up on the bed with us at about four o'clock and nothing short of an earthquake would get them back onto the floor. One of the dogs was draped over my left leg at the bottom of the bed and the other one was between us with her head on my pillow.

The second my eyes popped open, my thoughts replayed the scene that had invaded my restless night: my father's bombshell as he presented Suzanne Harper, his "precious one," his new wife. Dad had apparently thought a surprise visit was the way to introduce us.

Suzanne's image intruded on my sleep until there was no point even trying to close my eyes. I must have dozed off at some point though, because the ocean startled me awake, with a noise that sounded more like the roaring of Big Sur than the gentle lapping of our own Tampa Bay. The racket didn't cause the dogs to wiggle so much as an eyebrow.

Knowing we'd soon have several hundred guests in George's restaurant located on the first floor of our home, I dragged my leg out from under a sleeping Labrador and raised myself to a sitting position on the side of the bed. Holding my sleepy head in both hands, I wished again that Gasparilla weekend was ending instead of just getting started.

"Cheer up," George said. "Maybe a pirate will steal you away from all of this."

George was getting up as slowly as I was, so it took a few moments before we both realized what our noses were trying to tell us. Someone was already up and had made coffee. The aroma wafted in from the kitchen like the scent of a hot meal under the nose of a starving hobo. It was enough to get both of us to our feet. When I came into the kitchen, belting my robe, still rubbing sleep from my heavy, tired eyes, she was there. Suzanne Harper. My father's new wife. Despite my best intentions, I'm pretty sure I groaned out loud.

"Morning, Willa," she chirped in her sweet, high-pitched voice. "Fresh coffee in the pot. I found some eggs and cheese in your refrigerator, so we should have a baked omelet here in a few minutes. I hope you don't mind that I brought in the paper. I'm so excited about my first Gasparilla parade, I just couldn't sleep. This is all just so fabulous!" The enthusiasm was too much, too early.

Fortunately, she kept talking, so I didn't have to actually speak a coherent sentence. Suzanne's constant chatter reminded me of the roaring ocean sounds from my alarm, and I tried unsuccessfully to tune her out while I reached into the cabinet for my favorite "I hate mornings" mug.

Sitting at the other end of the kitchen table, I looked at Suzanne from my slowly awakening point of view. She was as beautiful this morning as she had been last night. Her long, artfully streaked blonde, curly hair fell attractively around shoulders that were wrapped in a lavender warm up suit with a designer logo on the pocket. The white tee-shirt under her silk jacket had the same logo, and molded to her slender but full-breasted frame. I, on the other hand, sat with my short auburn hair matted on my head and my green eyes barely open, feeling even less attractive than I appeared. At times like this, I envied the fifties sit-com moms, always dressed for breakfast in their pearls.

Suzanne had her makeup on, too, while I barely had my skin on. Her makeup was skillfully applied on her flawless complexion without excess, except for the lavender lipstick inside the purple lip liner on her full mouth. I hadn't ever seen such lipstick on a grown woman before.

And that was the problem. Suzanne wasn't a grown woman. She was all of twenty-three years old, if that. I suspected that, if I could see her midriff, I'd find a pierced navel. She was a sweet, engaging and, yes, loveable, child. Was that better? Or worse?

I put my head in my hands again. Jim Harper was a cliche'. He'd married a woman less than half his age. Hell, she wasn't much more than half *my* age. A trophy wife. I was having trouble thinking about how I would introduce them to all of our friends today. I might be thirty-nine, but my inner adolescent was alive and well, wailing, "How could you do this to me?"

George stumbled out to the kitchen behind me, saving me from having to make conversation before I finished my first cup of coffee. He was followed by both dogs. "Morning, Jim," George said as Dad came in shortly after that. Our tiny kitchen got so crowded that I mumbled a lame excuse and left without anyone really minding.

Attempting to stall as long as possible, I spent an extra fifteen minutes letting the shower's warm water run the full length of my body, all five feet, eleven inches of it. I am slightly taller than Suzanne, but not by much. I couldn't face the idea of dressing in costume, selecting instead a comfortable but casual dress and jacket. I lingered over my hair and makeup, but by seven-thirty, I'd forced myself downstairs to George's restaurant ready to start what would be a very full and lengthy day.

Members and guests of the social and service club George had founded, called "Minaret Krewe," were gathered everywhere, practically standing on top of each other. Minaret Krewe is one of the more than thirty "krewes" that participate in the annual events of Gasparilla month, and had been doing so for almost a hundred years. At least two of those krewes are all-women, one is Latin, there's an African-American krewe and even a set of Rough Riders. In short, something for everyone.

Minaret Krewe is named after our home, called Minaret because of the large, steel onion dome on the top. Today, all 250 members and their guests were having breakfast and beginning the day's drinking with mimosas, bloody Marys and several varieties of frozen coladas.

I saw the professional makeup artists, hired by the Krewe to transform the members into ferocious pirates and wenches who would be in today's parade, hard at work. Families allowed them to make the kids up, too. The boisterous beginning to a wild and crazy day that would carry over well into the evening had the added benefit of being way too busy for quiet chats with my father or his new bride.

By eleven o'clock in the morning, the now vicious-looking pirates had left to prepare for the parade down Bayshore Boulevard. The parade began when about seven hundred pirate members of Ye Mystic Krewe, in their barge made over to look like a pirate ship named *Jose' Gasparilla,* landed at the Tampa Convention Center and took over the city. Those who didn't want to join the madness on the Bayshore stayed at our house, upstairs, downstairs and everywhere, with televisions blaring the parade coverage on Channel 8.

George had arranged for non-stop food and refreshments throughout the day. Cuban sandwiches and Ybor Gold beer, brewed locally in Ybor City, were available in abundance. For those wanting a heavier meal, there were black beans and yellow rice, George's version of the Columbia's famous 1905 Salad, and several other Cuban dishes. Café con leche, the rich, Cuban coffee heavily laced with heated milk, flowed as freely as the beer. I'd had a cup of the coffee in my hand the entire morning.

Talking with everyone and generally playing hostess to the Krewe and their guests, I glimpsed only portions of the Parade of Pirates on television. Our local NewsChannel 8 anchor had dressed like a pirate and joined the parade route. From time to time, he interviewed a few of the half-million or so viewers lining the street. The floats were filled with pirates, wenches and local personalities, beauty queens, Rotary, Lions and Kiwanis members, politicians and sports figures. Local high school marching bands filled in between the other participants.

Most parade spectators were dressed in heavy coats, hats and gloves. Mother Nature, obviously out of sorts, had decided the high today would be forty-three degrees. What warmth the sun provided was more than eliminated by the gusty, cold wind. I shivered in sympathy, glad to be inside.

When I turned away from the television, Ron and Margaret Wheaton were standing next to me. "I'm so glad you could come," I said, giving them both a slight hug. "I haven't seen you in weeks, Ron. How are you feeling?"

Margaret, my secretary and good friend, looked tired and older than her sixty-something years. She is a kind person, always helping, never asking much for herself. At work, Margaret seemed to be handling her husband's terminal illness with compassion and very little fuss. But it was taking an obvious toll on her.

"I'm feeling as well as can be expected," Ron Wheaton said. He held my hand with little strength. "Thank you for inviting us here today. I don't go to many parties. Who knows how many Gasparillas I have left?" He said this without self-pity, but it was sad just the same.

Ron was dying of ALS, Lou Gehrig's disease. It's a slow, wasting of the muscles that would eventually kill him when the muscles that allowed him to breathe no longer worked. In the meantime, since Ron continued to be fully aware of himself and his condition, his mental depression was overwhelming. I could barely think about it, and I wasn't living with it twenty-four hours a day like the Wheatons were.

"He's doing much better lately, thank you," Margaret put in. "If he gets his rest, he can still square dance with the best of them." She put her arm through his and he patted her hand. Ron was a tall man, thin and frail. He smiled down on his diminutive wife with affection.

"Sure, honey, as long as I do it in my chair." He nodded to a wheelchair sitting over in the corner not far from where we were standing. "I get tired quickly," he said to me, by way of explanation.

"Well, just enjoy yourselves here today. There's plenty of food and drink. Too much, probably," I acknowledged as another guest captured my attention and I returned to my hostess role.

When I stopped in the Sunset Bar to chat with one of our local judges, I could see the television but I couldn't hear the reporter interviewing Gil Kelley, the current King of the Minaret Krewe, at the parade.

"What do you think of our Gasparilla parade, Pirate Kelley?" the reporter asked him. Gil's answer was drowned out by our shouting crowd inside the Sunset Bar. Whoever had done Gil's makeup here this morning had done a particularly good job; he had a wicked looking scar down the left side of his face with fake blood oozing out of it and one of his front teeth was blacked out, giving him a snaggle-toothed appearance. Gil's black pirate's hat, colorful yellow silk blouse, tight black pants and long sword were realistic enough. Like many Gasparilla costumes, his was an elaborate and expensive, if stylized, version of pirate wear. Gil's paunch was real, although it looked like part of the costume. His grey hair helped him look like a nasty old pirate instead of the president and majority shareholder of Tampa Bay Bank he was the rest of the year.

"Doesn't he look handsome," his wife, Sandra Kelley, said to me when she saw me watching Gil on television. Sandra herself was dressed in the twenty-first century version of a pirate wench's costume, an off-the-shoulder red blouse and a full yellow skirt that matched her husband's blouse. The number of Gasparilla beads around her neck were impressive for someone who wasn't out at the parade to catch them as they were thrown from the floats.

"Yes," I smiled down at her, "he certainly does. Or were you talking about Gil?" We both laughed. Neither the reporter nor Gil Kelley were particularly handsome men, although they once might have been.

"You and George are so good to have the Krewe here," she said.

"It's our pleasure. Are you having a good time?"

Sandra frowned daintily, with just a little downward bend to her black eyebrows over the bridge of her pert nose. "I was. Until he came in." She inclined her head toward a man I didn't recognize talking with Ron Wheaton.

"Who is that?"

"It's Armstrong Yeats. The one and only." The disdain in her voice was enough to convey her thoughts precisely. She didn't like the famous jeweler from the small beach community of Pass-a-Grille across the bay from Tampa.

"I don't know him."

"So much the better," she snapped. "Ron Wheaton shouldn't know him, either. If Yeats crawled back under whatever rock he slithered out from, all of Tampa would be better off."

Maybe Armstrong Yeats wasn't a model citizen, but the duo seemed to be having a pleasant conversation. Of course, Ron Wheaton is one of the kindest souls on the planet. He would have been nice to Jack the Ripper. You couldn't say the same of Sandra Kelley. At least, no one who knew her did. So, I took her venom with a side order of antidote as I excused myself to attend to our guests. Or so I said to Sandra Kelley. What I really did was head the other way when I saw my newly-minted stepmother headed in our direction. The absurdity of having a stepmother more than ten years younger than me hit me again.

The onslaught of guests, my lack of sleep and exercise and the stress of seeing Dad cozying up to Suzanne finally hit me. By early afternoon I was exhausted. I figured no one would notice if I ducked out for an hour, so I trudged up the stairs to our flat, dodging people seated and standing on every available surface, until I reached our bedroom. Thankfully, even though there is a television in our room, no one had camped out there. I locked the door and fell into immediate oblivion on top of the damask comforter.

When I woke and returned to the fray, it was dark outside and it seemed no one had missed me. I saw as many people in all the gathering places of our flat as had been there hours before. Maybe the faces had changed, but with all the makeup, it was hard to say. The crowd in the restaurant was still in full swing, too. George was serving dinner. He believed that enough food and coffee would blunt the force of the gallons of alcohol everyone consumed.

For all practical purposes, the jovial crowd was captive here. The parade was long over, but the thousands of people who had come to watch it were only slowly finding their way from Hyde Park to downtown Tampa, where the after-parade festivities would reverberate into the wee hours. An arts and crafts show, fireworks and the festival, featuring live stage shows, filled the downtown Tampa streets.

Those of our group brave enough to fight the crowds and the weather would start to head in that direction. They could walk downtown from here, of course, but it would be cold and exhausting coming back after midnight. George had hired a couple of vans to drive people back and forth so they could leave their cars in our lot. I was grateful I'd had a nap. This day wouldn't end for hours yet.

As I came down the stairs from our flat and into the lobby of George's restaurant, I saw Gil Kelley sitting with my new stepmother, obviously flirting with her. That's what Gil does with any pretty woman. Whether Suzanne was flirting back or not was hard to tell. She had her head tilted toward Gil and away from me, but I saw him laugh at something she said. Suzanne was very engaging and Gil would be totally captivated by her. I looked around for Dad and saw him standing talking to Gil's wife, Sandra. Poor Dad. Gil was getting the better bargain.

I wanted to offer George a chance to take a break, but I couldn't pick him out in the crowd. I walked around all the rooms on the first floor of this grand old house that had once been a private home looking for him, with no success. I finally found him in what had once been the sun porch and what we now called the Sunset Bar. George was sitting at our favorite table with Armstrong Yeats.

Yeats was good-looking for his age, which I guessed to be between sixty and seventy, but nothing to render women vicious with jealousy. He was fit, with the body of a martial arts expert, which is to say, lean and quick. He had a full head of dirty-blonde hair, worn in a pony tail. His eyes were a cloudy blue, not piercing or even remarkable. Whatever it was about him that raised Sandra Kelley's ire, it wasn't obvious.

I snagged a cup of café con leche on the way over to join them. George got up when I approached, as he always does when a woman joins his table. One of the things I love about George is that he treats me at least as nicely as he does everyone else, usually better. My friends all think George is perfect, but they don't have to live with him. Yeats was well back in the booth and made no effort to rise. "Willa, do you know Armstrong?" George said, as I slipped into the booth across from Yeats, our knees almost touching.

"No, I don't think we've met," I said, holding out my hand, which he shook softly, as if he wasn't used to shaking hands with women. After I sat down, there were a few moments of uncomfortable silence, until George smoothly rescued the situation. "Armstrong is a jewelry designer. He was telling me about the new jewelry he's entered in the Gasparilla Festival of the Arts competition. He hopes to win the grand prize."

"Really?" I said, looking at him with renewed interest. "I'd love to see your entry."

"The piece I'm entering is a pin. I call it Gasparilla Gold." He gestured to the picture he had pulled out of the pocket of his rumpled tweed jacket as he described the pin to me as if he was dictating copy for a catalogue, using his cocktail straw as a pointer. "It's quite large, about eight inches long. The pin is meant to be worn on the shoulder of a coat, on the outside of the lapel. The platinum dagger has semi-precious stones set in the handle, and a gold chain connects the scabbard to the knife. The dagger sits on top of a treasure chest filled with gold nuggets."

I'm not really a jewelry hound, but even I was impressed. "Can I see the piece sometime?"

"Sure. It's on display at my studio over in Pass-A-Grille. It'll be there until a few days before the art festival. Come over anytime," Yeats said. I handed the picture to George, who was about to say something when Dad walked over, peeked at the picture over George's shoulder, and folded his lanky frame into the booth with us. Dad, ever the salesman, whistled and asked, without a trace of embarrassment, "How much does something like that cost?"

George looked down at the table and I glanced away, too, so as not to show our amusement at Dad's trademark lack of decorum. Armstrong, though, looked completely offended.

"Well, it's not for sale, actually. The point of it is to win the competition, and then I'll return it to display in my store," he said with some hauteur.

Dad wasn't to be so easily deflected, though. "No, I mean, really. If you were going to sell it. How much?"

Seeing no graceful way out, Armstrong said, "Oh, probably about $175,000, particularly if it wins. Would you excuse me, please? I need to speak with Gil Kelley for a few minutes." He started moving toward Dad trying to get out of the booth, and Dad had no choice but to let him go.

"Somebody would pay $175,000 for that thing? Just to wear on your shoulder? Why, that would feed two or three entire families for more than a year!" Dad's awe was humorous, since he wasn't half the rube he was pretending, for the moment, to be. Dad knows that people are frivolous with money, even if he's not. Dad has always made money, managed it wisely and accumulated a sizeable net worth. He owns an insurance agency in New York, and his work has been his life. Whatever money he has, though, Dad lives quietly. Before Suzanne, he preferred the simple life. Based on all the status symbols she wore and the fashion show she'd given us since she arrived, Suzanne was about to change Dad's comfortable modesty.

While Dad continued his tongue-in-cheek marveling at the price of jewelry, I glanced over and noticed Armstrong Yeats and Gil Kelley arguing in the corner. The argument was heated. Yeats poked Kelley in the chest several times with his index finger as he spoke. Kelley's face was so suffused with color, I suggested George consider calling a paramedic, just in case he stroked out. George rose to break up the argument, but before he covered half the distance to the pair, Kelley stomped off into the dining room, leaving Armstrong Yeats to stalk out in the other direction.

Now, Dad and I were alone in the booth. It was our first private moment since I'd met Suzanne. I searched my mind's "social graces" data base for something acceptable to say, in the circumstances. Dad broke the ice. "How about those Bucs?" he said, with a grin on his face, and we laughed. We'd heard it fifty times today, or more. That's the standard greeting around Tampa since our football team had not just hosted the Super Bowl, but blown their chances of playing in it. They lost a wild-card playoff game on the road when the temperature was well below forty degrees. For half an hour, we discussed the merits of the Bucs, their inability to play in cold weather and the strengths of their opposition. It was a safe social topic that kept us from talking about his marriage or our own uneasy relationship. Fatigue and the easy talk relaxed me. I dropped my guard too soon.

Just when our conversation was threatened with an uncomfortable lull, Gil Kelley walked over, punched Dad in the shoulder and boomed loudly into one of those awkward silences that happen in a crowd, "Congratulations, Jim! Suzanne tells me you two are expecting! Didn't know you had it in you, you old dog!" I spit coffee all over me and the table. Which was just fine because it gave me the opportunity to excuse myself.

Later, I returned to the dining room where I saw Margaret Wheaton come out of the ladies room looking happy. She stopped to exchange mock consternation at the unruly crowd with a few other guests. I studied her as she slowly made her way over toward me, thinking my own situation was trivial by comparison to hers. "Keep your perspective. There will always be greater and lesser people than yourself," my mother once told me. Nowhere did that apply more than comparing myself to Margaret.

Since Ron Wheaton was diagnosed with ALS about a year ago, his illness had progressed slowly and steadily. I'm often oblivious to what goes on around me, but even I had seen Margaret become more and more exhausted. I attributed her fatigue to the stress of dealing with Ron. In the past few months, Ron had become weaker and less mobile. He was confined to his wheelchair much of the time and rarely went out. Ron would soon require twenty-four hour care. Yet, on the few occasions when I spoke to him on the telephone, he sounded as strong as he had ever been. I could only imagine the horror of knowing you would one day just stop breathing and not being able to tell your wife goodbye before it happened.

Margaret eventually broke away from her small group and made her way over toward me. I gave her a hug. A real one. Not that upper back patting that passes for greetings among Southern women. She felt small and frail to me and I marveled at how heavy a burden those tiny shoulders could carry.

"Can you believe this madness, Margaret?" I asked her.

She smiled and her face lit up a little more than usual as she nodded. "I love it, though. I've lived in Tampa my whole life and I never get tired of Gasparilla. When I was a little girl, Gasparilla used to be held downtown and it was the same time as the State Fair. I can remember going as a teenager and as a young bride. Gasparilla holds many good memories for me."

Before I could reply, we heard screams as if a thousand marauding pirates had landed at Minaret. Margaret and I and several other guests moved as quickly as possible through the crowds toward the noise. When we got to the verandah, we could see Ron Wheaton slumped over in his wheelchair, not moving, while Suzanne Harper, my stepmother, screamed at full volume, but not loud enough to wake the dead.

Chapter *Two*

Margaret turned her face into me as someone rushed over to Ron Wheaton's wheelchair and began to administer CPR, shouting "Call 911! Call 911!"

Over the heads of the small crowd pushing in on Ron's wheelchair, I saw George working his way through, trying to calm everyone down. Tampa's Police Chief Ben Hathaway, dressed in full pirate regalia as a member of the Minaret Krewe, heard the commotion and came forward, telling everyone to step back and give him room to work. It seemed too quickly, I heard sirens coming up the driveway. Soon, paramedics were out on the verandah, asking questions and trying to revive Ron Wheaton, but even the uninitiated among us could see that their efforts would be fruitless.

"Is he dead?" Margaret asked me.

"I can't really see much," I told her, trying to soften the blow. "I'm so sorry,"

"Don't be. It's a blessing," she told me. She continued crying softly and moaning against my shoulder.

I motioned to Chief Hathaway and to George that I was going to take Margaret into the smaller dining room to the left, where we could sit down. Margaret's happy memories of Gasparilla would be forever changed, now, and I was sorry for her. Margaret was one of those women who didn't deserve unhappiness in her life, yet it seemed to follow her like a black cloud.

After Ron Wheaton had been taken away by ambulance and Chief Hathaway was in charge of the scene, asking everyone not to leave because the police would soon arrive to take witness statements, George made a quick turn through the restaurant and came back to Margaret and me. Ron's death appeared to me to be by natural causes, but given the nature of a death in a public place, during an event filled with unknown spectators, the police would never know the names of people present if they didn't take them down now, just in case.

"How does it look out there, George?" I asked, while trying to get Margaret to drink a little water.

"In the front of the restaurant, people haven't even noticed that anything's happened. It's just nine-thirty. There's still a pretty big crowd out there and we've had sirens all day. I think there will be people who leave here tonight not even knowing that Ron died. If that's how you want it, Margaret."

Margaret nodded in response, and we took the nod to mean she wanted to keep her private life away from the public eye, which was so like her. As far as I knew, Margaret had led a quiet life. There was no reason to believe she'd want to change that now, even though her husband had just died a very public death.

"I'm going to take Margaret upstairs and put her in a guest room. Ben Hathaway can talk to her in the morning," I told George as I got Margaret to her feet and we made our way up the stairs to our flat. She followed, allowing me to take her hand and lead her without complaint.

I don't know if she was in shock or just exhausted and emotionally drained, but when I took her into the guest room, she lay down on the extra bed and fell into deep sleep almost immediately. I prayed she'd be asleep for several hours and closed the door softly as I left her there.

When I came into our living room, Dad and Suzanne were being interviewed by Ben Hathaway. I thought Hathaway was jumping to some pretty big conclusions, conducting witness interviews when a terminally ill man had just passed away. Maybe the Tampa Police Department wasn't as busy as they'd have us taxpayers believe, I thought. Surely, this was overkill.

For her part, Suzanne seemed more upset than Margaret had been. I poured a cup of coffee and stood in the doorway to listen as, between bouts of tears, Suzanne described finding Ron Wheaton on the verandah, while Dad held her and patted her shoulder, looking concerned. He obviously cared for her and showed as much. It was the most caretaking I'd ever seen him do and I was more than a little astonished that he knew how to comfort someone in distress. He'd certainly never demonstrated that with me.

"I wanted to go out for some air. I'm pregnant, you see, and I had gotten a little light-headed in there with all those people. I didn't know where Jimmy was," she looked at Dad, the man everyone called "Jim," and he said, "I'm so sorry, honey," as if not being by her side every minute was a capital crime.

"That's okay. You couldn't have known," she smiled, a little shaky, the purple lipstick long since chewed from her mouth and black mascara streaking from her racoon eyes. She looked far less beautiful and much more vulnerable than she had at six o'clock this morning.

Hathaway got them back on track. "About what time was that?" he said, as he wrote in the notebook balanced on his beefy thigh. We only had one chair big enough to hold Ben Hathaway. Whenever he comes to our flat, he always sits there. Now he was facing Dad and Suzanne seated on the sofa across from him.

"I don't know. About nine o'clock, I guess. I'm not wearing a watch," Suzanne sniffled.

"And then what happened?" Clearly, she needed prodding.

"I had trouble getting through the crowd, but I did make it to the verandah."

"Were the doors closed?"

"Yes. It was pretty cold outside even though there were a lot of people in the restaurant," she said, shivering as her body remembered that thirty-degree night out there. Dad pulled her shawl closer around her shoulders, over her pirate's blouse. She gave him a wobbly smile.

"Then what did you do?" Hathaway prodded again.

"There wasn't anyone outside, because of the cold, I guess. Anyway, I went out and it was sort of quiet, which I thought was great. It was so noisy inside the restaurant and I had started to get a headache," she almost whined and Dad patted her again while she laid her head on his shoulder.

"What happened next?" Hathaway was getting a little impatient. He didn't normally question witnesses himself. This was a personal favor to me and George. If Hathaway hadn't been here for the party this job would have fallen to a detective or patrolman, most likely. Hathaway's discretion was touching, and I appreciated it, even if I thought he was a little over zealous. He had no way of knowing how long he could find Suzanne Harper here in Tampa. But I felt this could have been done another time.

"I turned toward my right and I saw a man in a wheelchair. It startled me at first because I hadn't noticed him when I went out. So, I talked to him." I smiled to myself. Not because it was funny, but because Suzanne hadn't stopped talking since I met her. It would have been odd if she hadn't talked to Ron Wheaton, dead or alive.

Suzanne started to tear up again and Dad handed her another tissue. "And he didn't say anything." She was crying in earnest now, but continuing her story. "So I walked closer and spoke louder, thinking he just didn't hear me. But he still didn't say anything. I thought he might be sick or something, so I went around in front of him and I saw. . . ." At this point, she broke down completely and we all had to wait a few minutes for it to pass.

"What did you see, Mrs. Harper?" The question jolted me. It was the first time I'd heard Suzanne referred to by my mother's name. Something else to get used to.

"I saw he was blue. I just knew he was dead. And, I don't know what came over me, but I just started to scream and scream. I couldn't stop."

"Did you see anyone else outside, near Mr. Wheaton's wheelchair?" Hathaway asked her. She shook her head and continued to cry. Hathaway let her go, saying he'd talk to her more later if he needed to do so. She and Dad walked down the hallway toward their room, Suzanne still crying while Dad held her and crooned, "It's okay, honey. It's okay."

Although her distress was real enough, Suzanne was more emotional than the situation called for, if anyone had told her about Ron's condition and his prognosis. I've never discovered a dead person, myself, and Suzanne was probably more upset due to the raging hormones of pregnancy, but when I saw Ron he had looked peaceful. Not frightening in the least. But then, I had known he was going to die soon and Suzanne probably had not. Like Margaret, I felt it was a blessing that he'd gone now, and gone quickly. I was grateful that Margaret wasn't alone with Ron when he did. What a horrible experience that would have been.

Which is what I said to Ben Hathaway when we sat in the more sturdy chairs around our kitchen table over coffee and his interview notes a few minutes later. He looked at me quizzically until I told him about Ron's ALS. Hathaway had been treating this death like a crime scene in part because he hadn't known about Ron's medical condition and in part because he knew the urgency of getting the names of witnesses who were probably tourists and would soon be on their way back to wherever they came from. "If I had to guess, I'd say Ron Wheaton died of a heart attack. He had all the signs. But we won't know for sure until the autopsy comes back," Hathaway told me.

"Why do an autopsy at all?"

"We're required to do an autopsy when someone dies away from a hospital or under suspicious circumstances," he explained. "It's just routine."

Then, he added with a little too much enthusiasm for my taste, "And, it's always possible that he was murdered."

I couldn't have been more astounded. Maybe Hathaway really did need more work since Tampa's crime rate is down. He was certainly making a mountain out of less than a mole hill. "Who would murder Ron Wheaton? He was going to die soon anyway. What would be the point?"

Hathaway stirred more sugar into his coffee and considered his answer. "We don't have a lot of information right now, so I can't tell you whether Ron Wheaton was killed, let alone what the killer's motive might be. I'd say there's the usual possibilities: profit, revenge, jealousy, to conceal a crime, to avoid humiliation or disgrace. Or my personal favorite, homicidal mania. That's usually an easier one to solve."

"Is this cop humor or something?" I was a little cross with him, I admit. "Murder a man who soon wouldn't even be able to feed himself? What kind of a monster would do that?"

Hathaway looked at me as sympathetically as he could arrange the features of his pugnacious face. "Maybe someone who loved him very much and didn't want to see him suffer anymore. Did you ever think of that? We have way too many mercy killings here in Tampa, Willa. I think it's a part of having such a large, elderly population. Too often, it seems like the only way out of a terrible terminal illness is to end the patient's life."

He might just as well have slapped me. "What? I wouldn't even consider the possibility that Margaret could have murdered Ron, if that's what you're suggesting. Margaret loved Ron. They had been a devoted couple for more than thirty years. Even if she was capable of murder, Margaret wouldn't have killed Ron. He was the only family she had. She cherished every day he had left. We've discussed it many, many times. No. That is just not a possibility. Not at all." I told him with all the sternness I could muster, which is considerable.

"There's no point in arguing about it until we find out the cause of death, anyway," he said, unpersuaded. "Let's just wait and see."

Sunday morning, I awakened to the smell of freshly brewed coffee again. Not having the physical, emotional or mental stamina to deal with Suzanne two mornings in a row, I virtuously decided the best thing to do was to remember that I was supposed to be in training for the Gasparilla Distance Classic in three weeks and get my run in first. I dressed quickly and crept down the back stairs, with both dogs, sneaking away like an unruly child. I threw sticks in the water for the dogs to chase to tire them out as I stretched for my run.

We live on an island named Plant Key after Henry Plant, the railroad tycoon who built our home and the island, in the late eighteen-nineties. The island is eight miles around its circumference and I would do two laps today, for training purposes, not just to avoid my father, his child bride and her child-to-be. I'm not a fast runner. It would take me almost two hours to complete the sixteen miles.

I threw the sticks one last time and started out to the east, toward the rising sun, while the dogs were still in the water. If I get a head start I can sometimes stay in front of them for ninety seconds or so. Today, it took them only about sixty seconds to reach me, shake water all over me, and then leave me freezing in their wake as they bounded ahead.

While I ran, heavily and slowly, trudging along the hard packed sand of our beach, I dodged the cans, bottles and other trash left by the crowds from yesterday's party. I wasn't dressed well enough against the cold wind blowing in from the north, and I cursed my decision to sneak out of the house before I was properly prepared. The cursing didn't make me any warmer.

February is an iffy month in Tampa. Sometimes the weather is perfect—sunny, clear, highs in the 80s—for weeks on end. Other times, it's cold, windy, rainy and generally miserable. It wouldn't matter except that January and February are big months around here. In January,

Gasparilla preparations begin and the whole month of February is the party. Most events are held outside. So if the weather sucks, well, it spoils the party. Hundreds of thousands of tourists flock to Tampa for the Gasparilla Parade of Pirates and Pirate Fest, traditionally held on the first weekend in February. It's followed on the next Saturday night by the Knight Parade in Ybor City, the Distance Classic run for charity the next week and, finally, the Festival of the Arts on the last Saturday of the month. Except in years when Tampa hosts the Super Bowl. Then, everything moves up a week so we can get all that national media attention.

Because we live on Plant Key, right in Hillsborough Bay, we have no choice but to join in all of the Gasparilla festivities for the entire month. That's why the weather matters. We can't just turn on the fire, curl up with a good book, a bottle of wine, and unplug the phone. Instead, our home is flooded with diners at George's five-star restaurant.

Tourists are forever coming over the bridge, thinking that they can just use our beach, stroll around the grounds, and make a complete nuisance of themselves. People who live here know better, I thought, as I kicked the cans out of my path and farther on the grass to keep them out of the bay. No point in polluting the water even further with this mess. We could always pick it up off the island later. The bending over would do me good.

During Gasparilla month, we post a guard at the entrance to Plant Key and only allow guests with reservations, which are booked months in advance. For the invasion and parade, we have to hire private security because boaters pull up to our shores, beach their boats and get out. Just one guard at the driveway isn't enough. Most people who live along the Bayshore, Tampa's long and winding waterside drive, stay home in self-defense since it's impossible to go anywhere, anyway. And, to be fair, February is usually George's best revenue month, so we need to keep the doors open. Gasparilla month alone accounts for a third of George's annual receipts.

Having company in the house, as we did this year, makes matters even more complicated under the best of circumstances. But when old friends call and say they're coming, there's not much we can do. Hotels are booked to overflowing, so our guest rooms are their only option.

Allowing my thoughts to wander shortened the run considerably and I was back to the house after the first lap in what seemed like a few minutes. My feet wanted desperately to turn into the walkway and go upstairs for warmth, but I forced myself to keep running until I was so far from the house that it was better to continue than to turn back.

Which was a mistake, because then my thoughts returned to Dad and Suzanne. Suzanne pregnant. Dad, father to an infant, was just unbelievable to me. Jim Harper, as much as I have come to love him and accept his failings, hadn't been a great father to me. While Mom was alive he tried to be a good Dad. But he was just not comfortable around kids at all and certainly not around a little girl.

Jim Harper is really my step-father. He married my mother when I was five. She was a widow at the time, so he's the only father I have ever really known. Not that I know him all that well. He traveled a lot, brought me gifts and listened to my reading, but he wasn't like any of the television dads I saw. I never doubted that he loved me, although he didn't say so often. He was not demonstrative, not a "Mr. Mom" type at all.

Eleven years after they married, when I was sixteen, my mother died. Jim was so overwhelmed by grief and absolutely unable to cope that he gratefully sent me to live with my mother's best friend and her three children. That was twenty-three years ago, in which time we had forged an uneasy truce. I tried to understand how he could possibly have left me when I was already so bereft; he tried to understand how I could fault him for the way he dealt with his own grief. During our infrequent visits and phone calls, we did what all civilized WASPs do about everything–we didn't talk about anything of substance and we acted like we had no issues between us. But we both knew we did.

Dad now, a new father, was just, well, something I'd never thought about. Yet, last night when Gil Kelley hit him on the arm and gave him the "sly dog" routine, Dad grinned from ear to ear. His face lit up in a way I've seldom seen it. He looked positively radiant as he thanked Gil for his good wishes. George was quick to jump in with his congratulations, too. So far, I hadn't actually said anything to Dad or Suzanne about the baby and I truly didn't know what to say. I was tempted to just keep running, away from my home and my issues.

But I was really cold, now. The wind continued to whip around the island and was even worse on the west side as I came closer to the house again. This time, although the dogs could have easily done another lap, I put them into their run and trudged up the back stairs with a view toward a hot shower and hotter coffee.

If the weather didn't warm up before the Distance Classic, I might have to rethink this plan. I was running for my favorite charity, Young Mothers' Second Chance, a home for single mothers, and they really needed the money. But still, there had to be an easier way to capture the public's compassion—and their cash.

Later, in the kitchen, I found George sitting alone with coffee and the Sunday papers.

"Morning, Darling. I hope I didn't wake you," George said, without glancing up as I made preparations to brew my café con leche. He looked relaxed and happy, unshaven, hair mussed, like a man at home on a Sunday. Honestly, I thought, does nothing faze my husband? A man died downstairs last night and George seemed not to be troubled by it in the least. I envied him his tranquility and I felt worse for Margaret. I couldn't imagine my life without George. I was sure she felt the same way about her husband. I wouldn't believe she murdered him, no matter what Ben Hathaway suspected. Ben has been wrong before. I willed him to be wrong this time.

"Actually, I've been out running. Are you the only one up?" I waited for the coffee and heated the milk in the microwave.

"No. Your Dad and Suzanne went downstairs with a few of the others for breakfast. I decided to stay here and read the papers. Great news about your new sibling, huh?" he asked me, as he folded the front section over and looked up briefly.

"Sure." I said. "Wonderful."

"You don't like the idea of being a 'big sister' at the age of 39?" George turned his full attention to me now, in his concerned and compassionate way.

"No. Not really. Should I like it?" I snapped, a little more crossly than I had meant to.

"Sorry. No need to be so touchy." He sounded wounded. George and I rarely had personal disagreements, although we argue issues all the time.

I relented. "I'm sorry, too. I just haven't quite sorted out how I feel about this yet. Can we drop it for now?"

"Okay. This is a great story in the paper here today about how Americans are constantly reinventing themselves." He pounded on the paper with his index finger. "Did you see it?"

I sat down at the table with him and looked at the story he'd pointed to in the front section of *The Tampa Tribune*. I read the headline aloud, "*Change Your Identity, Change Your Life.* Well, that would be one way to do it. Seems a little far fetched, though. Who would want to do that?"

"You'd be surprised. Jim Harper is making himself over into a husband and father. Think of people who change their names for professional reasons, like actors and musicians. Or just because they don't like their names, they're too hard to spell or too hard to pronounce. Or maybe, they've done something illegal and they want to cover it up." George sipped his coffee and grinned at me. "There must be hundreds, if not thousands, of reasons to change your life or your identity."

He waited a beat or two, like a stand up comedian. "Like maybe your father has embarrassed you by marrying a woman half his age and getting her pregnant and then showing up at your house when you have several hundred guests to tell you the news?"

I had to laugh. "I don't think that would be enough to make me change my name and leave town, but it might be a motive for murder," I teased.

George relented. "Read this article later. It's quite interesting."

I looked at the *Tribune* article more closely. It was about a former member of the FBI who wrote a book telling ordinary people how to hide their assets and disappear. He was traveling the country giving seminars on the subject and had been in Tampa yesterday. Even with all the Gasparilla festivities, over 2,500 people had attended his presentation. The book had already sold over a million copies. Clearly, reinventing oneself was a more popular topic than I'd realized. I set the article aside to read later when Margaret came into the room.

The rest had helped her somewhat, although dressed in the clothes she'd slept in and with yesterday's makeup smudged around her face, Margaret looked far from her best.

"I can't really believe he's gone," she said to George and me, after we'd gotten her settled and fortified. The dry bagel she chewed slowly and washed down with coffee seemed to strengthen her somewhat but she still looked like an exhausted and bewildered shadow of dear, kind, petite Margaret Wheaton.

Some lawyers have office wives who partner with them at work as their spouses partner with them at home. I had Margaret, my office mother. She cared for me, watered my plants, dusted my desk, kept me from working too hard and others from over scheduling my time. Margaret even stood up to the CJ, my boss. She chastised me for antagonizing him, but when she thought he was out of line, she stood right up to her full height and went toe-to-toe with the old despot. Margaret had reserves of feistiness in her that would see her through her husband's death, even if they weren't apparent at the moment.

"We knew he was going to die, of course. We'd been preparing for it for months. He had a living will, made sure we transferred all the titles to my name. He gave me everything he had. So we were ready. We thought it would be the ALS. I'm glad he had a heart attack instead." She sounded anything but ready or glad. George reached over and covered her small hand with his large one. She stared at the plain gold band he wore on his ring finger for a while. Fresh, quiet tears, started down her cheeks again.

"What can we do, Margaret?" I felt as anguished as she was. I'm not good at death. I don't do funerals, wakes or memorial services, if I can avoid it. Death is a part of life's circle, I know. I even sort of believe in reincarnation of some kind. But the loss and sadness the living feel when a loved one dies is just too hard to watch and revives too many bad memories for me.

Watching Margaret's grief, I didn't believe she killed her husband. Nothing would make me believe it. Not even a full confession. Hathaway was just wrong.

But Margaret had to know what the police were thinking. So I took a deep breath and just said it. "Margaret, Ben Hathaway isn't convinced that Ron just passed away. He's checking that," I said quickly at her alarmed look toward me. "But he's checking other possibilities, too. He has to. It's his job."

She looked startled. "Other possibilities? Like what?"

George had looked up from his papers and listened intently to my answer. "Well, Ben has ordered an autopsy to see what caused Ron's death," I told her.

"Why?"

"Because it's the law," I said, as gently as I could. "They have to rule out other causes of death."

"Like what?"

I was uncomfortable with this line of conversation. "Well, like maybe suicide or homicide. I mean, not that that happened here. Just, that's the reason for the law requiring an autopsy."

Margaret shook her head, slowly, as if to say "no, no, no, no." "Who would want to hurt Ron? He was the kindest man in Tampa. He didn't have an enemy in the world. For all the years we were married, I don't think he ever raised his voice to me, even once." She kept shaking her head. "No. That's not possible. No one killed Ron. It's not possible."

Real tears and sobs began again, then, and I helped Margaret back to bed. Grief is like that, I remembered all too well. It comes in waves. Margaret would be alright again, but she'd have bad times, too, for the next few months. I hoped Hathaway would wrap this up soon so Margaret could deal with her grief and move on with her life.

Hathaway's suggestion was outrageous, I thought again. The woman just lost her husband. She wasn't a killer. I may not know everything, but I knew that much. Margaret didn't have anyone to help her except me, now that Ron had died. It's not that I'm all that experienced with killing, but I knew Margaret didn't kill Ron and I wouldn't let Ben Hathaway try to prove she did. Still, it nagged at me. Ben has been wrong before, but not that often.

When I came back from Margaret's room, I heard the front door to our flat open and Dad and Suzanne walk in, laughing and chatting, right past the kitchen and on to their room down the hall. George chuckled, "Afternoon delight, hmmmm?" I hit him in the arm and he yelled, "Owwwwwww!" loud enough to wake the dead. We were both still laughing when a couple of our other house guests came in to join us. We exchanged pleasantries for a while, spent the rest of the day being social and tried, unsuccessfully, to forget Hathaway's suspicions.

Chapter *Three*

Monday morning, as I drove over the bridge off Plant Key away from Minaret and turned right onto Bayshore Boulevard heading toward downtown, my favorite view of Hillsborough Bay unfolded. Some days I see dolphins and manatee on my way to work. My daily drive east on Bayshore, over the Platt Street bridge, toward the convention center and on to the old federal courthouse to my office is one of many aspects of my life for which I am truly grateful. I felt my mood lightening and I actually felt better, physically. Even though I was running late, something I detest in judges, especially myself, I tried to focus on the view as it sped past.

The old courthouse itself is Circa 1920, about twenty years newer than our house. As the most junior judge on the bench, I'm stuck in the least desirable office. It's the RHIP rule; I have no rank and no privilege. My courtroom and chambers are on the third floor in the back. Moving quickly from the parking garage helps me keep my schoolgirl figure.

Only slightly out of breath, I got to my chambers a little before nine and had to dig out my key to open the door when my repeated impatient buzzing failed to raise Margaret to release the lock. Margaret wasn't at her desk, but her computer was on, her chair was away from her desk like she'd just gotten up for a moment, and a cup of hot tea was steaming near her phone. Before she left our home on Sunday, I'd tried to convince her to take some time off, but she declined. She said she'd rather work. "I need to get on with my life, Willa. Let me do that, okay?"

I hurried into my office, dropped my minuscule purse into a drawer, and picked up my robe off the hook on the back of the door. I perused my pink telephone slips quickly before I went out into the courtroom and found one from the CJ, that is, the Chief Judge of the United States District Court for the Middle District of Florida. He'd called at seven-thirty this morning, knowing I wouldn't be here. I never get here much before nine. I'm not a morning person. The message, written in Margaret's hand, said CJ wanted to talk with me before I took the bench.

I was tempted to ignore him. If I went out right now, I'd be seated on the bench at eight fifty-nine, keeping my self-imposed rule of timeliness. The CJ isn't really my boss, although he acts like he is. I'm appointed for life and there isn't a darn thing he can do about it, as much as he'd like to. I inadvertently took his parking place my first day on the job and he'd been on my case ever since, a reaction more than a little bit drastic for such a minor infraction. I got the worst case assignments, the smallest chambers, the most meager courtroom budget. At meetings he ignored my suggestions and generally made it known, without saying so, that I was far from his favorite jurist. When his sister and brother-in-law both committed suicide a while ago, CJ acted like it was my fault. Then, when George was accused of murder, according to CJ, I should have resigned before the masses had a chance to impeach me. He's still pissed off that I didn't. My thinking was, hell, if Chief Justice Earl Warren could withstand an impeachment attempt, let 'em try and get me for nothing more than being married to a guy who was wrongfully accused. The CJ has aspirations to higher office and I've been his biggest supporter. Moving him to Atlanta would be a very pleasant surprise.

So talking to the CJ was never high on my list of priorities, and especially not when I'm already late taking the bench. Regardless of whether he acknowledged our true relationship, this was a *request* and nothing more. I could honor it. Or not.

But it would be good for me to take the high road, I reasoned, if he was ever going to give me a chance to move my office to the new courthouse with the rest of my colleagues. No point in creating trouble if it's unnecessary. So I picked up the phone, hoping he'd be busy. Unfortunately, CJ had left instructions to put my call through immediately. I sat down wearily in my chair and looked around at my minuscule office, decorated in what I call ugly green and uglier brown but a decorator probably once called "avocado" and "copper." The beat-up client chairs and this stupid platform my desk was on were put here by my predecessor, who was clearly a little Napoleon. I wondered when I would ever get to move. I refused to redecorate, although CJ had several times offered me the money to do it. I didn't want to give the impression that I was planning on staying here long enough to make redecorating worthwhile. Maybe if I could force myself to be a little more gracious to the CJ he'd find the money in this year's budget to let me relocate to the new courthouse with everyone else.

"Good morning, Willa," he boomed into my ear. Why is it that some people who are hard-of-hearing either shout at you or whisper? He continued right on through my greeting, "I understand you have Armstrong Yeats in your courtroom this morning." Really? I had no idea. I hadn't had time to prepare for my docket of conferences today and didn't know exactly what was scheduled. I'd been just a little preoccupied. Besides, one case begins to look like another after a while. The CJ knew more about today's calendar than I did.

CJ was continuing to shout, "I have personally known Armstrong for several years. I've bought a number of pieces of jewelry for my wife from him and I've always been completely satisfied. Most of South Tampa has bought from him at one time or another. There's not a damn thing to this case and you ought to dismiss it so you can get on to the real cases on your docket."

The CJ was so far out of line that if he hadn't been shouting I would have thought I'd misheard him. He wasn't really *asking* me to dismiss a case. He couldn't be. He took my non-response for consent, and said, "Good. I'm glad we got that resolved. You have over eight hundred cases on your docket, Willa. Surely some of them deserve your attention." And he hung up!

I was still nonplused as I walked out into the courtroom and took the bench to hear pre-trial motions on my first case, which I obviously knew very little about. The courtroom deputy called *Fitzgerald House v. Armstrong Yeats* and we were about to begin working when Margaret walked into the courtroom from my chambers, came toward the bench where I sat and handed me a ceramic mug filled with café con leche.

Seated at the defense table was a local lawyer, Armstrong Yeats, and his insurance adjuster. As Margaret looked over toward them all color drained from her usually placid, small, olive face. She stared at all three men, speechless, and just as I reached to take it from her, she dropped the coffee cup on the floor where it shattered into a thousand pieces. Just before she hit the floor.

The court security officer picked her up, carried her into my chambers and placed her onto the ugly brown couch that did nothing to enhance the adjacent ugly green chairs. Margaret could have simply fainted. Heaven knows she probably hadn't gotten much sleep or taken care of herself since Ron died two days ago. Yet, Margaret is a pretty tough little woman. She didn't faint when we found her husband dead and it was nothing short of amazing that she had now. I left one of my clerks to call the court's medical team and the housekeeping department while I went back out to the bench, stood in the position Margaret had occupied and turned to look out into the courtroom, just as she had done. I found myself looking squarely at the three men seated at the defense table.

Margaret had met the lawyer, the adjuster and Yeats before. What had caused her such discomfort? Today, Yeats looked much as I had seen him Saturday. He wore a business suit, which made him look somewhat more conventional. The style was recent enough, but the suit and its inhabitant didn't look like they were comfortable companions or even well acquainted. All in all, Armstrong Yeats wouldn't even rate a second look on the street, I thought. Margaret's reaction told me to wonder whether he had a totally different impact on older women.

Still thinking, I looked back into my chambers where Margaret was sipping tea, and in good hands. Knowing I had a courtroom full of work to do, I left her there and returned to the bench, making my way around the glass and coffee on the floor, vowing silently to ask Margaret about the entire matter later in the morning.

When the clerk called the *Fitzgerald House* case again, Yeats, his lawyer and his insurance adjuster were there looking pretty much the way they had a few minutes ago, except that Yeats looked even less comfortable. Fitzgerald House was present in the form of the chair of its board of directors, a bent, grey-haired, elderly woman who looked like my elementary school librarian. Her lawyer was young and inexperienced, probably because no more experienced lawyer would have taken this case.

I looked briefly at the case summary my clerks had provided to me. Privately, I had to agree with the CJ that this case didn't appear to deserve the court's time. Unfortunately, I don't get to make that decision. The case was a relatively small matter involving a business dispute between these two parties. Ordinarily, my view is that such matters should be resolved without my time or energy. However, anyone with the filing fee and a typewriter can file suit. It's called open access to the courts for the redress of grievances. Our government is founded on it. True, many cases were frivolous and got dismissed, and this one might, too, at some point. But we weren't there yet.

After a brief recitation of the facts by the young lawyer on behalf of Fitzgerald House, I tried to settle the case. Not because the CJ had asked me to, but because I try to settle all my cases. I tell litigants "all cases are settled. The question is whether you do it yourself or whether you let the jury do it for you." Sometimes litigants listen to me.

"No, Judge," the adjuster said in response to my suggestion that the insurance company simply pay Fitzgerald House the appraised value of the jewelry in dispute. An elderly widow had bequeathed the same to the charity in her will. "The widow knew full well the necklace and earrings were fakes when she bought them. They weren't even insured, which she surely would have done if she'd thought they were really worth a million dollars. No. This is just another frivolous lawsuit and we will win this case. And if we don't, it's because Mr. Yeats misrepresented the jewelry, which is an intentional act, and not covered by the policy anyway. We will pay no money to settle this claim." The adjuster was puffed up with righteous indignation, settling in for a long, cold trial.

I looked at Yeats and his lawyer. "You know how it is, Judge," Yeats apologized. "Insurance companies always want to collect your premiums, but you're never covered." He looked bleakly at the adjuster, who glared back. The lawyer was sitting, literally and figuratively, in the middle.

I'd dealt with this adjuster before. He would never budge. So I appealed to the board chair. Fitzgerald House is a museum, allegedly a modest home F. Scott Fitzgerald once owned and where it is claimed he wrote part of *The Great Gatsby*. I've always been a little skeptical of the claims. Scott and Zelda Fitzgerald used to spend vacations at the Don CeSar hotel near here on St. Pete Beach, and I've always felt a small connection to him.

Maybe the Fitzgeralds did own the little house in Palm Springs once. Beyond that, the connection to *Gatsby* seemed tenuous to me, based on what I've read of Fitzgerald's life.

"Can you afford a scandal like this?" I asked the board chair as kindly as possible. "And what if you lose? It's going to cost you a lot to take this case to trial. You could have to pay Mr. Yeats's costs, too. Does Fitzgerald House have that kind of money to risk?"

The board chair and her lawyer looked uncomfortable, but she answered me truthfully. "Judge, we believe we're right about this. I talked to the widow myself about the jewelry. Many times. She absolutely believed it was real. She thought she was giving Fitzgerald House a gift that would finally bring us financial prosperity."

The young lawyer inserted, with the righteous certainty only the young can muster, "We can't afford not to try this case in the face of absolutely no offers from the defendant."

"Well, then we have no choice but to get started. I'll take the plaintiff's motions first," I said, and we worked straight through all the motions until lunch. I recessed the matter for the day and went to take care of the pile of work on my desk, feeling exhausted already.

Margaret went out for lunch, which was unusual but not unprecedented. I didn't see her before she left, so I couldn't ask about her fainting spell this morning, but I was worried. I picked up the phone and called Chief Hathaway's office. He wasn't there. I left a message. I drummed my fingers on the desk, thinking about who could give me some answers. I picked up the phone and dialed Marilee Aymes. "Dr. Aymes' office," the receptionist said with as much enthusiasm as I display for over-cooked spinach.

"This is Judge Carson. Is Dr. Aymes in?" I asked, brusquely, and she agreed to check. I've learned that if you don't act important with these receptionists, they actually think they don't have to let you talk to the doctor. It's easier to call the CEO of Microsoft than to get past a physician's receptionist.

"What's up?" Marilee's office persona is about the same as her personal and private ones. For years, she was Tampa's only woman cardiologist and she was still the best. She's also brash, bossy, brusque and more than a little overbearing. I think she's a hoot, but George says I shouldn't be seen with someone so "unsuitable." I suspect he thinks she's unsuitable because she does whatever the hell she wants. To George, such conduct isn't becoming, honorable or appropriate. He can be awfully stuffy sometimes.

"Sounds like you're busy," I asked tentatively. This wasn't a conversation I wanted to have without Marilee's full attention.

"Always. But it's Monday. Everybody saved their heart attacks from the weekend for today. The waiting room is jammed. I'll be lucky to get done here by seven o'clock."

"So I guess a drink around five-thirty is out of the question, then?" I looked at the gold and platinum Cartier watch George had given me for our last anniversary. It was about two o'clock now. I needed to get home to my guests, but I wasn't impatient to do so. It was clear that Dad and Suzanne knew how to amuse themselves and George would be working until much later.

"Lemme look. Hey, girls, what's the wait look like?" she shouted to someone in the other room. "Umm. Ok. I could make it by six. How's that? Wanna meet at your place?" She asked me.

"How about Bella's? That's between here and there." I suggested a local Italian bistro with a nice bar and some quiet booths on South Howard, or "SoHo" as the area was now being called. She agreed and hung up without signing off. I called George's and left a message that I'd be later than usual, but home by seven-thirty at the latest.

I'd finished my tuna sandwich and now I wanted a cookie. Looking at my watch, I had just enough time to run down to the cafeteria to get one before my next conference. So, I picked up my purse and, preoccupied with my thoughts, made my way quickly past Margaret's empty desk and through the door to the hallway. Without watching where I was going, I literally bumped into Yeats, who had his hand on Margaret's elbow as they argued in hushed tones outside the door to my chambers. When I practically knocked them down, Yeats stepped away from Margaret and looked up, but Margaret was so engrossed she didn't notice I was there.

"But we're not young enough to waste any more time. Ron is dead now. Nothing will bring him back," she pleaded.

"Hello, Judge," Yeats said, loudly enough to interrupt Margaret and too loud for the quiet hallway of our surroundings.

"Hello, Mr. Yeats. Margaret." I nodded at them both. "Something I can help you with?"

"No, Judge," Margaret had composed herself. "We were just talking."

"You two friends?" I asked the obvious question.

"We were. Once. A long time ago." Margaret said. "I need to get back to work. Excuse me." She left us to return to the office. Yeats watched her go and continued to look uncomfortable standing there alone in the hallway with me.

"What was that about?" I asked him, not really sure I wanted to know. Margaret was all alone in the world. I didn't want to think she had any relationship, ever, with Armstrong Yeats. Based on what I'd heard this morning he wasn't the kind of man I'd want anyone involved with. If he had taken advantage of the widow in the *Fitzgerald House* case he might take advantage of Margaret, too. She had told George and me that Ron's life insurance and other assets would leave her financially well off. And she was particularly vulnerable right now. Exactly the kind of situation I had imagined the *Fitzgerald House* widow was in when she'd had her unsavory encounter with Yeats.

Margaret was unhappy and upset and trying valiantly to stay composed. Nothing good could come of any association between Margaret and Armstrong Yeats. I didn't have to know more about him to know that. I was in a position to rescue Margaret from herself, right now. So I went into what George calls my Mighty Mouse routine. You know, from the old cartoon where the mouse dresses up like superman and flies through the air singing, "Here I come to save the Daaaaaayyyyy." It's a bad habit that I've tried to break. George tells me, "Willa, if someone wants your help, they'll ask for it. You don't have to be everyone's hero. Some people don't want to be rescued, you know. If they want your help, they'll ask for it." I know that. But it's against my nature to turn my head when my friends are in trouble.

Maybe Margaret's wish right now was not to be rescued. But that could only be because she didn't realize what she was dealing with. If the fraud claims Fitzgerald House was making against Yeats were true, I didn't want Margaret involved with this guy, whether she thought she wanted to be or not. Especially until Ron Wheaton's autopsy came back and Ben Hathaway was satisfied that he'd died of natural causes. Nothing makes a cop more suspicious than a new widow with a man friend who has a questionable past.

"Margaret recognized me as an old friend, that's all. We were just catching up." Yeats said, like it was true. Maybe it was.

"Mr. Yeats, you are a defendant in a case in my courtroom. Please don't contact Margaret again until this case is over. After that, what you do is your own business." I told him, not as harshly as I could have. He shouldn't be having private conversations with Margaret about the case. Otherwise, litigants have social conversations with court personnel all the time. It's not a problem. But I was hoping he didn't know that, and that he wouldn't discuss it with CJ. If Yeats did as I asked, it might give Margaret time to come to her senses and decide on her own not to see him.

Beyond that, my staff isn't supposed to be personally involved with litigants in cases in my courtroom. It appeared that Margaret and Yeats had been arguing. That suggested more of a personal relationship than I could ethically allow. If any member of my staff did know Yeats personally, it would have to be disclosed to all parties and dealt with. I might even be required to recuse myself from the case, if the involvement had gone too far.

"Of course, Judge, I understand. I'm sorry," Yeats said as he turned off to leave the building. I watched him until he reached the elevator lobby, pushed the button and got in. My sweet tooth had evaporated, but I went quickly, bought my cookie and returned in less than fifteen minutes to finish my conferences.

After the last of the lawyers left, I should have spent the rest of my time on my work, but of course I spent the time dwelling on Margaret instead. What was Margaret's connection to Armstrong Yeats? Ordinarily, she wouldn't even know the man. Yeats traveled in circles that were way beyond Margaret's usual social life. He was a local celebrity, in a small town way. He'd been an award winning jeweler in Pass-a-Grille, the little beach community just south of St. Pete Beach in Pinellas County, across the bay from here, for at least as long as I'd been in Tampa. Yet I'd never met him before Saturday. Who was this guy and why had he upset Margaret enough to cause her to faint? Because, although there were other people in the courtroom when she collapsed, somehow I felt that Margaret was involved with Armstrong Yeats. I was concerned based on what I'd learned about Yeats today in the *Fitzgerald House* case.

Fitzgerald House claimed that the deceased widow hadn't just spent a million dollars on jewelry that Yeats sold her, she had spent every cent she owned. She believed, because he told her so, that the jewelry was "one of a kind," with a "special history." He told her the necklace and earrings had been designed by the legendary Tiffany's designer, Paulding Farnham and had belonged to Marilyn Monroe. He showed the widow pictures to prove it. Yeats sold the pieces to her as an investment that would increase in value more significantly than any other investment she could make. The widow died believing that she had left her favorite charity, operated by the little woman who was now the chair of the Fitzgerald House board and the widow's closest friend, a legacy.

When the widow died, Fitzgerald House had the necklace and earrings appraised to be sold. They had an actual value of about forty thousand dollars. They did look like the pictures of a set Marilyn

Monroe had worn to the Academy Awards in 1953, and they might have been. But if she'd worn these particular gems, they were fakes then, too.

Yeats' only defense so far was to admit that the stones were not real, but to claim the widow knew that when she paid him more than twenty times their value. He said Marilyn Monroe had actually worn the jewelry, and it had been costume jewelry at the time. As memorabilia, he claimed, the gems were actually worth a million dollars, and suggested that Fitzgerald House simply sell them. Yeats had counter-sued for defamation and damage to his business reputation caused by the claim.

Working at my desk, I got caught up in the *Fitzgerald House* file as the time passed me by. Margaret stopped to talk to me on her way out at five o'clock.

"What happened today, Margaret? What caused you to faint this morning? Are you alright?"

"Willa, I know you're trying to help," she stood in the doorway to my office with her purse in her hand and her coat on, tying a scarf around her head against the wind. Margaret got her hair done once a week and didn't touch it between beauty appointments. It always looked exactly the same. Her style was short, teased and varnished, not merely sprayed—a product of a bygone age. "But, and I mean this as kindly as I can say it, please don't interfere in my private life."

"Margaret, you're not yourself right now, and you know how much George and I care about you." I jumped in without really hearing her or letting her finish her sentence. "Ron's illness and his death has been so hard on you. The stress must be overwhelming. It's not a time for you to make any big decisions."

"I appreciate your concern. Truly. I do. But I've been on my own since I was a young girl, long before you were born. Let me handle myself." She said this in the same tone everyone uses to tell me to mind my own business, as she buttoned her coat and turned to go.

"If you need anything, you'll let me know?" I asked her.

She smiled her indulgence, "Sure, Mighty Mouse. I'll yell for help before I need it. Goodnight." She turned around to leave, but changed her mind. "There is something you can do for me, though. Talk to your friend Dr. Aymes and tell her not to sue Yeats, OK?"

"Why is Marilee Aymes going to sue Yeats?"

"You'll have to ask her. All he told me was that it was a big misunderstanding." This time she did turn and leave quietly. Margaret had no idea what kind of trouble she could be in. I had to help her, whether she wanted me to or not, I persuaded myself. Margaret was all the way out of the building before what she'd said actually resonated with me. When would Yeats have told Margaret anything about Dr. Marilee Aymes?

I had about an hour before my date with Marilee and I spent my time wisely. I turned around to my computer and accessed the files that are available to me as a U.S. District Court Judge. Computers made researching individuals fairly easy, although limited information was available without the consent of the particular individual in question. I could get access to certain FBI files if I needed to do so, but not without a good reason. Furthermore, I'm not allowed to investigate cases on my docket. So, all I looked for was whether there were any more cases involving Armstrong Yeats.

I punched in "Armstrong Eugene Yeats," after looking up his full name in the *Fitzgerald House* file. While waiting for the data to process, or whatever it does, I continued looking at the *Fitzgerald House* file. I'd have to know it fairly well for trial anyway.

A few seconds later, the computer came up with a list of cases involving Yeats. According to the screen, there were several closed civil actions in various jurisdictions. Some reflected Yeats as the plaintiff and some were claims against him. From this search, I couldn't discern the disposition of the files. Had Yeats ever been brought to trial? Or were all the cases settled? I'd have to look at the actual files to know and most of them were either in storage or over at the new courthouse. I saw one pending criminal complaint, *U.S. v. Armstrong E. Yeats* and according to the case number codes, it was also on my docket, although I hadn't had any involvement with the case yet. I wrote a short note to one of my clerks to pull the file for me and have it on my desk in the morning. I didn't have time to look into it further if I was going to make my date with Marilee Aymes. But I put it high on my priority list for Tuesday, along with a note to do a similar search on Ron Wheaton.

Chapter *Four*

I had about ten minutes to make it to Bella's. Fortunately, even with today's traffic, you can get just about anywhere in South Tampa in ten minutes. Ten years ago, you could do it in three. I picked up my purse, pulled my electronic key to my car out of the side pocket, skipped the ancient elevator ride and loped down the stairs and to the parking garage.

Minutes later I'd pulled onto Florida Avenue, a one-way street north, which took me past the new Sam M. Gibbons Federal Courthouse containing the courtrooms I lust after. I looked again at the killer palm trees out front, so called because one of them rolled off a truck during construction, landed on a worker and killed him. Not funny. I turned left onto Tyler and drove past the performing arts center where the marquee said Tony Bennett was performing. There was a crowd of twenty-somethings out front, lined up to get in. To see Tony Bennett. Go figure.

I pulled into Bella's parking lot at six o'clock on the nose. I love living in South Tampa. Everything is so close, so easy. Except finding a parking spot at Bella's on a Monday night in February. I finally found one at the far end of the lot, locked the car and rushed up to the front door. They had plastic walls up outside against the cold winds still blowing in the February chill and snow birds.

Bella's is cozy, with a large wood burning oven in the back. As I walked in, I was thankful for the oven's warmth. Like most nights, the bar was busy with the South Tampa crowd, while the tables were filling with diners of all ages. I looked quickly at the bar stools to see if Marilee Aymes was waiting there. She wasn't. Then I checked the booths along the bar side and saw her in the back. I waved the hostess away and maneuvered through the martini-drinking, upwardly-mobile, young professionals.

I ordered Bombay Sapphire and tonic with lemon. Marilee had a fairly hefty glass of bourbon on the table. It's not nice to make your friends drink alone. Besides that, the Queen Mother drinks gin and she's over a hundred years old. What's the problem?

Marilee was ensconced in the booth, her short, hefty body taking the entire bench on her side. She wore no make-up, a non-nonsense haircut, and a belligerent stare, a combination that made her a target of gossip and rumor around town. Add to that her tell-it-like-it-is style and it was fairly easy to understand why she was a guilty pleasure for people who cared about the opinions of others. That group had never included me. Being a federal judge, I'm appointed for life. I'll have my job unless and until I do something truly outrageous. That day may come, but drinking with Marilee Aymes didn't keep me from getting appointed and wouldn't put me over the line now.

After greetings, Marilee lit one of the new Gasparilla cigars. I declined her offer to join her in another of our shared vices. I came straight to the point, which is the best approach with Marilee.

"I'm here to ask you a favor from my secretary." It was a direct, but not elegant, start to the conversation.

"You're kidding, right?" Marilee interjected as she puffed.

"Let me finish. You know Margaret Wheaton, don't you? She's worked with me for years. She helped us with our pet project, Young Mothers' Second Chance, several times?" I explained Margaret's pedigree in terms Marilee would remember.

"That's right. A very nice woman. Doesn't her husband have some kind of terminal illness?" Everyone always remembers what's of interest to them. Sometimes, getting information from people is easy. I'd wanted to ask Marilee about Ron's death so I could head Chief Hathaway off at the pass if he kept going off in the wrong direction.

"Yes, that's right. ALS," I said. "Or, at least he did. He died on Saturday."

Marilee shook her head, finished her bourbon, and ordered another. "Nasty death, ALS," she said around her cigar. "The lungs lose the ability to breathe air. The victim suffocates, fully aware of what's happening. Makes you believe in voluntary euthanasia."

"Yes," I said again, startled that her thoughts were mirroring the police chief's suspicions without knowing the facts. "Chief Hathaway is suggesting Ron's death might have been a mercy killing. By Margaret."

"Couldn't blame her. If I had ALS, I'd kill myself. Wouldn't need anyone to help me," she said, as she knocked back another swig of bourbon.

"How would you do that?"

She eyed me speculatively through the purple haze of her cigar smoke between us. "Well, as a doctor, it would be easier for me to do than it would for someone who didn't have easy access to drugs. The nicest thing would be to inject myself with an overdose of morphine. I'd just go to sleep, rather peacefully, too." We sat quietly, both thinking about Ron falling peacefully asleep; Marilee thinking how much better that would be than the alternative at the end of the course of his disease.

I don't know what I was thinking. I'm not sure how I feel about voluntary euthanasia. Being a lawyer, I can argue all sides of the issue. But if I'd been in Ron Wheaton's shoes, what would I have wanted to do? And when would I have wanted to do it? Would it have been better to await my turn, living out my life until the last minute, experiencing all there was to this life before moving on to the next?

I knew Ron Wheaton was a religious person, like most Americans are. He and Margaret went to Hyde Park Methodist Church on Swann Avenue every Sunday for all the years I'd known them. Ron was a member of the administrative board; Margaret played the piano for the choir. Would his religious beliefs have made Ron less likely to take his own life?

"How far along was he?" Marilee asked me.

"Medically, I don't know. I saw him the day he died. He looked very thin, frail, like a strong wind could blow him down," I told her, taking a sip of gin.

"Was he ambulatory?" she puffed in my direction.

"He was walking, but he had a wheelchair nearby, which he used when he got tired. They found his body in it. On our verandah. After the parade on Saturday." The telling of it made me shudder. I recalled Ron's pale body in death.

"Then he probably had the dexterity to inject himself. Maybe he did. Make it easier on the wife," Marilee offered her brand of compassion.

"What else could he have been injected with?" I asked her.

"Almost anything in large enough doses will kill you. Cocaine, heroin, insulin, household bleach, even air, to name a few."

"Then again, he could have had a heart attack, couldn't he? He was the right age for it. He had a history of angina. Couldn't that explain it?" I asked her, hearing the hope in my own voice and thinking it odd to hope for such a thing as a heart attack. Everything's relative.

She nodded her head on her short, stout neck. "Yep. Saw three heart attack patients over the weekend myself and a couple more today. No reason he couldn't have been one of 'em. So, what's the favor?" she asked, reminding me of the second reason I'd asked her here.

"Margaret asked me to persuade you not to sue Armstrong Yeats. So I said I would talk to you about it. What's going on?"

"What do I look like, the answer woman? How should I know what's going on with that bony little troll?" she snapped at me, pounding her glass on the table to remind the bartender that she'd ordered another drink and it wasn't here yet.

"Well, are you involved in any lawsuits?" I asked her, feeling a little uncomfortable now. It was a fairly personal question, particularly for a doctor. Most doctors are fairly touchy about being sued. I used to defend doctors when I was still in private practice. I'd never met one who thought he'd done anything wrong. When I was a young lawyer, I had the chief of medicine say to me, "Willa, doctors are *never* negligent." If only that were true. More people die of medical errors in our country each year than heart attacks. Hospitals are places you go to die, it's been said. At least, you should keep your wits about you while you're there.

Marilee looked at me through narrowed eyes and a bigger cloud of blue smoke. I didn't mind the smoke. In fact, I was rather wishing I had broken my self-imposed rule about not smoking Partagas, my cigar of choice, in public. I took a second-hand whiff of pleasure. Bad habit, I know, and I don't have the Queen Mum to justify this one.

Marilee's bourbon arrived just as she was about to resume the glass-pounding routine, for which I and the rest of the patrons were no doubt equally grateful. She drank half of the bourbon down quickly. I had no idea how much Marilee drank on a regular basis or how well she held her liquor. And I didn't want to find out. I was still nursing my first gin, hoping the bourbon would make her more loquacious but not obnoxious.

"Several, actually, and perpetually," she said, jerking my thoughts back to our conversation.

"What?"

"Lawsuits. I'm involved in several lawsuits almost all the time. It's the bane of a cardiologist's existence. People with bad hearts and bad arteries just don't live without care and treatment. And sometimes, they die anyway. Or they have a stroke. Then, the family sues the doctor. Hazard of the profession." She dared me to contradict her.

In my experience, people sued other people because they were angry and felt cheated. I could believe Marilee's bedside manner left much to be desired and might easily get in the way of her medical skills. When a loved one died, she'd be the natural target of the family's anger.

"I don't mean to pry into your business. I had the impression that Margaret believes you're suing Yeats, not the other way around. Is that possible?" I was a little sorry I'd started this and wondering why I wasn't home, relaxing, with my own cigar. Then I remembered my child stepmother and that answered my own question. Maybe I was so interested in Margaret today because it gave me a legitimate excuse not to go home. That didn't bear thinking about.

"Anything's possible. But in answer to your question, maybe because I get sued all the time, I don't sue anyone myself. I usually try to resolve everything out of court," she said.

Then, she decided to give me a break. Maybe the bourbon was mellowing her some.

She lowered her voice and I bent closer to hear her over the dull roar of the bar crowd. "And I am trying to resolve a dispute right now with Yeats. Confidentially."

"So what is it?" Marilee might be the only person I know that I would ask so bluntly. In Tampa, no one asks anyone anything bluntly. Nor do we tell each other what we really think or how we're actually feeling. We tell everyone else what we think, but not the object of our affection, or rejection, or disdain. It's just not done. Bad form, you know. But it's okay to shoot them. Go figure.

Not Marilee, though. She was one tough cookie. Cool, strong-willed, and used to having her own way, all the time. Someone had once taken advantage of Marilee Aymes, but that was a long time ago and she'd spent a lifetime making sure it never happened again.

"That asshole," she hissed, her nostrils flaring and her mouth set in a hard line across her ample face. "He sold me a multi-color sapphire-and-diamond pinky ring for a gift a while back. Charged me over fifty thousand dollars."

"Wow. That's a lot of money for a gift."

Marilee ignored my comment. "I took it in to be appraised for my insurance and they said it was a fake. Can you believe that? I went right to Yeats and told him he'd give me my money back or I'd sue his scrawny little ass and make sure it got on the six o'clock news every night for a year. Do you know what the toad had the nerve to say to me?" With each sentence, her voice increased the volume until she could be heard plainly over the din of the bar crowd.

I shook my head and kept quiet.

"He said the ring was real when he sold it to me and whoever I gave it to must have had the stones switched. He threatened to sue me for defamation if I went public with this. And then the pony-tailed twerp offered me ten thousand dollars to settle!" With this last exclamation, she slammed her glass on the table so hard the ice cubes popped out onto the floor. The bartender, having learned his lesson the last round, rushed over with a fresh drink just in time.

"What are you looking at, Dad?" I asked as I approached him in the Sunset Bar at George's a little while later. I sat down across from him in the booth after I stopped at the bar and ordered a Perrier, thinking I might be careful about the drinking so I could avoid turning into Marilee Aymes in another twenty years.

"What do you know about the old masters?" My father responded.

"Not much. What I learned in the required art history classes as an undergraduate. Why?"

"I was thinking about how the smallest things can trip you up. If you want to embezzle from your bank, that is," he warmed to his subject, leaned back and clasped his hands behind his head. I saw he was drinking coffee. Which meant he was working.

Dad's insurance agency issued errors and omissions insurance, bonds against employee theft in banks, brokerage houses, art galleries, jewelry stores and other places where theft can be a serious loss to a business. As the selling agent, claims came to him from his customers for initial investigation before they were passed on to the carrier. He loved his work and always had interesting tales of larceny to report.

"Take the case of Miami's CenTrust Savings and Loan, for instance."

"Now there's an old case, Dad. You're too young to be wallowing in the glory days," I teased him.

"True. But seriously, when your Florida banking officials figured out that the bank's chairman had purchased a famous Rubens painting and two dozen other art-works for over $29 million, it didn't take long to discover where the money came from." Dad smiled a satisfied grin. "He's been sitting in prison for quite a while and is likely to be there a bit longer before he starts collecting art again." Dad thinks of himself as an all-American hero, a real John Wayne, one of the good guys who makes sure thieves go to jail.

"And this is relevant to our lives today, why?" I said, smiling, too. I guess we all get to create our own illusions, especially of ourselves. Jim Harper looked nothing like the Duke. More like Gig Young with salt and pepper hair, actually. He was taller than me by about two inches. He played squash and liked to ski, so he kept himself in shape. But Dad's crime-stopping role was strictly cerebral. He tried to out-smart those who stole from his clients.

Today, he had on a black cashmere turtleneck and a tan suede blazer. Grey slacks, socks and brown shoes completed the outfit. He reminded me of a black and tan Doberman; slim, sleek, and stealthy.

"I'm thinking about a new claim I got recently and how I'm going to prove that the bank's president has been embezzling for a long time. It'll be something small like that." We'd always been able to talk about work. It was one topic where we were completely comfortable and compatible. It was about the only topic we ever discussed.

"If I recall correctly, that Rubens sold for over eight million dollars not long ago. I'd hardly call that a small thing," I reminded him.

"True. But it's not usually like that. Usually, it's something smaller and easier. Like the guy who cheated on his expense report by claiming he'd been having dinner with the auditor and then the auditor caught it. Or the time we were looking through a stack of paid bills and we saw that some were folded in half where others from the same vendor weren't—because the folded ones were phony and the clerk was paying himself. That's the usual way we catch these things." He set aside his coffee cup and reached into the file sitting next to him on the bench, handing me an unsigned letter dated about six months earlier and postmarked in New York. "Maybe you'd like to help me with this one. Besides wanting to see you, it's one of the reasons I came here."

> *Dear Mr. Harper:*
>
> *I am a bank stockholder. I have reason to believe that the president is taking bank funds for his personal uses. I've asked him about this and he denies it. But he has a lot of perks for a guy with his salary and our stock isn't worth nearly as much as we expected. He has all the money in the world, but we never get any. And the bank is doing well. I'm elderly and don't have many assets. I need my money. Please look into this.*

I handed the letter back to him. "Won't this be a problem for you? I mean, if the president has been embezzling funds, won't you have to pay the bank on the bond?"

"Yes. But that's what insurance is for, Willa. It's important that my insureds feel like they're getting what they paid for. And this is a complaint from a shareholder. If you're a bank, you can't have many of those before you have the feds coming after you. My insureds expect me to take these things seriously and to investigate them right away. Whether or not there's anything to this complaint, the sooner we find out, the better."

"You must get hundreds of letters like this every month. Do you investigate them all?"

"To one degree or another, we do. The reason I'm getting personally involved in this one is that there's a lot of money at stake and the carrier is one of my biggest insurers." He put the letter back in the file. "And it gave me an excuse to spend a few days with you."

I couldn't help the warm glow in which his words bathed me, surprised at his expressed desire to visit. It wasn't something I'd heard him say often. "So you read this letter and you looked into it?" I asked.

"Kind of. I gave it to one of the younger guys to look into. And he didn't find anything. But one night, I was just flipping through the stuff he had accumulated and I came upon this." He reached across the table and handed me a list of transactions. I studied it for a while but couldn't make any sense out of it.

"What is this?"

"It's a list of transfers, all the deals the bank has done in the last ten years. Notice anything?" From the look on his face, I knew there was something to notice. But for the life of me, I couldn't figure out what it was. Accounting is not my strong suit. I like unraveling mysteries, but it's words that interest me, not numbers. I pay someone to do my taxes and I'd pay them to do all my bookkeeping if I didn't have George. He's the numbers man. He loves it. To me, numbers are Sanskrit, close to voodoo, cave drawings—well, you get the idea.

"I give up. What does it reveal, Oh Great One?" I asked with mock reverence.

"Let's take an example. Look here," he pointed to a transaction about halfway down the first page. "He moved $100,000 from Company A to Company B, both of which he controls. Then here, the first company shows a receivable on its books for $100,000 from Company B, but the second company shows no payable back to Company A."

"So what?"

"Where did it go?" He said, both hands palm up toward the ceiling.

"I give up. Where did it go?"

"Check the next page. The only $100,000 deposit recorded anywhere at the time was into the president's personal bank account. Voila'! Elementary, my dear Watson. He stole it. Plain and simple." Dad looked pleased with himself.

"Why didn't the big auditing firm catch that, if it's true?"

"Good question. Which is what I spent the day asking them. And you know what they told me?" He stopped again. His timing was almost as good as a stand-up comedian's.

"I'll bite. What?"

"They said they were never asked to compare all of the president's personal holdings to the bank records. They were only asked to audit the bank. Which they did. Quite competently."

"So how much are we talking about here? How much do you think the president has taken from the bank?" Which really meant how much had he taken from depositors and shareholders.

Dad answered me as he collected his documents back, put them in his folder and then inside his briefcase. "I'm thinking several million over the years," he said, almost nonchalantly, like several million dollars was gas money. To signal he was done working for the day, he ordered a draft beer and I ordered Bombay Sapphire and tonic with lemon, not lime.

"Who has several million dollars?" Suzanne asked, as she approached our table. Today, she was wearing another of her silk designer warm up suits. This one was silver and the underlying silk tee-shirt was bright teal. She wore silver flats with the easily identifiable Prada look, meaning they cost more than a good dinner for four at George's restaurant. I'd been wondering how she could hold up her left hand under the weight of the obscenely large diamond engagement and wedding bands she wore, but even the addition of the notoriously heavy diamond-bezzled platinum Rolex didn't seem to keep her hand from fluttering to her perfectly styled hair.

“That’s what I intend to find out, Darling. That’s what I intend to find out.” Dad’s determination made me shudder and think that I didn’t want to be in that bank president’s shoes right now. He not only looked like a Doberman tonight, he fairly growled, reminding me that Dobermans can be effective attack dogs as well as good for personal protection and defense. Like a football team, offense or defense just depends on who has the ball.

Chapter *Five*

Later Monday evening, George and I sat in the dining room of his restaurant with Suzanne and Dad, having put off the quiet family meal as long as we could. I was once again admiring the china, crystal and silver that George's inherited from his Aunt Minnie along with her house. The pieces were worn and well-used, which made us believe Aunt Minnie had had a wonderful life here, a tradition George and I intended to continue.

The four of us had ordered dinner, but I had little appetite for the heavenly Salmon with White Wine Sauce and fresh snap peas that was usually one of my favorite dishes. George's chefs had won so many awards that he couldn't keep all of the plaques on the wall in his small office off the kitchen, so he stacked them on the floor. George felt it was gauche to display one's achievements in the plain view of others, even if his competitors do so.

Salads, complete with the dried Traverse City cherries that George orders every year from American Spoon Foods were before us on the table and the talk had turned to sports, as it always did on social occasions with Dad. Suzanne and I were bored with the conversation, but our reactions to it were quite different. I was grateful that I didn't have to contribute, while Suzanne seemed annoyed that she was being excluded. Get used to it, I thought. Dad had about as much desire to discuss social topics that would be of interest to Suzanne and me as he had to discuss his deceased first wife. Which is to say, no interest at all and no intention of doing so.

It's not that I don't love Jim Harper. Just the opposite actually. I've loved him devotedly all my life. I've begged him to visit us, to stay a while, to leave those cold New York winters and enjoy the sunshine. Yet, I see Dad rarely. I wanted to get to know him better, to leave my adolescent feelings for him, both positive and negative, behind us. To forge a new, adult relationship.

Since Mom died, he had been rather scarce in my life. He'd loved mother deeply and just never seemed able to cope with her loss. Instead of the two of us helping one another through Grace Harper's death, his solution had been to run away and hide, leaving me to live with Kate and work things out on my own. We'd been wary strangers since, although I suspected he wanted to change our relationship as much as I did. It had been more than a year since I'd seen him briefly in New York the last time, and then we'd just had lunch.

All of which explains why I never know how to act around Dad. He's a good man, but he can't deal with emotional issues, so he ignores them. He never wants to discuss Mom and he doesn't want to hear anything remotely unpleasant. He only talks about work and superficial things: sports, the weather, vacations. He's a good guest though and entertaining.

Despite my unease, so far, Dad had been an excellent Gasparilla guest, I persuaded myself with the help of the wine. He'd been pleasant, fun, entertaining and the other guests liked both him and his beautiful, young wife. No one appeared surprised. In Florida, the February/December marriage is almost as accepted as in Hollywood.

I was the only one who seemed to notice how much younger Suzanne was and to find the relationship embarrassing. But then, I was the only one who saw in Suzanne what Jim Harper saw in her. I concluded I could work out my relationship issues with him some other time, and raised my glass of Stag's Leap Cabernet in a silent toast to my father. The wine was much too good to sour with a bad mood.

Suzanne, less tuned into the reactions of her new husband than I, waited for a lull in Dad's replay of last week's Super Bowl and jumped right in, with gusto. She started talking about the wedding, re-decorating Dad's apartment, the honeymoon, and finally got around to the new baby. Every comment she made, it seemed, was followed by "isn't that right, Jimmy?" leaving Dad no space to reply and forging into the next sentence without expecting one. By the time Suzanne took a breath, we were through with our main courses and the waiter appeared to take desert orders, which resulted in a few seconds of sound other than Suzanne's constant, high-pitched, meaningless prattle.

Since I'd been running eight to sixteen miles every day to train for the Gasparilla Distance Classic, I could eat with abandon. I ordered the Gasparilla Goldbrick, a sundae the chef created especially for the festival and makes only during Gasparilla month. It's golden vanilla ice cream, coated with butter toffee chocolate sauce that hardens into a sort of classy Eskimo Pie with crushed pecans on top. On the side of the pirate ship-shaped dish it's served in is a chocolate coin wrapped in gold foil. The coin is embossed with the face of the legendary Jose' Gaspar, for whom the month's festivities were named, on one side and his pirate ship on the other.

Like most signature dishes, once created by George's chefs, the Gasparilla Goldbrick is now copied all over town. But none of the copies are as good as the original. When the dessert arrived, I ate mine with gusto. Having a mouth full of sundae had the added benefit of excusing me from talking.

When Suzanne finally excused herself to go "to the little girl's room," with a kiss on Dad's cheek before she left the table, and George was called away to address a shortage of California wine he'd been experiencing since a fire burned all the stock in a Napa warehouse last year, I was face-to-face with Dad with nowhere to hide. Without the conversational cover of work to engage us, he didn't look any more comfortable about our forced unity than I did.

"I loved your mother desperately, you know," he finally said, playing with his wine glass and watching the light reflect off the crystal.

"I know, Dad."

"I waited over twenty years to remarry."

"I know."

"Suzanne makes me happy, Willa. She's bright and she's bubbly. She's as sweet as any girl I've ever known." He was almost begging me to like her, but he didn't look at me while he asked.

"Except one," I reminded him.

"Yes. Except for Grace," he sighed and looked up. "Grace was so much more than that. She was loving, kind, gentle." He skipped a couple of beats, "Quiet," he said, and we both laughed at his reference to Suzanne's unfortunate habit of prattling.

"It's just a coincidence that Suzanne looks so much like Mom, hmmm?"

He seemed uncomfortable again now, never one to honestly discuss things that were unpleasant to him. "No. Of course not. It's what drew me to Suzanne in the first place. I met her at a client's office in New York. She's an MBA, Willa, did you know that? She's not an air head."

I must have looked as doubtful as I felt. I'd seen no evidence to support that idea. "She was working on a marketing campaign that her company wanted some extra insurance for. I was selling it to them. We just hit it off," he said.

"It only took me about two minutes to realize she wasn't Grace, but, I don't know, something about her appealed to me. Is that so terrible?" He wanted my approval, asked for it, pleaded really. What could I do? My demons were not his demons, after all. He'd known my mother as an adult, and he'd loved her desperately. How long did I expect him to mourn?

But that wasn't it, really. It wasn't that he'd married that bothered me, although I would have appreciated a little notice and an invitation to the wedding. It was the choice he'd made.

I couldn't look at Suzanne without thinking of my mother. She looked nothing like Mom, in truth, when you studied Suzanne carefully. She had freckles and blue eyes like Mom, but where Grace Harper had been delicate and willowy, Suzanne was impish and childlike. There were other differences. Suzanne was taller, broader, had more physical substance than Mom had. And the personality difference was so striking that it jarred me every time Suzanne opened her mouth. Mom was a nurse and Suzanne's expertise is sales. That said it all.

I knew Grace Harper wouldn't be one bit satisfied that her husband had stayed single and alone all these years. Grace expected Jim to remarry, told him so and told me so, too, before she died. Nor would she be happy with me if I was less than kind to Suzanne or to Dad. Grace would want me to try at least, and a lot harder than I had been trying so far with Suzanne.

I reached over and took Dad's hand where he had laid it open on the table between us like he used to do when I was a child, like he was offering his heart to me, too, gently and without insistence, letting me make up my own mind but letting me know what he wanted.

"I feel blessed to have another chance at happiness at my age, Willa. I know I wasn't the best father to you. I'm hoping to do better this time, to learn from my mistakes. I'm older now. Wiser, I hope. Will you help me?"

"That's a little unfair, isn't it?" I wasn't really pouting.

"I was five when you married Mom. I needed a father, too."

"Yes. And I wasn't good at that then. I was young. Just getting started in my career. And I made the biggest mistake a man can make. I thought I'd have more time. It never occurred to me that Grace and I wouldn't be together forever."

"Me, neither," I told him.

Before I could say or do anything else, George and Suzanne returned to the table. They both noticed our clasped hands and smiled hugely. George clapped Jim on the back and Suzanne gave him another kiss.

Then she sat down quietly and allowed everyone to talk pleasantly for another hour. She and George discussed the stock market's recent plunge. She told me how much she admired our federal judiciary, explaining intelligently why she felt so. I recognized, with a guilty twinge, that Suzanne must have been nervous about meeting us; unsure of her reception. Empathy is a sign of maturity. Maybe I was developing some.

When Dad reached over, took her hand, and suggested they go upstairs to bed, Suzanne said, "Good night, Aunt Willa. I so hope our baby has that cute little gap between her two front teeth that you have. Good night, Uncle Georgie. See you in the morning." Dad at least had the good grace to mouth the words, "I'm sorry" as he herded her out the door, leaving "Uncle Georgie" and me at the table.

George had some things to do in the restaurant's kitchen and I didn't want to go upstairs, so I wandered into the Sunset Bar looking for some quiet time to think.

I picked up a Bailey's Irish Creme and a cup of coffee and took it over to my favorite booth, which was always reserved for me. One of the perks of being married to the proprietor. Just as I started to contemplate the vagaries of the universe, Marilee Aymes sat down across from me with a drink and a cigar. Since I was an outcast from my own flat, I broke my self-imposed rule and joined her in a satisfying Partagas.

I looked at the cigar, smelled it, tasted it and wondered not for the first time whether fifteen dollars was just too extravagant for something that would intentionally go up in smoke. According to the propaganda, Partagas cigars come from the Dominican Republic and are made from tobacco originally from Cuba. Hand rolled, of course, and aged until just the right flavor was to be experienced. It was the aging, along with the Cuban tobacco, that made the limited reserves special. I lit this one with a sigh of pleasure.

"Penny for your thoughts," Marilee said to me. Then, with a grin and the type of self-deprecating humor I liked her so much for, she said, "Since Yeats got through with me, a penny's all I have. I was supposed to meet the little toad here, but he hasn't shown up. I'll sit with you while I wait for him."

I was searching for a safe topic of conversation. I really did not want to talk to Marilee about my father and Suzanne. But I wasn't going to tell her that, either. "I was thinking about Gil and Sandra Kelley," I said.

"Really? Whatever for?"

Because I'd seen them in the dining room at dinner, I thought. "Do you know them?"

"Sure. Knew Senior Kelley, too. He was a regular fixture around town. A philanthropist of the first order. And a really decent man. I liked him a great deal. His funeral was very, very well attended, so you know how folks felt about him."

I hadn't known know Senior well. I think George did and had a lot of respect for him. Senior dined here a few times, we attended the same parties, he belonged to the right clubs, gave to the right charities, had his picture made with the right people. I'm told the bank prospered under his guidance. Since George's restaurant is a large depositor and we're the type of high-profile couple bankers like to get to know, Senior made it his business to eat here, just like his son, who succeeded him as president when Senior died, ate here.

Then, being Marilee, she had to spice up the conversation. "Sandra's been telling people that Senior stole money from the bank."

"Why would she do that?"

"Who knows, where Sandra is concerned. That woman is as vindictive as a rattle snake. Maybe Gil's been having an affair again. But I've heard her say it myself. And heard about it from several folks in the last two weeks."

"Do you believe it?"

"That Senior was a thief? Hell, no," Marilee said, re-lighting her cigar. "But he might have used the bank's money on the theory that it was his anyway. He owned the bank, you know. Or at least he did until it went public in the late 1970s."

Marilee and I pondered in silence a while. Senior had been a wonderful, courtly Southern gentleman. I knew, but wasn't about to say, that Gil, a man of only modest success in town, must have been a great disappointment to his father. Whereas Senior had been honest, hardworking and straightforward; Gil was a party boy, more interested in having a good time than living the staid banker's life. I'd heard that quite a few Old Tampa depositors had left the bank when Senior died. George only continued to deposit there out of respect for Senior and concern for Sandra. The Kelleys had been posted at the club for failure to pay dues a few times. George was worried that they were having financial problems. And he felt pretty secure in that Federal Deposit Insurance on his accounts.

"My favorite story about Senior's character was why he sent Gil away to Miami to learn the business back in the fifties." Marilee puffed her cigar and drank her bourbon straight while she told me. "Gil was a pretty wild kid around here in his high school days and his momma petted him like he was the future king of England. She had lost a couple of babies and Gil turned out to be an only child. She treated him like a miracle and Senior indulged them both." She paused for a swig and a puff before she continued.

"Gil got into a bunch of minor scrapes that his daddy had to get him out of, but nothing that would have sent him to jail. Still, when he went off to Duke and then on to Florida for his MBA, the local mamas were pretty glad to have him away from their girls. Even then, he was a ladies' man, flirting with any female in a skirt old enough to drive and young enough to walk unassisted." Marilee lifted her glass to the bartender and he brought her another bourbon. I could see she was just getting wound up, so I ordered another Bailey's Irish Cream on the rocks and more coffee, but I was sipping slowly and listening carefully. "Anyway, when Gil came home from school, he started up to his old tricks."

"Like what, specifically?"

Marilee looked at me with one eye open, peering through the amber liquid in her glass. "Gil had a pretty rip-roaring summer that year. He dated several local girls, bedded a few, crashed a couple of cars, stayed out late, drank, gambled and just generally sewed his wild oats, as Senior put it to the local cops more than once."

"Was he actually arrested?"

"I doubt it. In those days, Tampa cops didn't arrest a guy like Gil Kelley. But they picked him up and brought him home and Senior felt obligated to smooth it over. Until Gil went too far."

"In what way?"

"Well, it turned out that one of the many local girls Gil had taken a shine to was the daughter of the McCarthy citrus empire. You've heard of those folks, haven't you?"

"Hasn't everyone?" McCarthy had sold out to one of the big conglomerates right after we came to Tampa, for several billion dollars. They made everything from orange juice to sausage.

Every grocery store in America had examples of McCarthy labeled products in their produce, meat and dairy isles. In Tampa, you could hardly buy anything else.

"Yes. Well, old man McCarthy was fit to be tied. Threatened to pull all his money out of the bank. He wasn't about to have his daughter messed up with the likes of Gil Kelley. No-sir-ee-bob." Marilee slapped her glass down on the table and ordered another bourbon. This had to be her standard practice for getting served, I guess. It worked. The bartender scurried over with another bourbon and I made a mental note to get someone to drive Marilee home later.

"So what happened," I asked her, impatient for the punch line.

"Mariam McCarthy got pregnant, that's what happened. And Gil Kelley 'borrowed' some money from the bank to send her to Paris for an abortion. Or at least that's the story that made the rounds at the time. Senior found out about it and shipped Gil off to Miami for two years until old man McCarthy could get over it and find his daughter someone else to marry." Marilee finished her story with the bulldog look I've seen on her face a thousand times. The one that said she was telling the truth and if you didn't believe it, well, then, that was just your problem.

But I believed her. And I felt sorry for Mariam McCarthy. "What happened to her?"

"She stayed in France for a while, but then she came back to live in Tampa and married Ozgood Richardson. Didn't you know?" The CJ's wife? Had a torrid affair with Gil Kelley? Hard to believe, even if they were both young and foolish at the time. Actually, it was hard to believe Mariam McCarthy Richardson had ever *been* young and foolish. All the times I've been around her, she's been about as interesting as paint dust. I couldn't believe she had suffered a broken heart at Gil Kelley's hands, but I did believe that if she had, she'd be mortified to be living in the same town with him. And I also understood why Kelley was a reluctant member of the Tampa social scene. He wasn't welcome at many clubs and parties. Old Tampa has a long memory and wouldn't have condoned such behavior, even in a young man. Especially if Mariam Richardson was there to put the kibosh on it.

Marilee and I talked for another hour or so before I got one of the waiters to drive her home and gave him cab fare back. Then, I went in and talked to George for a while before going up to bed with a great deal on my mind and hoping that all of our house guests had already retired for the night.

Chapter *Six*

Tuesday morning, the *U.S. v. Yeats* file was on my desk, along with stacks of other files, mail and stuff that had spontaneously generated in the night. I looked at the notes I'd left for myself on what I'd planned to do today. A few years ago, I started making a list at the end of every day for tomorrow's work. It was the only way I could make any sense of my workload. Otherwise, I'd start the day with a plan and within minutes, be completely overtaken by the waves of work that flowed into my office as the tide overflows our beach. While the tide ebbs and flows on a regular daily cycle, my work remains for years. Since I became a judge, I understand the story of Sisyphus on a personal level. The Greek who was condemned to forever push the boulder up the hill was a perfect mascot for judicial work.

Today's project list said "No. 1-check Ron Wheaton's history; No. 2-Review *U. S. V. Yeats* file." While my ancient government issue computer was coming up, to use my time wisely, I pulled the *U.S. v. Yeats* file over toward me and took a look at it, once again lusting after the new courthouse where the judges had much newer, faster computers.

The second I started reading the *U.S. v. Yeats* file, I forgot about my computer search altogether. Yeats was being prosecuted for conspiracy to commit fraud, money laundering, witness tampering and fraud. What was surprising was the number and caliber of people who claimed to have been fleeced by this rather ordinary man. People who should have known better. Educated people, who were obviously wealthy to have paid Yeats the millions they claimed, but must have had more dollars than sense.

The indictment charged that Yeats had sold, cleaned, cut, appraised and consigned diamonds and other jewelry to the listed twenty complainants, and countless unnamed others. All along, the indictment said, Yeats had given his customers cheap imitations. When sued by fleeced customers, Yeats counter-sued for slander and reached confidential settlements for less than his customers' losses, so complaints about him never spread.

Like Fitzgerald House, several of the complainants were also involved in civil suits against Yeats. Many of the complainants were names I recognized and a few were people I knew personally: celebrity golfers, performers, national and local businessmen. The claims were eerily similar. In paragraph after paragraph, the indictment named individuals who had bought jewelry created by famous designers, now deceased. The most frequently mentioned was the award winning Paulding Farnham, one of the world's most talented and artistic designers of fine jewelry. At the Paris Exposition of 1889, Farnham had received the gold medal for his Tiffany & Co. jewelry designs. In part due to Farnham's exquisite designs, Tiffany's became the leader in the field of fine jewelry and silver.

In several paragraphs, Yeats was alleged to have sold copies of Farnham's award winning, twenty-four karat gold-and-enamel orchid brooches, and other pieces of Farnham's original work, to unsuspecting customers. In some instances, the original designs are now featured in public collections at the Metropolitan Museum of Art, the High Museum in Atlanta and others, the indictment said. But Yeats told his customers that Farnham created designs for private customers as well, selling his copies as Farnham's originals. Because Farnham left Tiffany & Co. in 1908, when he was just forty-eight years old, the claim that he continued to create one of a kind jewelry for many years thereafter was certainly plausible. People who should have known better believed it.

Yeats had sold a pin consisting of a cluster of white tigers to a famous illusionist. It was made of diamonds in several colors. The diamonds were later determined to have been treated with radiation, and so were less valuable than the illusionist believed. On other pieces, Yeats was alleged to have inflated the weight and value of the stones, charging his customers several times the market price for such jewelry.

A particularly unbelievable allegation concerned a 40-karat cubic zirconium that cost less than two hundred dollars. The stone was given a celebrity name and sold by Yeats for over a million dollars. As authentic looking as these manufactured stones have become, it was still hard to believe someone would part with a million dollars without a valid appraisal. Human folly among the wealthy was more rampant than I'd realized.

In all, the indictment claimed that Yeats had fleeced customers for a total of more than $170 million. Punitive damages and recoverable attorney fees would also have been available in civil actions based on each individual fraud. If convicted in the criminal case, Yeats faced up to 165 years in prison in addition to a potential order to make restitution. No doubt about it, if Yeats was convicted, his pampered lifestyle would be over. Prison would not be kind to anyone used to the finer things, to put it mildly.

If Yeats could make restitution, the criminal case might be pled down to lesser charges or dismissed altogether. The complainants might be persuaded to go away quietly if they got their money back. The negative and outraged responses I'd gotten from Yeats's insurance adjuster to my suggestion that the insurance company pay to settle the Fitzgerald House case, suggested that Yeats would not have any better luck getting money for the claims in the criminal case. Where would the money come from?

So Yeats must be desperate to find enough money to settle these claims. Where would he get $170 million? Tampa isn't Palm Beach. That kind of money would be hard to come by here.

The assistant U.S. attorney assigned to the *U.S. v. Yeats* criminal case was someone I'd known for years, and always considered an astute lawyer. Briefly, I considered picking up the phone and dialing his office, but decided against it.

Judges are not supposed to seek or obtain information about cases on our dockets except through the litigation process. Because this was a criminal case and would be tried to a jury, I would have a little more leeway than if I was to sit in the trial as the finder of fact. I considered how to discover what the federal "fraud squad" had learned about Armstrong Yeats. The only way I would feel comfortable investigating now was if I transferred the case to another judge, or if both of the parties consented. That was about as likely as rain in the desert.

I could think of no appropriate way to learn more about Yeats and I was out of time to think about it further. The *U. S. v. Yeats* case was up for a pre-trial conference in two weeks and I'd learn more about it then. But now, both my law clerks stood in my doorway with lists of questions, the computer flashed to tell me I had mail, all four buttons of my telephone were lit up with phone calls holding for my attention and Margaret reminded me of my afternoon calendar. My "to do today, first thing" list was buried under a mountain of paper. I didn't give Ron Wheaton's computer check another thought.

The rest of the week passed swiftly and uneventfully. Fitzgerald House requested a short adjournment of the trial, which I granted, giving them time to resolve the case. I'd been required to make some pretrial rulings that would give certain advantages to Fitzgerald House. Perhaps Yeats and his insurance company would agree to settle the case.

I called Ben Hathaway several times, but he wasn't available to speak to me. Apparently, the Tampa police chief had a few things on his "to do" list, too. I was grateful that he hadn't called back because no news meant he didn't have the results of Ron Wheaton's autopsy. I allowed myself to be lulled into complacency on the investigation, thinking there was nothing to investigate.

I tried to talk to Margaret several times, but she remained uninterested in my help. She seemed to be dealing with Ron's death just fine, and I even heard her singing in the office several times. Margaret looked better, younger and happier than I'd seen her in months. I knew she was a bereaved widow, but someone who didn't know her history would never have guessed that she'd just lost her husband. Margaret didn't even plan a memorial service. She said she was the only family Ron had, and she didn't need a memorial to remember him. I feel the same way about funerals. The point of them is to provide closure for the living, I'm told. They do nothing for me but make me sad. I didn't find Margaret's decision bizarre.

Margaret took a couple of days off at the end of the week, citing the need to resolve some problems with Ron's finances and life insurance. I didn't wholly believe her, but I felt she was giving me a clear message to stay out of her life, so I allowed myself to be deterred and occupied by a couple of applications for emergency temporary restraining orders and my other cases.

Dad's investigation was moving relentlessly forward. He'd left a note on the refrigerator door before I got up Wednesday morning saying he'd found a paper trail taking him to Miami to investigate the bank and would be out of town. Thankfully, he'd taken Suzanne with him. He was due back Saturday and I looked forward to hearing about his progress. It gave us something to talk about besides the baby, Suzanne and my hurt feelings.

Dad and Suzanne offered to get a hotel room at the Marriott Waterside when they returned on Friday. Both George and I prevailed to keep them at Minaret, if for no other reason than to avoid the awkward explanations the move would require. After being around her for several days, Suzanne continued to make me uncomfortable. Every time I saw her, Suzanne and Dad's obvious affection affected me like fingernails on a chalk board. I was probably acting like the spoiled child I must have been once, but it was going to take me a while to get used to the idea of Dad having a wife and a baby. It would have been a little easier to deal with if Suzanne wasn't so good-natured, obviously in love with Dad, kind to everyone and just generally so damn likeable.

My soul mother, Kate Austin, had gone on an extended vacation to Italy before Gasparilla started. She was the only person who could give me some objectivity on this thing with Dad since she had been there since he and Mom married. Without Kate to discuss everything with, I was adrift in emotions that likely had no basis in reality. Dad had known Kate would be in Italy this month, which made me wonder whether he'd chosen to bring Suzanne to Tampa now so that he wouldn't have to deal with Kate and me at the same time. I couldn't imagine that Kate Austin, who had been my mother's best friend, would approve of Dad's marriage any more than I did. I tried to call Kate in Italy a couple of times, but she was always out of her room. I'd left messages, but she hadn't called back.

George was certainly no help. He kept telling me that Suzanne was Dad's choice and I would do well to accept her, unless I wanted to alienate Dad further. Men can be so obtuse sometimes. Of course, I knew that. But knowing and doing are two different things. I would come to terms with Suzanne in my own way, but the marriage was still too new, too much of a shock, to resolve itself so neatly in a few days after almost twenty-five years of the status quo.

George removed the restaurant's money from Gil Kelley's bank and redeposited it elsewhere after hearing Marilee's story about Gil's youthful and distasteful indiscretions. Sandra Kelley's allegations about Senior, which George had heard from a couple of other sources, caused further disquiet. George didn't believe Senior had embezzled from the bank, but he felt it was better to be safe than sorry. Besides that, if Marilee's stories were true, which George didn't wholly believe because they came from Marilee, he didn't want to be associated with Gil Kelley anyway.

Between my personal life and my work, I had little time for Margaret. And that was before Friday, when, for the first time in my life, I got served with a subpoena. I was commanded to testify before a panel appointed by the Judicial Counsel, who seemed to investigate judges at the drop of a gavel in Tampa these days. We'd had several of our state court judges resign under pressure from The Florida Bar's Judicial Qualifications Commission. We all knew the JQC was investigating alleged improprieties by other judges. Ranging from allegations of gambling using county computers, to sexual misconduct with subordinates and case fixing, the investigations were alarming. But the state JQC investigations hadn't reached the federal judiciary. Until now.

The process server came into my chambers respectfully enough. He asked me my name and handed me the folded subpoena in an envelope. As he left, I removed the subpoena and began to read it. I was being called to testify in the matter of a confidential investigation into allegations of misconduct by one of our federal judges. The judge remained unidentified, since the investigation was confidential until charges, if any, were filed. But whoever had put the subpoena in the envelope had enclosed a copy of an article from the *Tribune* reporting the story of sexual harassment allegations by two female magistrate judges against "an unnamed federal judge." Someone had penciled the letters "CJ" in the margin.

According to the newspaper account, the "unnamed judge" had made "unwanted passes" at the magistrate judges, left suggestive messages on their answering machines and asked them out on dates. In writing, yet. All the women judges were being subpoenaed to testify. If more instances of harassment were found, the investigation would be spread to other women in the courthouse, including law clerks and support staff.

The old geezer! Who'd have thought he had it in him? Truly, I didn't. I wasn't fond of the CJ, and I was surely annoyed at his refusal to move me to the new courthouse, but I knew his wife. I didn't think he'd dare look for a date at work or anywhere else. Men are often falsely accused of sexual harassment and it's a hard claim to defend. The CJ struck me as dumb enough to leave messages to women which could be traced, but smarter than to try to date women he worked with. Besides, I knew both of these magistrate judges. While they were somewhat strident and opinionated, I didn't believe they would falsely accuse the CJ. Among other things, they did not have the luxury I had of a lifetime appointment. They liked their jobs. If, as the paper said, they were complaining, it was because they had something to complain about.

What was it with men and sex, anyway? Did the recent impeachment of a United States President teach them nothing? I was figuratively shaking my head over this development while remaining sure that there was more to this story than met the eye. The CJ had a number of detractors and he was unpopular with the junior jurists. I figured there was a hidden motive in this story that I'd have to wait to learn.

Part of me just rebelled against everything. I felt both exhaustion and an overwhelming need for solitude. I was tired of the "George Knows Best" show, Dad's mid-life crisis, Suzanne's sweet disposition, constant smile, extended fashion show and incessant twittering, and most of all, tired of worrying more about Margaret than she was worrying about herself. I was even tired of Kate's absence. If I wasn't running ten miles a day, I would probably have strangled someone that week. It was a good thing that Margaret didn't need my help and compassion, I thought on my drive home Friday night along the Bayshore toward Plant Key. Help and compassion were in short supply with me right now and they didn't seem to be on the immediate horizon, either.

Such was my mind set as I drove across the Plant Key bridge in the dark at 6:30 Friday night, with a full briefcase, a head full of troubles, and a heavy spirit in need of care. The tranquil vista of Hillsborough

Bay was obscured by February's early nightfall, the avenue of palms was dark as pitch and Minaret blocked the lighted downtown Tampa skyline from my view.

Our house, Minaret, is a grand old building. It was built in the 1890's when Tampa's richest citizen, Henry Plant, wanted a family home. Plant was constructing the Plant Hotel, now the University of Tampa, which he believed would be a Mecca for the rich and famous. When they came to the hotel, he wanted to show off a fabulous home as well. He wasn't going to be outdone by his rival, Henry Flagler, who had created such a magnificent hotel in Palm Beach.

Before he could build his house, Plant had to build Plant Key itself. When the Port of Tampa channels were being dredged to allow passage of freighters, Plant persuaded the Army Corps of Engineers to build up enough land mass for Plant Key at the same time.

Plant made his island oval shaped with the narrow ends facing south toward Bayshore and out into the Gulf. It's about a mile wide by two miles long. Plant also built (you guessed it) Plant Key Bridge which connected Plant Key to Bayshore Boulevard, just east of Gandy. Marine life ecosystems weren't a priority then. If you had an island, you had to have a way to get there, didn't you?

I pulled under the portico and let the valet park Greta, my Mercedes CLK convertible, and grabbed my briefcase out of the trunk. I prepared to trudge up the front stairs to our flat with all the enthusiasm of Marie Antoinette on her way to the guillotine. So lost was I in my own thoughts that I ran right into the broad back of Chief Ben Hathaway, standing in the doorway, waiting for a larger party in front of him to be seated.

Ben turned around saying, "Hold on a minute, there, partner—Oh, Willa, it's you."

"Sorry, Ben. Didn't see your tail lights. What seems to be the hold up?"

"I don't know. Looks like round two of the drunken revelers you had here last Saturday to me." I looked through into Aunt Minnie's tastefully decorated foyer.

When Aunt Minnie lived here, the house was a private home and these were her secretaries, breakfronts and sideboards. Even the small butler's table between the upholstered camel-back sofas in the center were Aunt Minnie's pieces, and they were filled to capacity with small children climbing over the arms and the graceful backs. The soft blue fleur de lis wallpaper had been restored to match its former gilded excellence. Even using modern materials, the wallpaper wouldn't hold up long after we scrubbed off the sticky paw prints prevalent about three feet off the floor.

Would Aunt Minnie be pleased to have her beautiful things returned to usefulness or horrified that strangers came into her home for lunch and dinner seven days a week? I felt sure she'd be horrified at the disrespect those unruly, excited children were showing for her furnishings tonight.

"Good Grief!" I said, turning on my heel. I left Hathaway there waiting for a table, retraced my steps back down the stairs and around to the back entrance. I'd forgotten that Minaret Krewe would be here in force for the pre-event party to celebrate tomorrow's Knights of Sant' Yago Illuminated Knight Parade in Ybor City. The grounds were quickly filling up with cars and guests. I put my head down, watched my path, and carefully made my way around the house in the semi-darkness.

I heard them before I saw their shadows. Two men, close together, speaking softly. I couldn't see them clearly. They were too engrossed in their conversation to notice my approach. I recognized the CJ's voice, raised in stage-whisper anger. "Damn you, anyway. Why the hell did you have to come here? And why now? I already told you I don't have any more money." CJ shoved the smaller man roughly. He whispered something I couldn't hear before he pushed back. I was uncomfortable standing there, silently stopping in my tracks, inadvertently eavesdropping. I couldn't hear the smaller man. Whatever he said angered CJ further because CJ gave him a push hard enough to challenge his balance.

"Forget it!" CJ said. "Just forget it! It won't happen! Go crawl back into the hole you came from and leave me alone!"

The smaller man righted himself, said something further, walked around out of my sight and behind a parked van. CJ stood there a little longer, raking his hand through his hair and muttering curses loud enough for me to hear. Then he turned and saw me standing, watching. Not knowing what to do, I simply continued to walk toward the back of the house. As I passed CJ standing in the shadows, I said, "Good evening. Anything I can help you with?"

"No, thank you," he said. I'm not sure whether he realized I recognized him or not. I kept my head down. CJ didn't stop as he walked past me, but he was close. I could feel his heavy breathing and the anger that blew off him like radiating heat from an out-of-control bonfire. I marched directly up the back stairs and into the flat without another word, but I was trembling so hard it took me three tries to unlock the door.

Inside, our Labradors, Harry and Bess, were laying by the door waiting for anyone who happened to come in so that they could immediately lick them to death. Bess is black and Harry is yellow. Like their namesakes, Harry and Bess Truman, they're fiercely independent dogs, thoroughly devoted to one another. We got them originally for protection and guard dogs because so many strangers come into what is, after all, our home. Of course, anyone who spends five seconds with Harry and Bess realizes what useless guard dogs they are. They do have big barks and that counts for something, at least to strangers. We still pay the alarm company every month, just in case.

Both Harry and Bess were wild to get out. I went over and let them out the back door. If they found the CJ and scared him off the property, so much the better.

"What was that all about, I wonder?" I said to no one as I sat heavily onto the couch to gain a little self-control. I'd recognized Armstrong Yeats as soon as I'd seen him standing there. It was the second time the CJ's connection to Yeats had been thrown in my path. I worried that their connection to each other somehow related to Margaret, and I didn't know what to do. I would have gone downstairs and found Chief Hathaway, but I didn't want to give him any more reason to upset Margaret. At least, that's what I think my motivation was.

George would be working until well into the night. I was beginning to feel like a prisoner in my own home and I couldn't wait for Gasparilla month to be over so that I could get some of my life back. I decided to eat scrambled eggs in the kitchen rather than face the crowd downstairs again. George wouldn't even notice I was missing. Tomorrow night would be another long one as we kept the restaurant open until the wee hours of the morning for folks going to the Knight Parade. I felt entitled to a quiet dinner before the onslaught.

Dressed in yellow pull-on knit slacks and a matching sweatshirt with brightly colored fish on the front, I sat at the dining room table and ate my infamous "Eggs a'la Willa." I'm not sure exactly what I put in the eggs. It's never the same thing, but just whatever we happen to have that isn't growing mold. This time, the final result was heavenly, and I don't even like eggs. Pumpernickel toast and hot tea completed the meal, which I thought was fine enough to support a great French chardonnay. Not that it matters what I eat with a great French chardonnay. I intended to think about Margaret, Yeats, the CJ and Ron Wheaton. I meant to figure out what the connection was between them and why I felt so uneasy about it all. But by the time I finished my eggs and wine, I could hardly keep my eyes open and called it a night.

I slept fitfully and my dreams that night were vivid snapshots of one disjointed scene after another. Ron Wheaton was walking around Minaret, kicking up his heels every now and then, square dancing at the

Minaret Krewe Gasparilla Ball with Sandra Kelley as the Queen, wearing a sparkling tiara, diamonds dripping around her neck. Gil Kelley with his King's crown, leering after my step-mother, who sported the swollen belly of her near-term pregnancy, giving her lanky frame the look of a pencil carrying a basket ball. Dr. Marilee Aymes in my courtroom arguing that Sandra Kelley should be executed for embezzling from her husband's bank. And, just to be sure I recognized these as nightmares, the CJ in a cartoon version of prison garb, peering at me from behind the bars of our holding cell in the old federal courthouse.

When I sat bolt upright in bed, my heart pounding wildly, I was grateful for whatever awakened me, although it took me a few seconds to figure out what it was. I thought I heard the cannons on the Jose Gasparilla firing off just as they had on the day of the Pirate Parade, when Ron Wheaton had died and Chief Hathaway suggested Margaret could have been a mercy killer. Once I came fully awake, I realized it was still dark out and the cannons wouldn't sound again until next year's parade. So what woke me up? George was snoring gently in the bed beside me, exhausted from the party tonight, for which I had never made it downstairs. Both dogs were sleeping peacefully, too. Why did I wake up? And then I remembered the final snapshot in my dream. Margaret Wheaton gleefully injecting her wheelchair-bound husband with a lethal dose of morphine.

Chapter *Seven*

My Saturday began early, since I couldn't get back to sleep after my last nightmare. If a real noise awakened me, I never learned what it was. Otherwise, it must have been an over-active imagination, or messages from my subconscious, or something. In any event, when I woke up at four o'clock, it was pitch black out and cold in our flat. I wrapped myself in the warm terrycloth bathrobe that George had bought me for Christmas from the Don CeSar hotel. The robe was pink, like everything else associated with the hotel, and had an emerald green crest on the pocket. I snuggled my feet into the matching lamb's-wool lined slippers and headed to the kitchen.

Temperatures were still well below normal for February. Our nineteenth century home was long on charm, but drafty and short on heat. When we renovated the house, we did the best we could with insulation. But the old clapboard siding had cracks in some places that gave old man winter free passage.

Both dogs and George were sleeping soundly and the rest of the flat was quiet. I went into the kitchen and started my tea ritual, the one I use when I want to calm my nerves. I'd picked up my journal on the way through the den, too.

I'd started journaling recently at Kate's suggestion. She gave me a black spiral-bound journal with Andy Melon's words on the front, "When your heart speaks, take good notes." I was resistant to it at first, but now I found writing in the journal to be a comfort. Kate, who is more than a little metaphysical, feels strongly that keeping a journal is a way to reach your inner guidance, whatever that is. I just feel it helps me to organize my chaotic thoughts.

I still didn't believe Ron Wheaton had been murdered, Chief Hathaway's suspicions, Dr. Aymes's suggestions and my over-active dreams notwithstanding. But I'd found during a spot of trouble George had been in recently that it helped me to figure things out if I wrote them down.

After the kettle heated, I poured the hot water over chamomile tea in my mother's Royal Albert tea pot and covered it with the rose tea cozy she'd loved. This ritual with Mom's tea things comforts me somehow. While waiting for the tea to steep, I carried everything in on a tray to my favorite chair and ottoman in the den, where I lit a small fire in the fireplace. The last piece of the ritual is to select one of the animals from my Herrend zoo to share my contemplation.

I studied the animals inside the curio on the wall in the living room. The zoo had been Aunt Minnie's. I think she had a Hungarian admirer at one time. He gave her a beautiful set of Queen Victoria china and the whimsical porcelain figurines painted in the technically difficult fishnet pattern. Judging from the many animals in her zoo, the relationship must have lasted for a while. Aunt Minnie gave all the animals Hungarian names that she left in the inventory we received when George inherited the house.

To the extent Aunt Minnie's ghost or spirit still lives with us, she must be pleased that I admire her zoo and George is adding to her collection. Whenever a particularly special opportunity arises, George orders an unusual piece from Hungary to give me. The animals are now available here in the states, but all of Aunt Minnie's pieces, and mine, were specially made for us.

Tonight, I chose Szabo, Aunt Minnie's blue cat, stretched out and laying down, looking as if she was as content with life as a cat could possibly be. I settled in with her, hoping she'd pass some of that tranquility on to me, picked up my journal and began to write down everything I knew about Ron and Margaret Wheaton. I found I needed to shorten my musings because I'd known Margaret for ten years and I knew a lot about her.

For instance, I knew she was an only child, like me. That made us feel closer to one another. I'm technically an orphan, I guess, since both my natural parents are dead. But I don't feel like an orphan. James Harper adopted me when he married my mother. I was five years old and he is the only father I'd ever known. Kate Austin was my mother's best friend and has been my soul mother since I was sixteen, the year Mom was diagnosed with the breast cancer that eventually killed her.

But Margaret felt like the orphan she was. Both of her parents had died when she was young. She didn't marry Ron Wheaton until she was twenty-five. Ron had adored Margaret. That much was obvious to anyone who ever saw them together. Although she was grateful for Ron and felt affection for him, when she married, Margaret's heart had belonged to another. She'd never told me much about him, but once, when another friend had been having marital problems, Margaret said, "Not everyone has the storybook marriage you have, Willa. Some of us can't have our one true love. We've had to make the best of what we've been offered."

It's one of life's ironies that everyone always assumes my life is so perfect. People feel free to accuse me of being beautiful, rich and, most dismissively, *lucky*, as if such luck was a personal affront to the speaker. Margaret had done so that day, telling me that my life was blessed in a way few lives are, that I should be grateful. What she didn't say, but I heard, was "more humble."

The truth is that I feel attractive enough, most days, although I'm far from beautiful. We live comfortably, but George and I both have full time jobs, and not just because we want to contribute to the world, except in the sense that we have to pay cash for groceries, like everyone else. I am lucky, though not in the way people accuse me of.

The most significant thing that's ever happened to me was that my mother died of cancer. While she was ill, we spent as much time together as we could: I wanted to savor every moment of the life she had left. Mom wanted me to go to school and the truant officers insisted that I go at least half a day. But the last few months of her life, they let me stay home.

That was such a glorious time. She taught me how to make bread, arrange flowers, put on a dinner party. She told me all of the secrets a mother imparts to a daughter about dating and dealing with men.

Mom and I had our own little world then. Dad was traveling, as he always had, even at what was clearly the end of his wife's life. On some level, I never forgave him for that. But on another level I was glad for the time it gave mother and me to be together. Maybe that was his present to both of us.

It was while Mom was sick that she told me she'd wanted to be a lawyer instead of a nurse. And I promised her that I would do what she had not done. Eventually, Mom died and her husband never came home. I was sent to live with Kate, graduated from high school and then went directly to the University of Michigan.

What doesn't kill you makes you stronger. I know now that I was lucky to have loved my mother for 16 years, and to have had her unconditional love while she lived. She sent me into the world with that, the love, desire and support necessary to make something of my life. Every time I think of her, I think, "I could be better," not just as a lawyer, or a woman, but as a person. She believed that what's important is how you live your life, how you treat others. She taught me always to do my best and to help those who need it. It was a hard lesson to learn at 16, but I learned it, and it sustains me. It also gets me into trouble. Mighty Mouse does save the day, but it's not easy.

Of course, I am grateful for my life. But anyone who really knows me understands that things are not always what they seem. And that was the remark I'd snapped at Margaret at the time, causing her to stop talking. I cursed my impatience now, because I missed the opportunity to learn more about Margaret Wheaton's relationship with her husband, why she married him and what had happened to the love of Margaret's life.

Ron Wheaton was a janitor and later, maintenance supervisor, for Hillsborough County Schools. He was a big man, capable and well liked, from all accounts. He and Margaret didn't travel in our social circles for the most part, but when we did see them at events or around town, Ron was always pleasant to me. We invited Ron and Margaret to Minaret on the day of the Parade of Pirates, just as we invited almost everyone we know. Before he was diagnosed with ALS, both were active members of Minaret Krewe. They would come to the parties every year and celebrate until the wee hours. Ron was a party person, even then, and so was Margaret.

After his diagnosis, Ron deteriorated fairly slowly for an ALS patient, but it was just too much of a struggle for them to socialize as they once had done. Indeed, I was surprised when they showed up for the Minaret Krewe party last week.

Ron's condition had gotten much worse than Margaret had led me to believe. He was mostly confined to his motorized wheelchair which he could still maneuver himself but couldn't get out of without help. They had twenty-four hour care at home, where Ron slept in the guest room in a hospital bed most days. I'd been pleased they had come because Ron wouldn't allow visitors to the house. He hated people to see him so debilitated, unable to care for himself and dependent on Margaret.

I refilled my teacup, poked the fire and gazed at Szabo's peaceful countenance, imagining I could hear the ceramic cat purr. Returning to my journal, I recorded all the curious behavior I'd witnessed this week, from Margaret, the CJ, Gil and Sandra Kelley, Marilee Aymes, and

Armstrong Yeats. Was there a connection between them all? And, if so, what was it? Did it have anything to do with Ron Wheaton's death? Or to Yeats's legal problems? As I wrote these questions down in my journal, I felt better.

Asking better questions is the first step to solving problems of all kinds. I knew the answers would be revealed to me in due time. Thinking about everyone else left me free to ignore the issues I was facing with Dad and Suzanne, too, although I knew I'd have to do something about that soon.

The chamomile tea wasn't making me sleepy, and I'd written about all I knew of Ron and Margaret Wheaton. The sky was slowly beginning to lighten in the east. I made a list of all I had to do today. Yet another celebration this evening was scheduled here before and after the Knights of Sant' Yago Illuminated Knight Parade in Ybor City. Whatever it was that caused George to think having a Krewe named after Minaret and sponsoring them every year would be a good idea, I can't imagine. Yes, the Krewe did a lot of good works for the community and George was always wanting to "give something back," but really--we could just have written a check or something.

Which made me smile. After all, I was the one training for the 15K Gasparilla Distance Classic next weekend just to raise money for Young Mothers' Second Chance. A small light dawned in my head--that was another thing I knew about Margaret Wheaton. She sits on the board at Young Mothers' Second Chance. She told me once that these women and their babies were her own children and grandchildren, since she and Ron had never been blessed with a child themselves. I reopened my journal and wrote that down, too, where I'd previously written in "Children—none."

I closed my journal, and as I set it aside it fell to the floor. When I bent down to pick it up, I found the article from the *Tribune* George had brought to my attention last Saturday. I picked it up and returned it to my journal, promising myself I'd read it after my run. I returned Szabo the cat to her place with the rest of my zoo, the tea things and my journal to the kitchen table, and began the day.

I dressed in a long-sleeved tee-shirt and long cotton pants, pulled out my light-weight gloves and a headband to cover my ears, and left George snoring while the dogs and I crept down the back stairs. It was too cold to throw sticks into the water for them today, so we started to run. Within seconds they were so far ahead of me that I could barely see them in the gloaming. They wouldn't leave the island, though, so I wasn't worried. It was peaceful to run in the pre-dawn without the dogs trying to lope around me every step of the way.

I did my two laps around Plant Key, then let all three of us back upstairs, heading directly for the shower while Harry and Bess had their breakfast. I could hear voices in the kitchen and noticed George was out of bed as I walked through the bedroom and our dressing room to the shower.

I missed my weekly golf game during Gasparilla month. Usually, I spend every Saturday morning at Great Oaks Country Club, playing golf with my former law partner and whoever else we could get to make up a foursome. With every Saturday taken by one festivity or another, golf was impossible. Yet another reason to look forward to March, I thought, smelling the ginseng shower gel that promised to deliver energy today.

When I toweled off and dressed in black jeans, topsiders, lime green socks and a matching lime green sweatshirt, I spent about two minutes with the blow dryer, which is all it takes to dry my short auburn hair. I applied light makeup and quite a bit of concealer over the dark circles under my eyes, shrugged and faced the day.

By the time I made it to the kitchen, George was alone, reading the paper and drinking coffee in his white pajamas and the royal blue silk robe he favors. I smiled as I noticed the blue silk scuffs on his feet, too. How many men dress like that these days? Damn few, I figured, given the casual look that has become so popular with the Generation Xers.

I'm an old-fashioned girl. Give me Cary Grant in his silks anytime over those rugged Xers with their hip hugging pants, tight shirts and scratchy, unshaven faces.

"Morning, darling," he said, eyeing my journal on the corner of the kitchen table and the left-over tea things. "Manage to run your cares away?" George knows me too well.

"Not all of them," I told him as I made my café con leche and Cuban toast. Usually I don't eat breakfast, but I'd been up so long this was practically lunch time. "Where is everyone?"

"We should talk about Jim and Suzanne, you know. It's not the kind of thing that's going to go away by itself. In fact, I'd say we're soon going to have even more to think about," George told me gently.

"Like what?" I was still fooling around with the toast. It takes longer to toast half a loaf of Cuban bread than you might think, even if you don't put the cheese on it, which is the way I eat it.

"Jim told me they want to have several children. This isn't going to be the only one. You'll have a much bigger family than you expected. It's something you're going to have to deal with."

This wasn't altogether surprising, really. Suzanne is young and she told me she loves children. I expected her to want more of them, at least in the abstract. These things have a way of working themselves out once the reality of three a.m. feedings sinks in.

"I know," I told him.

"Then why are you so resistant to the whole thing? I'd think Jim's happiness would be important to you. Isn't it time for you to show him what you're made of?"

"Funny. I thought I was." I took the toast from the oven and added the cheese, returning it to the broiler.

"Meaning what, exactly?"

"Jim Harper wasn't much of a father to me. He thought of me as 'in the way' when Mom was alive and he wanted her all to himself. And he just left me alone for years after Mom died. If it hadn't been for Kate and her family, I'd have had nothing resembling a normal life." I put the cheese toast on the plate and sat across from him at the table.

"All of that was years ago, Willa. People often attempt to repeat their lives and improve on the job they did the first time around. You have the ability to be a hero, here. To show Jim, Suzanne and everyone else that you're a bigger person than most. To live up to everyone's expectations of you. Including your own." George was attempting his personal brand of gentle persuasion. What he meant was I had a chance to live up to his standards. To George, it was always of utmost importance to do the right thing, the honorable thing; to go one's own way; "to thine own self be true" and all that. George thinks the only one we have to please is ourselves, and that we should have exacting standards for our own behavior. This, of course, leads to constant disappointment when others don't behave as well. Such as one's wife when her father marries a woman half his age and begins to act like the father he never was.

I said nothing as I ate my toast and reached for the front page of the *Tribune*. After a few moments of silence, George got up, put his dishes in the sink, and kissed my head as he walked by to get dressed for the very long day we had ahead of us.

A short while later, the telephone rang twice and I got up to answer it. "Is that son-of-a-bitch Jim Harper there?" A woman's voice. One I recognized.

"Hello? Sandra? It's Willa Carson. Dad's not here right now. Can I help you?" I thought I heard growling from Sandra Kelley in response.

"Yes, you can help me. Did you know your father was in Miami snooping around Gil's bank this week?"

"Not really, I . . ."

"You can tell him that we don't appreciate him suggesting Senior was a thief. Gil is damned upset about it, and so am I. You can tell him that for me." She was breathing heavily as she spoke to me in loud, angry tones.

"I'm sorry. I don't know anything about this, Sandra, but I'm sure you both are upset. I'd heard that you were suggesting Senior had embezzled money from his bank, though. Didn't you expect people to take you seriously about it?"

"You just tell Jim Harper to keep his nose out of our business or he'll have someone else to answer to!" she actually shouted at me. Just before she slammed down the phone.

I looked at the receiver and then replaced it as George came back. "She hung up on me," I said.

"I figured that. If I was an eavesdropper, I could have heard the entire conversation from the other room," he said. "Actually, I did hear every word she said. You can't have thought she'd take it well--Jim going into her husband's bank and asking questions about thefts by Senior Kelley."

I frowned at him. It was okay for me to be upset with Jim, but I didn't like Sandra Kelley's tone. I'd always thought she was more than a little unstable.

"Do you have any idea what your Dad's been doing in Miami?" George asked.

"He didn't really tell me. He mentioned last week that he was doing a bank investigation. I didn't realize he meant Tampa Bay Bank."

Chapter *Eight*

I had a few hours before the hordes descended on George's restaurant again today, so I decided to take a trip to Pass-a-Grille and see The Armstrong Yeats Studio for myself. Driving over the bridge from Plant Key to Bayshore Boulevard, I turned left and then right onto Gandy, headed due west. As I drove, I assured myself the visit was not unethical.

Yeats had invited me to come over. I didn't intend to speak to him. And I wasn't sitting in a bench trial, I rationalized. Nor did I intend to rely on what I learned to make a decision in any case. Besides that, based on what I'd read in the *U.S. v. Yeats* file, I was the only person in Tampa who had never seen the studio. Some people, like the CJ, would say my visit had the appearance of impropriety. But so did smoking in my office, which I sometimes did, too. Nothing I said convinced me to turn the car around.

Gandy Boulevard begins at the Bayshore, runs for about five miles as a busy commercial highway and then becomes a bridge connecting Hillsborough and Pinellas counties. Gandy Bridge is the third and southernmost bridge connecting the two counties and helping to form the Tampa Bay Metropolitan Area, as the Chamber of Commerce likes to call it. Until the advent of crass commercialism joined the counties in their search for tourist dollars, sports franchises, and business development, the two counties couldn't have been more separatist. Today, we're just one big happy family. Or so the *Business Journal* would have us believe.

In any event, I passed the beach areas where the thong-bikini clad hot dog vendors used to stop traffic--literally--until they were banned as "unhealthy." Those women had looked mighty healthy to me, but I easily believed they were a traffic hazard. The fifty-million tourists who visit us every year, stop on the entrance ramps before merging on the freeway, turn right from the left hand lane and drive the wrong way on Tampa's many one-way streets make driving a death defying experience. We don't need one more traffic problem. My opinion had absolutely nothing to do with my personal appearance in a thong-bikini. Really.

Once I reached I-275, I could put the pedal to Greta's metal and speed down to exit 4, the Pinellas Bayway. For a mere fifty-cent toll each way, this little stretch of highway connects St. Petersburg with St. Pete Beach, just north of my eventual destination. Between here and there is Eckerd College, the road to Fort DeSoto Park, and quite a few golf courses next to high-rise condominiums. All of that passes before the Intra-Coastal Waterway that separates the mainland from the barrier islands, including St. Pete Beach and Pass-a-Grille, further south.

The Bayway ends right at the doorstep to my favorite famous old hotel, the Don CeSar. The Don was built in the 1920s and, as I said, was a vacation spot favored by Scott and Zelda Fitzgerald, among other flapper era swells. During World War II, the Don served as a hospital for recuperating RAF pilots. A recent multi-million dollar renovation brightened up its pink and white birthday cake exterior.

The insurance conglomerate that was the Don's current owner created a spa and resort that welcomed guests who would visit for a few hours instead of a few weeks. A sign in the lobby said, "You don't have to stay here to play here." That philosophy had done much to return the Don's financial situation to the pink, too. We'd been invited to several weddings and parties here the last few years, and they were always beautifully done.

I turned left at the Don and drove under the second floor entry way, traveling at the staid twenty-five miles an hour required on Pass-a-Grille Way, down to Eighth Avenue and the business district. Being a Saturday in the middle of the high season, there was no hope of finding a good parking spot. I cruised up and down the short one-block street a couple of times before resigning myself to the ravenously hungry parking meters at the beach side on Gulf Way. Over staying the meter here can cost thirty dollars or more. The local paper boasted the amount of increased revenue the town collected from over parked tourists each year.

I walked back to Eighth Avenue from the Gulf side and realized that I might never have really looked at these little shops before. There weren't many of them, but the shops they had were quite nice. A hair salon with a small lending library; an upscale sportswear store; two gift shops that didn't have a single pink flamingo in the window but displayed pottery, oil and watercolor works by local artists.

On the south side of the street was the famous jeweler, Evander Preston's place. The beautifully painted Chinese red doors had a door bell on the left doorjamb and a sign beneath it listing Preston's "hours of availability."

On the north side of the street was Armstrong Yeats' Gallery. It wasn't as impressive as Preston's, but it had the same look about it. Yeats' door was painted a bright green and his doorbell had a sign listing his hours. He was open "by appointment" on Saturday from ten until two o'clock. It was eleven-thirty. I pushed the lighted nose of a Newfoundland, hearing the discreet chime of the bell inside.

A woman opened the door. "Welcome," she said, "have you been to Armstrong's before?" When I told her I hadn't, she said, "Only the jewelry is for sale. Everything else is for your viewing pleasure. Please look around and let us know if we can help you."

As I said, I'd been to Preston's shop before, so I expected Armstrong Yeats' copy to be similar. Yeats displayed an eclectic collection of autographed and personalized lithographs, hand- thrown pottery, brass sculptures and, on the walls, a few photographs of himself with celebrities.

A poster of Steve McQueen on a turquoise and white Harley Davidson inscribed, "Armie—let the good times roll, Steve," was perhaps the most valuable. But there were similar pictures of Yeats with Donald Trump, Ted Kennedy, Jimmy Buffett and other celebrities with ties to Florida.

The jewelry itself was avant guard in most respects. It was behind glass, on the walls and in jewelry cases near the discreet cash register. I wasn't too surprised to see that there were several different artists credited with designing the jewelry as well. One entire wall of jewelry was devoted to designers Yeats employed who had, at various times, won the Gasparilla Festival of the Arts' Emerging Artist Award.

When I'd been looking for about twenty minutes, the rail-thin hostess who'd greeted me returned. "Is there anything I can help you with?"

"I'm unfamiliar with Mr. Yeats' work. Can you tell me a little about it?"

She handed me a small brochure with Armstrong Yeats inscribed in gold calligraphy on a bright green cover embossed with the head of a Newfoundland, a large, black dog that closely resembles a St. Bernard. "This tells Armstrong's story and gives you some examples of his work. He's probably most well known for nurturing new talent and allowing promising young designers to create new pieces under his tutelage. Armstrong and his protegees have won many national art prizes. The piece he plans to submit to the Gasparilla Festival of the Arts is in this display."

She directed me to a glass case in the middle of the room. "This is Gasparilla Gold. Isn't it fabulous?"

The piece was even more spectacular than it had looked in the photograph Yeats showed us. It sparkled in the center of a white background. It was smaller, though, than it had looked in the photo.

"Do you think this piece will win first prize?" I asked her.

"Oh, we hope so," she gushed as she clasped her hands together as if in prayer.

I looked briefly at the brochure she'd given me. "I see Mr. Yeats is also well known for collecting and reselling 'jewels of the world.' What is that, exactly?"

"Let me show you," she said as she led me to another cabinet on the opposite wall. "Here are several examples of what you're talking about. As you can see, this is a picture of Princess Grace of Monaco, wearing a sapphire necklace. And here, below the picture, is the necklace. Here's another one; a picture of Princess Diana with a pearl ring on her pinky. The ring is right here," she pointed to it as if it wouldn't be obvious to anyone.

"This is amazing. How did Mr. Yeats acquire such wonderful pieces? Aren't they dreadfully expensive?" And, I was thinking, aren't they assets that could be attached to satisfy some of those claimants in the criminal case pending against Yeats?

She smiled her own Grace Kelly smile, a slight bending of the lips with evident amusement. "Oh, Armstrong knows absolutely everyone."

I looked at the pieces more carefully now and asked, "Does Mr. Yeats have any jewelry worn by Marilyn Monroe?"

"I'm sure he must have. He knew Joe DiMaggio quite well. I would be surprised if Joe didn't sell Armstrong some of her pieces. I could ask him for you, if you'd like to leave your card."

"Hmm," I said. "How much would something like this Princess Diana ring cost?" The question was indelicate, but this was a store, after all, where things were for sale.

She gave me the look that said, "If you have to ask, you can't afford it" and coughed a little behind her hand. "Armstrong makes all sales of his 'Jewels of the World' himself. You'd have to discuss that with him. Would you excuse me for a moment, please?"

I wandered around a while longer. There really was something to see in every nook and cranny. I started to wonder how I'd been in Tampa all this time and had never known this place was here. Or that its occupant was so well known. I don't usually think of myself as isolated, but maybe I was. Partly, it was that I don't wear jewelry that much, myself. What I do wear regularly are a few good pieces that were given to me, mostly by George. Although I find it very interesting and beautiful, my usual lifestyle doesn't have much room for elaborate jewelry. I look at the constant streams of catalogues that make it to my mailbox at the office, but otherwise, I'm woefully ignorant on the subject.

When the sales lady, or whatever her title was--curator?- –didn't come back after a while, I decided to take my brochure and leave. I couldn't stay gone from home forever. Even with a few hundred people around, George would surely notice. But this had been a nice break for me. I took advantage of it just a short while longer. I zipped my jacket, turned up the collar, and stuffed my hands into my pockets. I walked on the beach from Eighth Avenue up to about Seventeenth and back. Then, I returned to the Hurricane restaurant and went inside.

The waitress seated me on the second floor balcony overlooking the Gulf of Mexico. She took my order for a grilled grouper sandwich with lettuce and tomato, claimed to be the best in the bay. I reached into my pocket and pulled out the bright green Armstrong Yeats Gallery brochure while I awaited my lunch. The brochure was sealed with a gold crest sticker in the shape of Newfoundland, and I recalled that I'd noticed the same crest on the door of Yeats' shop. Pulling the sticker open, I then had a sort of envelope that had five flaps and a few four-by-six cards inside.

On each of the cards was an example of jewelry creations by several of Yeats' protegees, with both the designer and the pieces described on the back. The flaps of the envelope contained short comments about Yeats himself. Mostly promotion pieces about his training, awards and commitment to creative jewelry design.

The "Jewels of the World" were mentioned only in a short paragraph that said: "Armstrong is pleased to be able to offer select customers a limited number of truly special Jewels of the World owned by the most gracious women of our time. By appointment." I didn't see anywhere in the promotional material that said the jewels might be faux.

What I did see were several pieces of jewelry I recognized as belonging to a number of Tampa socialites. For instance, the diamond and black pearl drop earrings set in platinum were worn by the Queen of Ye Mystic Krewe last week during the Parade of Pirates. And the last time the CJ and his wife had been at the cancer foundation fund raiser she'd worn the large Atocha coin set in diamonds and sapphires on a platinum chain around her neck. The prices for these pieces weren't listed, but I'd bet my greatly devalued stock portfolio that they weren't cheap.

When my sandwich arrived, I put the brochure aside and spent a fairly leisurely forty-five minutes enjoying the Gulf, the sand and the sunshine. I left reluctantly, walked down the beach and back to where I'd parked Greta--only to find a neon green envelope holding a parking ticket on the windshield.

When I returned to Minaret, the members, friends and family of Minaret Krewe had already begun to fill George's again for makeup and pre-festivities revelry. It was too cold to put Greta's top down, even with the heat on. I pulled her over to the side and surreptitiously slipped the electronic key to the valet on my way through the front door. The valet would park Greta later, after he took care of the paying guests.

The makeup artists were again set up around the lobby and the perimeter of the dining rooms. Pirates and wenches in various stages of preparation wandered around, carrying drinks and unlit cigars. Some had heavy, gold-tone coins in small bags hanging from their waists, and most had the brightly colored beads they would throw to the crowds later draped around their necks like Floridian stoles.

I noticed Gil Kelley and his wife Sandra making the rounds, gleefully preparing the men and women who were brave enough to participate tonight in what the weatherman was calling one of the coldest nights of the year.

By the time the parade was in full swing, the temperatures would be down into the high thirties. These costumes were clearly meant for warmer weather and I saw some of the women, in particular, attempting to find a suitable wrap for their bare shoulders and legs.

When George and I had agreed to be in the parade tonight, I'd had no idea it would be so cold. But we couldn't demur now, so I trudged upstairs to find my costume and to hope I'd saved some long underwear from my prior life in Detroit. When we lived in Detroit, we'd have considered forty degrees in February a heat wave. I smiled to myself as I thought of the whining I was doing over a little cold snap and picked up the pace up the stairs.

A short while later, I'd donned my wig of long, red ringlets covered by a bright blue bandana, which was bound to keep me warm. Half your body heat escapes through your head, Mom used to say as we bundled up for sledding or ice skating. I was counting on that bit of folk wisdom tonight. I'd found some pink silk long underwear in the back of the dresser, and they didn't show under the flounce skirts and petticoats of my wench's costume. Short black boots completed the outfit, which I normally wear with sandals or no shoes at all. Not tonight. Inside George's restaurant, I was actually getting a little too warm.

The pre-parade preparations were in full swing when I returned to the party downstairs. I'd done my own makeup, accentuating my lips with deep red lipstick and my eyes with dark brown liner and blue shadow. I felt I looked as good as Margaret Wheaton, who'd had hers done by the professionals. Of course, I was over twenty years younger than Margaret, but she looked young enough tonight. As she stood talking with Sandra Kelley, I thought they must have been made up by the same artist. They looked enough alike to have been sisters. Armstrong

Yeats joined them and they had an animated conversation that might have been a quarrel, or could have been just the fun and spirit of the evening.

George came up behind me and put his arms around my waist while nuzzling his chin into my neck and pinching the big hoop earrings I had on against us both. "Ahoy, wench!" he sneered in his best pirate accent, which still sounded a lot like a mid-western banker. "What're you doin' later this evenin'?"

"I'm open to suggestions," I told him, laughing, as Dad joined us, a glass of something dark and foamy in his hand.

"Are you two a threat to my health and safety this evening?"

"Perhaps, sir. Perhaps we are." George told him. "You might want to return to the safety of your home."

"Exactly my plan, dread pirate. I have a big thick file to work through and I've just come in from outside. I think a good seat in front of the television is the best place for this boy tonight." He raised his glass and turned toward the Sunset Bar.

"Landlubber!" George shouted after him as we all got into the spirit of the thing.

Shortly afterward, buses were loading the costumed ones to drive down to Channelside where we'd get on the float and prepare to join the parade.

George and I stayed around to be sure his staff had everything in hand for the next phase of the celebrating, which would go on while the parade was winding through historic Ybor City and then afterwards, when the buses returned us to George's for late night snacks and coffee. Our float was about number ninety-one in the procession, so we had some time to avoid going out in the cold.

Dad wasn't the only one staying in tonight. About thirty would-be revelers had settled into the Sunset Bar with the television on to watch the parade in the comfort of seats, food, drink and most of all, warmth.

Suzanne was sitting with Dad, all cozy in a booth. I bid them goodbye and boarded the last bus.

Channelside was a fine example of Tampa development. When we moved here, the land around the cruise ship dock was nothing short of an eyesore. Filled with abandoned warehouses and flat lots holding old beer cans and trash, it wasn't a credit to the chamber of commerce. Today, the area houses the Florida Aquarium, Garrison Seaport, Channelside Shops, a movie theater, and is just a short walk from Tampa's fabulous hockey arena. The only thing Tampans could find to complain about now is the increased traffic. On the evening of the Knight Parade, that complaint was more than justified.

When we got to the float, it was already fully loaded with members of Minaret Krewe in costume and weighted down with beads, coins and candy to throw to the crowds. People were warming up and the body heat on the float made the cold more bearable. I was getting a little warm, myself, but not enough to make me want to take off my long underwear.

Making my way to my assigned station, I was surprised to see Margaret Wheaton and Armstrong Yeats on the back of the float. I waved to Margaret, but she didn't see me. She was too involved in her conversation with Armstrong, as he held her arm and no doubt regaled her with tales of his celebrity customers. I scowled at the scene. Neither Margaret nor Armstrong were Krewe members. Why were they here? And together? There was no one for me to ask.

The float, a replica of Minaret, the Krewe's namesake, had been funded and built years before, when we first founded the Krewe. The float required some sprucing up every year, but was mostly unchanged. The Minaret in the middle, a banner with the Krewe's name on the front, and the shape of a pirate ship made it fit into the overall theme of the parade. George and I took our places at the front of the float next to Gil and Sandra Kelley, this year's King and Queen.

"We seem to have some non-members on the float tonight," I leaned over and said to Sandra Kelley, who was standing on George's right.

"Really? We probably had some people cancel out because of the cold and got some volunteers. The more the merrier, right? You don't own the Krewe, Willa. George just sponsors it." The loud music someone had added to the float last year emanated from the miniature Minaret. The small tractor that would pull all of us along started up. I couldn't talk to Sandra over the noise, keep my balance, and prepare to throw away the beads and candy given to me all at the same time. The conversation would have to wait, but I definitely intended to have it. I didn't like Sandra Kelley's short temper and angry threats against Dad. Unstable or not, I didn't think she was dangerous. She just needed to understand that her behavior wouldn't be tolerated. Not by me, on my own behalf or for Dad.

Chapter *Nine*

The illuminated Sant' Yago Knight Parade has been following the Parade of Pirates for more than forty years. The group that sponsors it, the Knights of Sant' Yago, has about 275 members and claims to have roots in the ninth-century Spanish Brotherhood of the Royal Order of St. James. Like most of the clubs, or "krewes" that participate in the various Gasparilla events, the Knights use the revenue from the parade for good works. In this case, to fund renovation of historic club buildings in Ybor City, community projects and scholarships. Mostly, their aim is to promote the Latin heritage in Tampa.

The parade route has been changed several times, but this year it wound down Channelside Drive, over to Ybor City, down Seventh Avenue and terminated on the east end of town at 22nd Street. Wall-to-wall people lined the sides of the narrow streets from curb to storefronts. Most of them raised their arms and their voices as every float went by, seeking to catch whatever booty was thrown out to the spectators. The bars were open, selling beer and soft drinks out of barrels, both inside and out on the sidewalks.

By the time we got to the end of the parade route, I was hoarse from yelling to George and the others over the noise of the music and the crowd. My arms were tired from throwing beads and coins to the spectators. The long underwear I'd so happily put on at the beginning of the night had turned into a cocoon of hot skin that had me sweating like I'd just completed a marathon at the head of the pack. George had to get back to the restaurant and I was grateful to be one of the first ones off the float, onto the bus, and back at home. I thought if I didn't get a shower, I might die of heat exhaustion.

I peeled all the pirate wench garb off and threw it in a heap on the bathroom floor, hoping never to see it again. Beneath the steaming shower I began to feel a little revitalized. Once out, I managed my quick change: hair (three minutes), makeup (two minutes), clothes (three minutes). Usually I can do the clothes faster, but it took me a while to decide on the medium weight, long-sleeved pink cotton dress and jacket from Fresh Produce. I had been very warm in my costume, but it was still only about forty degrees outside.

Back in the fray, I saw that most of the revelers had returned and were making their way through the buffet line. Everyone looked a bit worse for wear. I approached George and suggested he go upstairs and change, offering to play hostess while he was gone. I was making my way around the tables of seated pirates and wenches, deliberately taking my time, and avoiding the tables where the CJ and his wife were sitting, as well as where Sandra and Gil Kelley were holding court. George could deal with them when he returned.

Dad and Suzanne were seated in the small blue room that was originally a parlor and where dining was more intimate than what was now George's main dining room, but was once the ballroom. They saw me and waved me over to join them, which I found myself curiously happy to do. Maybe that was because they had a free chair.

Dad smiled while Suzanne squeezed my hand when I sat down. They shared the details of their television viewing experience with me, telling me all about the Knight Parade as if I hadn't been one of the participants. It was actually fun to hear Suzanne's take on the whole event, so childlike was she in her enthusiasm.

When Dad excused himself to wash the bar-b-que sauce off his fingers, Suzanne took the opportunity to bend my ear about her latest shopping experience for "Elmo," the name she and Dad had humorously given to my soon-to-be sibling until its sex was determined. She described the layette, toys, wallpaper, paint and accessories until my eyes glazed over. Being Suzanne, she never noticed how little I contributed to the conversation. I almost missed it when she uttered a startled, "Oh!" and allowed a momentary lull into her stream of chatter. "There's that police chief, Willa. I don't want to talk to him again. Sit up straight so he won't see me," she said as she crouched down across the table from me.

"Why don't you want to see Ben Hathaway?"

"I just don't want to tell him the same story over and over again, that's all. He keeps asking me if I saw anybody with Ron Wheaton out on the verandah, and I didn't. I wish I had, but I didn't even know he was there. Until I found him alone and not breathing." She shuddered again, remembering the experience which had upset her so much last Saturday.

"I've been thinking about the same thing, Suzanne. I tried to remember seeing Ron with anyone else during the party, but there were so many people here, I just don't recall."

"Well, I didn't know him at all, so I wouldn't have thought anything about it, except that he was in that wheelchair and I felt bad for him. I had talked to him a little bit. He was with that nice Armstrong Yeats. And since I didn't know very many people here, I went over and talked to both of them for a while. They were discussing Mr. Wheaton's wife, and I don't know her, either. Both of them were talking about how nice she was, how kind and loving. I remember because I thought that it would be wonderful if Jimmy felt that way about me after thirty years. But that was the only time I saw Mr. Wheaton before he died." She had started her chatter again and I tuned her out. I'd seen Ron and Margaret talking with Armstrong Yeats earlier in the day, last Saturday, too. But that was earlier in the day. Surely Hathaway had been able to determine who Ron was with just before he died. I determined to find Hathaway and ask him.

When Dad returned, I left them to continue visiting with our other guests. By the time I'd made it all the way around the dining room, the crowd had started to thin out. The buses were again available for those not ready, willing or able to drive home. When I looked at my watch, it was after midnight. Feeling I'd done more than my duty today and that it had been a very long time since I got up at four o'clock this morning, I waved goodbye to George, went upstairs and fell into oblivion.

When I finally returned to the land of the living, it was late Sunday morning and the flat was empty. George was gone to parts unknown, leaving me with two sleepy dogs, an empty coffee pot and papers strewn all over the kitchen table.

Cherishing the unexpected gift of peace and quiet, I made my café con leche and settled in the den with it and the four papers we get every Sunday morning. They were a jumbled mess, so I tried to sort them out before I started reading them, not wanting to get my current events from four cities mixed up. Then, I started with the *Tribune*, although I expected all the coverage to be about the Knight Parade yesterday and the festivities before and after.

I spent the rest of the morning this way and then decided I needed some exercise, so I'd go to hit a bucket of golf balls. I'd been off the course for two weeks now and I was getting restless. When I'd dressed in light weight slacks and a sweater, I snuck down the back stairs, leaving a note for George on the kitchen table, the place we'd decided all notes would be left after a fiasco a few weeks ago.

The short drive to Great Oaks, the country club where I play golf, invigorated me as it always does. As I approached the large, plantation style club house, I realized, as I always do, how amazing it is that such a beautiful 36-hole golf course is nestled right in the center of South Tampa. Actually, it was the only place to play golf that didn't require a twenty-minute drive, so most golfers in South Tampa were members there. Fortunately for me, Great Oaks has a very liberal admissions policy: anyone who applies gets in. As a federal judge, I can't belong to any discriminatory societies, and I wouldn't anyway.

It was about two o'clock in the afternoon by this time and all the serious golfers would be off the course and back home. I went into the pro shop for a bucket of balls and asked to have my clubs brought around. In no time, I was out on the driving range, the bright Florida sunshine warming the still cool temperatures, and not a soul around. My idea of heaven on earth.

After a few stretches to warm up, I began hitting the balls, five strokes with each club through all the clubs in my bag. Soon, the repetition of the swing allowed me to trance into a deep meditative state that gave me a chance to examine my issues.

I was avoiding the obviously more important issue of Ron Wheaton's death in my home, but just now I needed to come to terms with the new family I would soon be getting. George was right that I had nothing to say about all of this and I could either choose to be closer to my new family or more estranged from it. Living half the country away didn't seem to be as much estranged from my Dad as I would be if I didn't accept Suzanne.

I believed in my heart that Suzanne wouldn't stay with Dad long. She'd get bored with his empty conversation, tired of his low-key life style, angry with his failure to emotionally connect, and leave him heartbroken one of these days. Until that happened, if I wanted to have any kind of relationship with my father, I had to accept Suzanne. Of course, after she left, there would be the problem of half-siblings to cope with, too.

Unlike some adult children in my situation, I wasn't worried about my inheritance because I never expected to get one. I'd long ago told Dad I wanted him to spend all his money, prepay the funeral and put the last five dollars toward the party he'd be at when he died a happy old man at the age of 102. I was only kidding about the "prepay the funeral" part.

George and I had done fairly well in the stock market riding the long-term bull for the past ten years. George's restaurant was profitable and I had a very decent salary from my job as a U.S. District Court judge for the rest of my lifetime, or as long as I wanted it. I knew Dad had made a provision for me in his will and that Suzanne could get him to change it, but that was a long way down the road and I truly didn't care.

It would have been easier if I hadn't finally realized that Suzanne was such a nice kid. While her nervousness had made her early conversations and behavior seem vacuous and tedious, once she began to feel more comfortable around us, I noticed the character Dad loved. Suzanne was truly likeable and everything about her now made me want to take care of her. I'd enjoyed talking with her this past week about a variety of subjects—where I could get a word in. In some ways, living in New York City had made her sophisticated beyond her years. She looked smart, well-educated and savvy because she was. I couldn't honestly say Suzanne would be bad for Jim Harper. Indeed, he was lucky to have attracted her.

What I was worried about, truly, was me. That I'd refused to face this until now was typical of my Pollyanna attitude toward most of life. I was worried about being displaced in Dad's affections by Suzanne and, worse, by his new children. His own natural children. Which I wasn't. I know this isn't particularly noble, or even novel. It certainly wasn't a mature attitude. Maybe deep emotions never are.

People call me strong and intrepid. I think they mean it as a compliment. And most of the time, I am. But the one Achilles heel I have is a deep, abiding, fear of abandonment. It's not rational. I've considered going into analysis about it, although I never have. Usually, it doesn't affect my daily life, so I can ignore it. But when it rears up and slaps me, I'm forced to pay attention.

This was one of those times. I rarely talked to Dad, saw him more rarely, and thought of him almost never. Yet, he is my Dad, with the emphasis being on the word "my." Now, he'd be her husband and their dad, too, for I had no doubt there would be at least one more after this child. That thought caused me to hit the last ball over one-hundred yards--with a pitching wedge.

It took two buckets of balls to get through all the clubs in my bag and the stuff in my psyche, but afterward, I felt stretched, limber and relaxed for the first time since Dad showed up with Suzanne. And I'd come to terms with my fears so that I could face my emotions and stare them down. At least, I could do that at the driving range where my resolve wasn't being tested. That challenge was waiting for me back at Minaret when I returned to get dressed for an evening at the performing arts center to see a revival of *Oklahoma* with George, Dad and Suzanne.

"Sandra Kelley called the house looking for you," I told Dad as we shared a glass of cheap--but not inexpensive—white wine at intermission.

"I know. She told me when she bitched me out at the Knight Parade. She said she was pretty rude to you."

"You could say that," I told him wryly. "But, if she was rude to me, she was positively offensive about you. What's going on?"

Instead of answering my question, he asked his own. "Why don't you tell me the local view of Gil Kelley?"

"You already know that Gil inherited Tampa Bay Bank from his father, who acquired it by marriage to Gil's mother. The bank was owned by the family until about 1990 when they sold off some shares. George would know more about that than I do. Gil tried to sell some of the shares to George at the time, but George didn't think it was a sound investment. I don't know who bought into it."

"I do. And I want to ask you about those other shareholders. But for now, I just want to hear about Gil Kelley."

I sipped my wine, thinking about what to tell. Most of what I knew about Gil and Sandra Kelley was second-hand information. Things I heard at George's parties, fund raisers and on the golf course. The only first hand knowledge I had about Gil came from one Saturday afternoon a few years ago when he was at Minaret waiting for George. I later learned he wanted George to buy shares in his bank, but at the time, I didn't know anything about Gil except that he was a local banker. George had been a banker in Detroit before we moved here, so I thought Gil Kelley was making a social call. Comrades in arms and all that.

Anyway, I had gone downstairs to greet him and he not only hugged and kissed me, he tried to stick his tongue down my throat. I pulled away from him and would have slapped him silly, except that George came in right at that moment and I didn't want to make an already bad situation worse. I found out later that Gil Kelley had done something like that with every woman I know. And I stayed clear of him ever after. I'd never told George why I didn't want to be alone with Gil Kelley, but George has a built in radar for quality people. He never liked Gil and we didn't discuss it. Gil and Sandra Kelley had joined Minaret Krewe, but they just never made it to our list of friends. Since I hadn't told George about my Gil Kelley encounter, I wasn't going to tell Dad about it now. So I repeated the gossip I'd heard from Marilee Aymes instead.

"Why are you so interested in Gil Kelley, Dad? It's not that he's been flirting with Suzanne so shamefully, is it?"

"Maybe," he grinned. "But that's not all. I believe Kelley has either personally embezzled several million dollars from the bank and its depositors, or he's covering up for someone else who's done it. I think it's been going on for years, and I plan to prove it."

"What evidence do you have so far?" I asked, just as the lights flickered and the chimes sounded for Oklahoma's second act.

"I'll tell you about it later. At this point, I've reached a few dead ends. I'd like your thoughts," he said.

As we were returning to the play, Larry Davis, a lawyer with one of Tampa's better law firms, approached me. "Willa, I'll need about an hour of your time tomorrow, if you can manage it. I can come over to your office," he said over the chimes calling us back to our seats.

"I've always got time for my friends, Larry, but my calendar is very full. What's up?"

"I'd rather not discuss the whole thing here, but I was Ron Wheaton's lawyer and my firm did his estate plan. He came to see me about a month ago and changed his will."

"Yes?"

"The new will names you as his executor."

I couldn't have been more surprised if he'd told me Ron had left me all his money. I knew Ron, but we weren't confidantes. Ron hadn't called or said anything to me about being the executor of his estate. "Does Margaret know?"

"I haven't told her, and I don't believe Ron did, either."

"Maybe I'd better come to see you, then. I don't want to upset Margaret until we have this figured out."

Chapter *Ten*

Monday morning came with the precision of a universe still on its axis, time moving inexorably forward, as it normally does. I have always been fascinated by the concept of time travel. Many times I've wanted to go back and change mistakes made during my course in Life 101. It would be fun to travel to other times and other cultures. I could see Mom again, know my grandparents, be present when great world events occurred. I like the theory that everything in the universe now exists in the same time zone and that's why deja vu happens--that you get a glimpse of other things going on in the space-time continuum simultaneously with your life. For me, though, time marches forward, seconds at a time, to be sure, but steadily forward, leaving me no choice but to continue along with it.

Although her husband had been dead only a week, Margaret had arrived at the office before me and there was a waiting room full of fashionably monochromatic grey-suited, grey-tied, lawyers there as well. I nodded to them all, acknowledged them with the traditional, "Counsel," and strode forward into my chambers to prepare for the long queue of pre-trial conferences scheduled today. My law clerks and the court reporter came in right behind me and we started to work. Four hours later, the last of the day's matters was being discussed between the assistant U.S. Attorney and defense counsel. The case had been transferred to my courtroom from Miami by a judge who'd said the defendant couldn't get a fair trial there. This is often a euphemism for "I've got too many cases on my docket and now I have a legitimate chance to get rid of one, so I'm going to do it." Use this ploy too many times and other judges were likely to start returning the favor.

I was zoning out when the case started, so I missed the initial statements by counsel and was more than a little shocked when I heard the assistant U.S. Attorney say a word I hadn't heard in my courtroom before today.

I held up my hand in the traditional "stop" position, palm out, and said, "Whoa, there. Come again?"

"I said, the Defendant, Mr. Aielo, was a member of a Philadelphia Mafia crime family in the 1980s, your honor. He's being charged with Federal murder and robbery there in the death of a housewife."

"Mafia?" I repeated the foreign word again. "You're kidding, right?"

"No. I'm serious as a heart attack, Judge."

"This is outrageous, Judge," the defense attorney broke in. "Mr. Aielo is a legitimate businessman. He owns six popular night clubs in Miami. Before the case was transferred here, several of his customers put up their personal property to secure a $15-million bail bond. What kind of criminal has those kinds of friends? The way our society works is that when someone comes from a rough neighborhood and turns his life around, becomes successful, they become a target. This is a vendetta by the U.S. Attorney, nothing more."

"Is this some kind of career case or something?" I asked the people's lawyer. "Because I'll tell you, Tampa is not Miami. We don't have a Mafia mind-set here. Do you think you can make a Tampa jury understand what you're talking about?"

"We haven't had Mafia running things here in more than twenty years, Judge, that's true. But there was a time when the mob flourished here. There was a lot of illegal gambling, money laundering, loansharking. Mob guys were gunned down in the streets in the 1970s.

Several high-profile cases were tried and mobsters sent to prison. There was even a Tampa mobster who was involved in the cases that resulted in the movie, *Goodfellas*." He was attempting to impress me with a side to Tampa history I hadn't known. It didn't work.

"Well, all of that was before my time. I doubt our jurors will have such long memories. Even so, why would I want to keep a case like this? Shouldn't Mr. Aielo be tried in the state where his crime was allegedly committed?"

Now, I had the chance to transfer the case to another court, and I was sorely tempted to do it. Here on the bench in the Middle District of Florida, justice is too often delayed and denied in our courtrooms by the sheer volume of the work. The CJ, who has the moral responsibility to resolve this problem, to his credit, had been working to get us more judges. But so far, we were just slugging along as best we could. One case less would be a welcome gift, but would not lower the level of the water enough to cause me to transfer the case without good reason.

"Judge, Mr. Aielo is a Floridian now. It would be a real hardship on him and his businesses to send him up to Philadelphia. And these are Federal charges. Surely the court can apply the law as well here as they can up north," the assistant U.S. Attorney argued.

"Why shouldn't I grant the State of Pennsylvania's request for a transfer, then, counsel? Surely, you have enough work to do down in Miami without this file? And," I said, turning to the well-known celebrity defense counsel, "surely you would be defending Mr. Aielo in Philadelphia as well? Mr. Aielo fled Philadelphia in what, it says here 1986? Haven't the people there waited long enough for justice?"

Both of them started to sputter at once, leading me to believe both the cases in Miami and Philadelphia had strong possibilities of success.

They argued a while longer over the various interests of the people of Miami versus the people of Philadelphia while I snuck a surreptitious glance at my watch. It was one o'clock already. How time flies when you're having fun, I thought sourly, as I took the matter under advisement, told them I'd review their briefs and issue an order shortly. Then, I shooed everyone out of my chambers and sat down behind my desk for the first time that day.

Margaret had brought me my usual working lunch of tuna salad on white with chips and a Diet Dr. Pepper. It sat invitingly on the right of my desk and today's newspapers were folded neatly on the left. Pink slips were piled in the middle, the voice mail light flashed on my phone, the message that I had e-mail waiting was in the middle of my computer and the mail was piled a foot high above the in-box. In other words, it was a typical Monday.

As I ate the sandwich, I flipped through the pink slips first. Three from the CJ. I threw those in the trash can with a small, rebellious smile. Messages from several of my colleagues on the bench about committee meetings and such. I scribbled answers to their questions on the slips and put them in a pile for Margaret to return their calls. We rarely talked to each other, my colleagues and I. Instead, our staffs called back and forth, relaying our questions and answers. We called it successful delegation. It was better than voice mail or e-mail because we didn't have to actually do it ourselves.

After that exercise, I had three pink message slips left. One from Police Chief Ben Hathaway, with a note to "please call back," and no clue as to why. One from Dad containing the same notation. And one from George that said, "Check the *Tribune*. Metro. Page three." Curious.

I took another bite of my sandwich, pulled the newspaper over toward me, started flipping through it, looking for the Metro section, as I cradled the receiver to my ear with my shoulder and waited for Dad to answer the phone. This is what they call "multi-tasking"--doing three or more things at once--and I'm a master at it. What woman isn't?

Just as I swallowed, Dad answered the phone and a small item in the Metro section, on page three, caught my eye.

LOCAL MAN FOUND DEAD AFTER PARADE

Sanitation workers cleaning up after the Knights of Sant' Yago Illuminated Knight Parade found the body of Pass-a-Grille artist Armstrong Yeats on Sixteenth Street in Ybor City early Sunday morning. Few details were available at press time, but it appears Yeats may have fallen and hit his head on a sharp piece of broken concrete. Yeats was taken to Tampa General Hospital where he was pronounced dead.

"Hello? Hello? Anyone there?" Dad was saying. I was so dumbfounded by the *Tribune* that I couldn't answer. He must have heard something, though, because he said, "Willa? Is that you? Are you alright?"

I got it together enough to answer him in a few seconds. "Uh," I said. Not brilliant, but enough to keep Dad on the line.

"Is something wrong? Willa? If you don't answer me, I'm coming right over there. I see on the caller ID where you are." He was starting to sound stern now, although it could only have been a few seconds since he picked up the phone.

"Yes, Dad. I'm here. Just a second." I took a swallow of my Diet Dr. Pepper to wet a throat suddenly too parched for speech, took a slow calming breath or two, and put the receiver back to my ear. "Okay. Sorry. I was just eating my lunch when you picked up the phone. Something must have gone down the wrong way." Not an entirely truthful explanation, but not really a lie, either. I try to make it a point never to lie, even white lies that are meant to save other's feelings. George believes lies diminish both the people who offer them and the people who accept them. It's one of the things we agree on. It's harder to tell the truth and still be tactful. Sometimes I fail the second half of the equation. But I still try not to lie, even if it gets me into trouble, which the truth often does.

"What's up?" I asked him. "You called me."

"I did?" he sounded genuinely perplexed.

"According to this pink slip here on my desk, you called at three-forty-five this afternoon," I told him, still distracted.

"Willa, it's only two-fifteen," he said, gently.

"Yes."

"How could I have called you over an hour from now?"

I was not really listening. Or looking at the pink slip, either, apparently, which clearly said this message had come in last Friday.

"Willa? Are you sure you're okay?"

"Yes. I was just reading the paper. It says that Armstrong Yeats died over the weekend. I guess I'm a little preoccupied." I was thinking about Margaret and how she would react to this news; about the Fitzgerald House case, and what would happen to it; and most of all, about the man, Armstrong Yeats, who was becoming such an interesting phenomenon to me and whose studio I had visited for the first time just two days ago.

"Really? I wonder where Gil Kelley was at the time of the murder?" Dad sounded sarcastic. He was single-minded in his pursuit of Gil Kelley. To him, if it related to Kelley, it was a worthwhile conversation. Otherwise, not. I told him I needed to make some more calls and would see him at home tonight.

Then I looked at the message slip saying Ben Hathaway had returned my call, made sure he had called today, and punched his private number. He picked up on the third ring, sounding harried and rushed, "Hathaway here."

"Willa Carson, Ben. What's up?" I asked for the second time in the last ten minutes.

"Just a second, Judge," he said, covering the receiver with his hand and talking to someone else in muffled tones. I gathered up the rest of my sandwich and tossed it in the trash, collecting my thoughts and waiting. I heard what sounded like a door closing and Ben Hathaway was back on the phone.

"Sorry about the wait, Judge. I'm in the middle of two homicide investigations here. I'd like to come by and ask Margaret Wheaton a few questions about the death of Armstrong Yeats and her husband."

"When?" I squeaked.

"Now," he said. "I'd like to hang up, get in my car, and be there in ten minutes. Is she there?"

I actually hadn't seen Margaret since I walked in this morning. "I don't really know."

"Can you check?" he asked me, with barely suppressed impatience.

I buzzed her and she answered. "Yes, she's here." I warned him, "And so am I." I didn't have much time to talk to Margaret before Hathaway arrived. She came in the room and I took a critical look at her for the first time since I'd seen her on the Minaret Krewe float Saturday night with Armstrong Yeats. The night Yeats died.

To hear Hathaway tell it, Margaret was some sort of Dr. Jack Kavorkian, the physician convicted of helping terminal patients commit suicide. Or maybe he thought she was another Lizzie Borden, killing men for her own personal reasons. No one could look the part less. Sitting in one of the ugly green client chairs in front of my desk, she appeared tranquil and relaxed, the same Margaret she always was. She'd been somewhat happier the last week or so, her face a little softer, fewer lines around her eyes. I imagined her improved mood was because she didn't have the burden of dealing with her husband's illness every day. I told her that Ben Hathaway was coming over to talk to her, but not why he was on his way. We discussed business until we heard the buzzer at the door, impatiently seeking entrance into my chambers. I got up and let him in.

Hathaway is a big man, but he moves quickly. He blew into my reception area like a wind storm and walked right past me into my chambers before I had a chance to point and say, "she went that-a-way, chief."

Perhaps he was worried that I'd sent Margaret off somewhere to avoid him. And I might have, except that I wanted to hear what she had to say as much as he did.

"Mrs. Wheaton," he nodded to her as he sat in the other ugly green client chair across from my desk, pulled out his old- fashioned notebook, the small one with the spiral on the top, and rested it on his wide thigh. I closed the door to my chambers and sat behind my desk, my hands folded in my lap, watching them both closely.

"Where were you on Saturday night between the hours of midnight and three a.m.?" was his first question, after the preliminaries. So that's when Yeats died, I thought, and made a mental note to recall where George and I had been, too.

"I was in Ybor City, on the Minaret Krewe parade float. Why?" Margaret looked a little bewildered at this question.

"The parade ended around eleven. I'm talking about after that."

"Oh. Well, I had coffee with Armstrong Yeats at Joffrey's down on Seventh Avenue, afterward. Why?"

Again, he ignored her question and asked his own. "How long were you there with Mr. Yeats?"

"I don't know. A half-hour or so, I guess. Why?" She was embarrassed to admit she was with Yeats in front of me. I'd specifically asked them both not to speak to each other, which they'd ignored and flaunted their disregard on the float Saturday night. I'd seen them together myself and done nothing. Now, I was sorry I hadn't attempted to enforce my own advice.

As before, Hathaway ignored her question and asked his own. "When was the last time you saw Mr. Yeats?"

"About eleven-thirty, I guess. Some friends came along and invited him to go to a party. I got on the last bus back to Minaret because I was tired and wanted to go home. Why?"

This was the fourth time she'd asked this same question and this time, Hathaway answered it. "Armstrong Yeats was found dead on

Eighteenth Street, near the corner of Seventh Avenue, early Sunday morning," he told her, bluntly and without much finesse, I thought. She broke down completely, sobbing and wailing. She crumpled onto the floor. Everyone in the office could hear her, which would embarrass her beyond redemption, once she regained her composure.

Ben and I tried to comfort Margaret, to get her off the floor, but she wouldn't stand. Finally, he picked her up and put her on the couch in my office, while she was still crying like I have never observed a person cry before in my life. I was too shaken to do much besides cover her with the afghan which always stayed there since she'd knitted it for me. I locked the door connecting my chambers to the courtroom and Ben and I left Margaret, crying more softly now, and went out into my reception area to be alone.

"I guess that answers that question," I told him, bitterly. He had the grace to look sheepish. "I'm shocked at you, Ben Hathaway. I never would have thought you capable of taking advantage of a woman that way."

"You knew he was dead, too, Willa," he accused softly back. He was right, of course. I could have told her about Yeats before he arrived and she would have at least been somewhat prepared. I didn't tell her because I wanted to see her reaction when Hathaway revealed the news as much as he did. Now that I'd seen it, I was grateful I wasn't there alone when she learned Yeats had died. I was also ashamed of myself. How could I have thought for one second that Margaret would hurt anyone? Based on what? Nightmares and an overwrought psyche? Unbelievable.

"Now what?" I asked him. "Surely, you don't think she killed Yeats, after that reaction? She couldn't have known."

"You don't think that was the reaction of a guilty person being found out?" he asked me, as if he believed that, which I knew he didn't.

I ignored the question. Two could play at that game. "Like I said, now what?"

"Now, I find out who did kill Armstrong Yeats. And why. And hope that his death isn't tied to Ron Wheaton's somehow."

"That's the second time you've suggested that. Do you know more about Ron's death? Was it murder?" I wasn't going to let him sneak out without at least telling me what was going on.

"We're not releasing that information, Willa. Let's just say the autopsy's back and we have good reason to suspect Ron's death wasn't by natural causes."

"What reason?"

He studied me for a minute before making his decision. "Will you keep it to yourself?" I nodded. "Ron Wheaton had three times the amount of insulin in his body than it takes to kill a man in his condition. It didn't get there by itself."

"I thought you couldn't detect insulin on autopsy. I had a case in my courtroom about that several years ago."

"That was true, once, because we believed that insulin dissipated quickly from the body. But now we know that the acidic conditions in the body at death preserve the insulin and the formation of lactic acid in the muscles after death prevents insulin breakdown. There's no question that Ron Wheaton died of insulin overdose."

"How long does it take an overdose of insulin to kill someone?" I asked him, making my mental pictures of the night Suzanne found Ron Wheaton dead on our verandah repeat themselves.

"The reaction time is from five to sixty minutes," he replied, letting me reach my own conclusions.

"Meaning someone killed him while he was a guest at George's last Saturday night?"

"Exactly," he said.

I thought about it a little while and then asked, "Where was he injected?"

"I'm not releasing all of the details at this point. Let's just say it was in a location where someone else could have done it. We'll need a list of everyone at Minaret for the party. We've already started to repeat the interviews we did that night. I'm going to want to talk to Suzanne Harper again. I'll interview you and Margaret myself, when she pulls herself together. And Willa," he said, as he turned the door knob to leave, "keep Margaret here for a while. We have a search warrant for her home that I'm about to execute. No point in upsetting her further."

I grabbed his arm and said, "Not without me present, you won't."

"Oh, really? And just why would I allow you to be there?" he was already walking through the door as I turned back to my office to get my purse and car key. I stopped to tell my clerks to look after Margaret, cancel the afternoon pre-trial conferences, and to lock up at the end of the day. Hathaway had about a fifteen-minute head start on me when I hurried out the door and hopped down the stairs, two at a time.

Chapter *Eleven*

It only took me about fifteen minutes to catch up with Hathaway. When I arrived at Margaret's home on Coachman Street, just off the Bayshore, past Bay-to-Bay, there were two police cars on the street out front and the front door was closed. I parked in the driveway, went around back and tried the door. It wasn't locked. How convenient, I rationalized. I was meant to be here. Besides, Margaret or her lawyer could be present as the police executed their warrant and, since they weren't, someone had to protect her interests.

I heard Ben Hathaway directing officers to search here and there in Margaret's modest house. It didn't take me long to find him. "What have you found so far?" I asked him.

He gave me a sour look. "Why are you here?"

"Owner's representative," I said. "May I see your warrant?" He grunted in a way that meant, "Yeah. Sure." But he handed me the warrant and didn't ask me to leave. Maybe he wanted someone to report back to Margaret. Or maybe he's just given up trying to make me do things he knows I'm not going to do. In any event, he turned back to the officers conducting the search.

I glanced at the warrant quickly and saw that they had the right to search the entire house looking for insulin, syringes "and any other evidence" that Margaret Wheaton did or had reason to administer a lethal dose of insulin or any other drug to Ronald Wheaton last Saturday.

They had started in the obvious places: the bathroom medicine cabinet, the bedroom that was still furnished as Ron's sick room, the kitchen where I had seen other medications on the counter when I came through the back door. A photographer was making still pictures of the house and another was taking video of the search. I was torn between running back out to Greta for the small disposable camera I kept in the glove compartment to take my own photographs, and staying to watch the search. I figured I could get copies of the police photos later and make my own pictures after they left, so I stayed to watch.

The officers found and bagged several syringes, but they all appeared new to me, not used. Then they found a plastic container near the sick bed labeled "sharps," which they bagged unopened. Margaret had clearly not been up to the task of dismantling the last remnants of Ron's illness. The room was tidy and clean, but still full of the accouterments of a long-term sick room. Hathaway and I watched as the officers took all of the prescription medication with Ron's name on the label and a few bottles that looked like over-the-counter medication. Margaret's medicine was left intact and there seemed to be quite a bit of it. I didn't know she took so many drugs on a regular basis. I made a mental note to ask her about it. I also noticed an officer dusting for finger prints in all of the rooms. Randomly, as if Hathaway didn't have anything in particular he was looking for, but thought he might get lucky.

Finally, after they'd done all they could, they picked up their things and left. I stopped Hathaway as he was about to walk out the front door. "What did you find?"

"Nothing much, I'd say. No 'smoking gun' at any rate. I'll have to wait until everything is analyzed to be sure."

"Let me rephrase," I said, lawyer like. "What were you expecting to find?"

Hathaway appraised me and made up his mind, again for reasons he didn't deign to share, to answer my question. He raked a weary hand through what was left of his hair, chewed more furiously on the toothpick he'd been holding between his teeth in a death grip similar to the one he unleashed on unsuspecting T-bone steaks, and said "I thought we'd find the insulin and a set of syringes to inject it with. I thought we might find some financial evidence of a motive for killing him. A journal. A letter to someone. Something like that. But we didn't."

"So what do you think? About Margaret, I mean? Do you really suspect that she killed her husband?" I didn't mention my nightmare the other night. There was no reason for me to ask him his opinions if I was going to credit my subconscious.

"Yes, that's what I think. But I'll grant you I'd have a hard time prosecuting her for it. He was going to die anyway. A long, terrible death. I've checked up on it. That ALS he had is a terrible thing. For all I know, he asked her to do it. Or maybe he did it himself. I understand he still could operate his hands somewhat before he died?" I nodded yes and he went on, "So I figured they were either in it together; he did it himself to spare her; or she did it to spare him. I'll admit to you, though, that this Armstrong Yeats thing has thrown me a curve."

"You think the two deaths are related?"

He looked at me like I was one brick short of a load. "Of course, they're related. I don't believe in coincidence. Especially when I'm investigating homicide."

"I'm sorry, Ben. But I honestly don't have any idea what you're talking about. Give me a hint."

He tilted his head to one side as if to say, "Ok, I'll humor you this time," and then told me, "Margaret Wheaton's husband and her lover are both dead within a week. Do you mean to tell me you don't think the two deaths are related?"

For the second time today, I was stunned to speechlessness. I tried to ask Ben another question, but no sound came out of my mouth. I choked on my own saliva and then coughed myself into the kitchen for a glass of water. Ben, who is an uneasy friend of mine, followed me into the kitchen to help me along. When I'd finally gotten ahold of myself again, I managed to ask him, "You think Margaret and Armstrong Yeats were lovers?"

"Willa, really. What planet do you live on? I've gotta go. Give me a call if you want to share information sometime. I figure Margaret will talk to you. Eventually. And that may be the only way we ever solve this thing." He said, as he turned around and walked out of Margaret's house.

I stayed around for a little while, convincing myself that Margaret would want my help, now that Yeats was dead and Hathaway had targeted her as his number one suspect. I'd need to get her a lawyer, soon, and I was preoccupied with thoughts about that as I walked back out to Greta for my camera.

When I returned, I took pictures of every room in Margaret's house, the medicine cabinet, all angles of the sick room, the bottles of medication on the counter, even the dishes in the kitchen sink. I didn't know what these pictures might do for me, but I'd been helped by this procedure before, so I tried it again. Sometimes, things are hiding in plain sight, but I just can't see them because I don't know what I'm looking for. I hoped that would be the case with Margaret's house because the more I tried to resolve the conflicting sides of Margaret Wheaton, the less sense all of this made to me. I locked the back door on the way out.

From my car, I called Marilee Aymes. Once again, the receptionist threatened not to let me talk to the doctor, but I insisted. She put me on hold for several minutes, which I used for thinking. I knew Margaret was diabetic, of course. We've talked about it many times. Whenever someone brought in a great desert for a party; when people send me Godiva chocolates, some of my favorite things; when she was invited out for drinks with colleagues.

Margaret was a type one, insulin dependent diabetic. Her mother had the disease, too. Margaret was very careful of her diet. Although I'd never seen her do it, I knew she injected herself three times a day, and had done so for years. She kept her daily insulin supplies in her purse. But shouldn't she have had more at home? Why weren't they there? Was it because someone had used them to kill Ron?

So Ron might have had access to the syringes and to the insulin. But could he have injected himself? And if he did, why would he kill himself at Minaret on Gasparilla? The insight, which seemed like such a lightning bolt when it had hit me while I was standing in Margaret's house, now presented as many questions as it answered. What did Ron Wheaton and Armstrong Yeats have in common? Margaret.

"Yes, Willa? What do you want? I've got an office full of patients here." Marilee finally came to the phone, bringing her usual gruff manner with her. I asked Marilee Aymes the question and she thought about it before she responded to me.

"Sure, he could have done it. His ALS wasn't that far gone."

"What would have happened to him, if he'd injected himself?"

"Depends on how much pure insulin he injected. Too much, and within minutes he would have been in a hypoglycemic coma. Not long after that, he'd have been dead. Probably about thirty minutes. Less if he hadn't eaten in a day or so. Anything else?"

"Just one more thing. Where on the body would you have to inject enough insulin to kill a man?"

"Insulin has to be injected under the skin, or it can be given in an IV. Enough to kill would leave a pretty big lump under the skin, so somewhere on the body that has the ability to take a big lump." She was impatient to hang up, and I was impatient to let her.

I was speeding now, needing to get there before Hathaway figured it out, too. I parked the car, jumped out, and ran. It didn't take me long to find it. In the azalea bushes about ten feet from where Suzanne found his body.

The killer must have thrown the syringe there after he injected Ron with pure insulin. I picked it up carefully with a plastic bag I'd grabbed out of Margaret's kitchen and brought with me for that purpose. Then, I zipped the syringe up inside the bag and looked at it.

Now what? If I didn't give this syringe to Ben Hathaway right now, I would be obstructing justice instead of just the bit of tampering I'd already done. I ignored the CJ's voice I could hear in my head, warning me that I was putting my career on the line again. Obstruction of justice is definitely an impeachable offense. The syringe might have the killer's finger prints on it. Or it might not.

I looked around in the bushes for a pair of surgical gloves. If the killer had worn gloves, he took them with him when he left. But if Ron had injected himself, his prints would be here. I put the syringe in my pocket and went back out to my car, where I stored it in Greta's glove box.

It was a ten-minute drive back to the old federal courthouse. I parked Greta in my customary spot, across two spaces, and walked pensively back through the courthouse to the ancient elevator. I could have taken the stairs, but my spirit was dragging, so I just waited. The elevator took longer to arrive than my drive in from home. Another interminably slow ride up to the third floor reminded me why I never got in this elevator. I've seen entire pregnancies come to full term in less time.

I pushed the buzzer seeking entrance to my chambers rather than dig out my keys. No one answered the door. When I looked at my watch, it was only four-thirty, so I kept buzzing. Eventually, all the way back in the library, one of my clerks heard me and came to let me in. I thanked him and made my way into my office, expecting to see Margaret in exhausted sleep on my couch. Which is just where she was.

Before waking her, I made us a pot of hot tea, making a little noise at the same time so that she might wake up by herself and not be startled. When I brought the tea back to the couch, she was sitting upright, more than a little sleepy still, and looking quite bewildered. I gave her the tea, liberally laced with lemon and a dollop of whiskey, for fortification. We sipped in silence until I thought she was gaining composure.

"Margaret, Ben Hathaway wants to arrest you for murder. He's been searching your house. It's time to let me help you. Will you do that?" I spoke gently to her because she looked so small and fragile and just plain old, sitting there with the afghan she'd made me wrapped around her small shoulders. Without her glasses on, her eyes looked smaller than usual. She blinked at me as if she didn't quite understand what I was saying.

"Margaret." I touched her on the arm this time and said, still gently but more insistent, "Do you understand what I'm saying? You need a lawyer." Ignoring the warning bells going off in the self-preservation section of my own mind, I told her, "You need to let me help you. If you don't, you're going to be in jail soon. Ben Hathaway thinks you killed Ron. And Armstrong Yeats, too."

She continued to stare at me with eyes that widened to the size of saucers, completely bewildered. Then, she began to cry again, but more controlled tears this time. I put my arm around her and we sat there for quite a while until the tears stopped. "Let me take you home with me for tonight. I'll call a lawyer to come over and talk with you in the morning." She didn't resist. When I got her home, I gave her a sleeping pill and put her to bed in one of the guest rooms. For the second time in as many weeks, and the only times in all the years I've known her, Margaret Wheaton spent the night at Minaret.

Once I got her settled, George and I moved into the den with our drinks and my first Partagas of the day. It took about an hour to explain everything, but afterward, George furrowed his brows and suggested I call Olivia Holmes, the lawyer who had successfully defended him on a murder charge. I had mixed feelings about hiring Olivia for Margaret's case. For one thing, I doubted Margaret could afford to pay Olivia's fees and I didn't think it was appropriate for George and I to pay them. Besides that, Olivia was a little too flamboyant and self-assured to deal with Margaret, who had been quite intimidated by Olivia when she was representing George.

We considered some other possible choices and decided to discuss it with Larry Davis, especially since I'd completely forgotten about my appointment with him today. Besides, Larry had a temperament closer to Margaret's, as well as a large firm that could afford to wait for Margaret to pay her legal bills. And Larry was unusual in that he specialized in both probate and criminal law. Margaret would need a lawyer with both of these specialties. Larry might decline to represent Margaret because he had represented Ron, and Margaret was a suspect in Ron's death. But since I didn't believe Margaret had killed Ron, I was hoping Larry would agree to do the work.

I placed the call to Larry Davis myself. After I'd outlined the situation briefly, he agreed to stop by Minaret on his way home. Dad came into the den with Suzanne and his evening beer and joined us.

Suzanne looked at our somber faces. "Somebody die in here, or what?" she asked.

Chapter *Twelve*

Larry Davis has rapidly disappearing brown hair and a portly build. He wears thick glasses that conceal his hazel eyes. A piece of tape wrapped several times around the bridge of his glasses kept the two halves together. One of his five kids must have broken this pair, too. He's got bad feet, so he wears Rockport shoes that get replaced every ten years, whether they need to be or not. They rarely, if ever, get polished. His suits are always old and brown or green. He told me once that brown and green suits don't sell as well as other colors so he can buy them marked down at the end of the season.

Tonight, Larry had his jacket over his shoulder and too-short shirt tails had crept out of his trousers in the back. His tie acted as a bib and had several meals represented in spots all over it, which we could see even in the dim light of the early evening. In short, Larry looked the same as always: dumpy, happily married, happily poor and a loveable father of five.

We told Larry our limited information about the deaths of Ron Wheaton and Armstrong Yeats, Chief Hathaway's comments about Margaret as his most likely suspect and the results of the search of her house today. Larry had a few questions of his own, which forced me to tell him what I'd told George earlier: exactly how Margaret had behaved after she learned that her husband of thirty years had died as opposed to how she'd taken the news of Armstrong Yeats's death. The contrast was obvious and supported Hathaway's assumptions. We all saw that. But I refused to believe Margaret was a killer.

"Things are not always what they seem," I said, to the room at large.

"But sometimes they are," Larry replied quietly. "It's not smart to overlook the obvious, especially if you're a police officer. Most criminals are just not that smart."

"You're telling me," Dad chimed in. "Did you hear the one about the bank robber who passed his hold up note to the teller written on one of his own bank deposit slips, including his name and address? Or the guy who called in to report the theft of his heroin stash? I could keep going, but the tales of dumb crooks are legendary. They could make a good stand up comic routine."

"But we're not dealing with a criminal. We're talking about Margaret," I said. Only George seemed to understand me, but he and I were the only ones who knew Margaret well. I could see from Dad and Larry's response that someone who didn't know Margaret at all might believe she had killed two men in the past two weeks. That was a bad sign. It meant Hathaway could probably arrest her and the State Attorney could easily get a grand jury to indict. I had been right to insist that Margaret needed a lawyer. I just wasn't sure how much Larry was going to be able to help her under the circumstances.

"Let's not panic yet," Larry was talking to all of us. "All they have right now is opportunity. They're having a big problem with means for both deaths and motive on Yeats. Even the motive Hathaway hypothesized for Margaret killing Ron is weak."

"I thought you said it was believable," I scolded him.

"It's believable," he replied. "But it's not likely. I've defended mercy killers before. Usually, the killer is the husband. Most wives don't feel as desperate when faced with the care-giving responsibilities. They're still a ways from arresting Margaret. But we do need to get some facts from her and get ahead of the police. Do you think we can wake her up and talk to her now?"

"I don't think that's a good idea. As much as another twelve hours will put you behind, Larry, I think you'd better wait until in the morning. Why don't you come over here early, say around seven-thirty? We can talk to Margaret then," I suggested.

"All right. In the meantime, I'll call Hathaway and see if I can get him to tell me anything else. Are there any witnesses I can interview?" Larry didn't sound pleased at the forced delay in his investigation, but Margaret hadn't even agreed to let him represent her yet, and I wasn't completely sure that she would do so gracefully. Particularly if she couldn't pay his bill.

We talked about everyone who was on the Minaret Krewe float during the Knight Parade. We told Larry that neither George nor I had spoken with Armstrong Yeats that night because we were on the front of the float and Yeats was on the back.

"I talked to him," Dad offered, surprising us all.

"When was that?" Larry was taking notes.

"Probably about midnight, I guess. He was with a group of people over on Seventh Avenue. The group included the Kelleys."

"Was Margaret with them?"

"I don't know. I've never met Margaret, have I? If I saw her, I might remember. There were probably six or eight folks. Men and women."

"What did you talk about?" Larry asked.

Here, Dad started to look a little embarrassed. He turned to Suzanne, who was being blissfully quiet for a change, and asked her to go make him some coffee. When she'd left the room, he turned back to Larry and answered the question.

"I wanted to return some jewelry he'd sold me last week," he said. He went on to explain that he'd bought Suzanne a gift from Yeats's shop after George introduced them. It was a diamond and emerald slide for her Omega necklace. Then, when they were in Miami this week, Dad saw the same slide in the window of a costume jewelry store.

"So I had the slide appraised and the appraiser told me the stones weren't real," he finished. Dad was embarrassed. The fraud buster should know better. He would consider it a personal failure that he'd been duped. George and I just listened.

"What did Yeats say about it?"

Dad cleared his throat. He was getting redder and cast his eyes down. His voice was steel. "He said no. We got into a shoving match. I pushed him down and would have continued the fight, but his friends broke us up and I walked away while he was still laying there."

"Did you say anything else to him?" Larry insisted.

More embarrassed now, Dad said, "I shouted that I'd sue him."

"Did he respond to you?"

Dad cast his eyes down and looked chagrined. "He said, 'take a number.'"

Armed with his list of potential witnesses to contact this evening, Larry was preparing to leave with a promise to return early tomorrow to interview Margaret. He asked to see me for a minute privately. We moved into the den, alone, and closed the door, leaving the others having cocktails without us.

"I need to discuss Ron's will with you, Willa. I've got to tell Margaret about it in the morning and you need to hear it first."

"I know. I'm sorry I didn't get to your office today, but I had just a little bit of distraction. Let's do it now."

"I was hoping you'd suggest that, so I brought things with me." Larry pulled out a thin file and began to tell me about its contents. "I've known Ron and Margaret Wheaton for a long time."

Larry explained that he had prepared wills for the Wheatons when he first started his practice. Then, about a year ago, when Ron was diagnosed with ALS and they knew he would die before Margaret, the Wheatons came to see him for financial planning advice.

"We drafted Ron a new will and helped them arrange their financial matters so that Margaret would inherit everything they had as simply and reasonably free of taxes as we could make it," he said.

"I'm confused. I thought you said Ron had named me as his executor?"

Larry nodded. "About two months ago, Ron came back to see me by himself. He said he was worried about Margaret. He was afraid that, after he died, someone would try to take advantage of her and would take her money. He wanted to restructure his estate so that Margaret would have someone else looking after her best interests. He specifically wanted you."

"But why? Margaret has a good head on her shoulders. She's been handling everything very well, I think. Why would he do that?"

"That's all he told me." Larry tried to talk to him further about it, especially since he knew Ron was depressed. Ron had never suggested suicide before. He wouldn't say anything more except that he knew I would take care of Margaret.

"And he left this safety deposit box key for you. He said to give it to you after he died." Larry handed me a small envelope. "It's a box in the downtown branch of AmSouth Bank. I've arranged it so that you can go over there and open it whenever you're ready. But do it soon. Margaret probably has a few thousand dollars in her checking account and not much else. She'll need money and to have this all resolved as soon as you can get around to it."

Larry left me, bewildered, holding the key in its little cardboard envelope. Was Ron Wheaton worried about something in particular, or was he just being overly protective of Margaret when he changed his will? I had known that Margaret was somehow involved with Armstrong Yeats before he died, and I didn't like it, then or now.

Maybe Ron had known, too. If Yeats had been Ron's concern, it was not something we had to worry about any longer, now that Yeats was dead. I would go to the bank as soon as I could get there and hope that

Ron had left me some explanation for his actions in that safety deposit box.

After Larry left, George and I discussed the facts as we knew them for a while longer before my growling stomach led me to suggest that we go downstairs for dinner. Dad and Suzanne joined us.

"Just what do we know about this Yeats character, anyway?" Dad asked when Suzanne left to powder her nose. After George had given him the thumbnail sketch of Yeats' credentials, I told them both about my visit to his gallery in Pass-a-Grille on Saturday.

"According to the CJ, almost everyone in South Tampa except us had dealt with Yeats at one time or another," I said.

"But I dealt with him, Willa," George responded. "He was recommended to me by several of our friends. I took some of Aunt Minnie's estate jewelry over to him for cleaning and restoration once. I thought he did a good job. That's when I saw his gallery and first became familiar with his work. Then, I bought your anniversary gift from Yeats two years ago. The platinum Minaret pendant with the tourmaline and diamonds in it."

"Really? I had no idea. Was he reasonable to deal with?"

"Well, the cost of the restoration work was not out of line, based on what I'd had done before. I can't say the pendant was cheap, but I thought it was reasonable at the time," George said. "Our insurance agent didn't demur when I told him to add the pendant to our homeowner's policy at the price I paid for it. But I've never had it appraised."

"Based on my experience, maybe you should," Dad told him. "Maybe you should have all of the jewelry Yeats touched appraised."

George was looking alarmed now. "Why would I do that? Yeats had a sterling reputation. Everyone we know has bought from him at one time or another. I feel terrible about what happened to you, Jim. I even recommended him to you. I had no idea."

I told them about the Fitzgerald House case, how Yeats had sold fakes to the widow and passed them off as "jewels of the world," and collected a million dollars from her. I also told them about the allegations in the criminal case. I thought the civil cases might proceed against Yeats' estate, but the criminal case would now be dismissed.

After hearing about the claims against Yeats, George was champing at the bit to go to his safety deposit box and get Aunt Minnie's old jewelry out for appraisal. Of course, the bank was closed.

George got up to call another jeweler to schedule an appraisal appointment while Dad and I finished our coffee. "I thought this was such a sleepy little town. In all the years I've worked in New York, there's never been a murder in a place I was sleeping. What kind of a city have you moved to here, Willa? " he teased me, but weakly.

In truth, I was more than a little shocked myself. We have relatively little crime here in South Tampa. The "police blotter" is printed in the South Tampa News every week and it's usually a few petty burglaries, one or two "throwing deadly missiles" and three or less "criminal mischiefs." Deaths happen all the time around here. Indeed, the second highest volume of export from the Tampa Airport is dead bodies, after tropical fish. All those retirees who come here to live their last days in the sun return to their northern homes to be buried in the cold when they can no longer feel it. I guess the theory is that if the departed are close by, the loved ones will take better care of the graves and remember them longer.

Ron Wheaton's death in George's restaurant had upset me more than it seemed to upset Margaret. I had to acknowledge that. She returned to work two days later and seemed to be almost lighthearted about it all. I thought she was just putting on a brave face, but maybe she was happy that Ron had passed out of the way.

I went to a memorial service for a minister's wife where a Dixieland Jazz Band played "When the Saints Go Marching In," because both she and her husband felt that the best of life comes after death. I had put Margaret's behavior down to similar feelings, particularly in light of Ron's terminal illness.

But, what if it was something else? Could Margaret have killed him? Or at least, known he was planning to kill himself? I had to at least acknowledge the possibility.

Armstrong Yeats's death, from what I'd heard about it so far, could easily have been an accident. A fall, hitting his head, probably resulted in a subdural hematoma which was eventually fatal. In the Ybor City crowd Saturday night, it would have been easy to be jostled to the ground, with no one ill-intentioned. Laying undiscovered on a side street north of all the main action for several hours wasn't outside the realm of likelihood, either. Not on such a cold and busy night. By the wee hours, most people would have tired of the struggle to stay warm and have gone home. So far as I knew now, Yeats was a casualty of a few too many drinks and a few too many people on a busy and cold night.

Although Dad admitted to pushing Yeats down, I wasn't about to disclose that to Hathaway as an alternative theory of murder. When Dad left Hathaway, he was on Seventh Avenue, not Eighteenth Street. Yeats yelled back at Dad from the ground. And Yeats had friends with him who would have taken care of him then. No, Dad wasn't responsible.

If Hathaway's investigation pointed in Dad's direction, I'd deal with that problem when it arose. For now, I wouldn't believe Margaret had pushed Yeats to his death, either. She wasn't physically strong enough to kill him, even if she'd wanted to. And I was certain Margaret had been surprised and devastated by the news that Yeats was dead when Hathaway told us so today. Margaret didn't kill Ron or Yeats. No doubt about it in my mind. Well, almost no doubt.

Chapter *Thirteen*

I had four days left to train for the Gasparilla Distance Classic. The race is one of the biggest running events in Florida, often voted the best race and among the top ten races in the United States. The Gasparilla Distance Classic Association has donated more than $2 million to local charities and sponsors other running events.

If I finished the race, Young Mothers' Second Chance would collect $10,000 from the corporate sponsors I'd lined up. If I won, which was highly unlikely, Young Mothers' would get $20,000. But I could place in the first five finishers and if I did, the moms would get a five-figure check.

It was a powerful motivator to haul my butt out of a nice warm bed the next morning before daylight and pull on my running clothes. When the dogs and I got outside, I was tempted to go back upstairs for my polar fleece, but I resisted and started my run at a slow, loping pace to warm up. By the time I got to the north end of the island, I was freezing, so I stepped up the pace. One lap, I told myself, just one. I could do one lap. I'd have to do more in the classic, but I hoped it would be warmer.

I struggled through the entire run and finally made it back to the house. Harry and Bess beat me back and had plunged headlong into Hillsborough Bay. They were frolicking around in the water as if it didn't contain ice cubes. Figuratively, of course. I had to stand around, stomping my feet and watching my breath come out in huge white puffs while they worked off their excess energy.

Margaret was up and about when I returned to the kitchen after a long, hot shower. She and George were having coffee and toast in the kitchen. It was about seven o'clock and Larry Davis would be here in a half hour. I wanted a turn at asking Margaret my own questions first.

Looking her in the eye, I told her I'd asked Larry Davis to take on her case. "Thank you, Willa," she said, surprising me by accepting my decision. "I've known Larry for years, of course. His parents were always kind to my mother. If I have to have a lawyer, I have a lot of confidence in him." Her comment startled me. Larry hadn't said he didn't know Margaret well. But I'd assumed he didn't know her because he'd acted like he believed she was capable of murder. Which I thought preposterous. I'd assumed our difference of opinion was based on his lack of knowledge.

"I'm sure he'll be able to make payment arrangements with you if you need them," George told her.

Margaret's response was another surprise. "That shouldn't be necessary. I'll collect Ron's life insurance soon and then I'll be a rich woman." Then she said with some quiet irony, "that is, if they'll pay it to a woman suspected of killing him." Which, I knew, the company would never do. Like many states, Florida law prohibits killers from profiting from their own actions. The insurance company would stop payment faster than a stock broker can say "profits."

"Since you didn't kill him, it shouldn't be a problem," I said. "You didn't kill him, did you?"

"No. I didn't kill him. I wasn't sorry that he died, though I do miss the man I spent half my life with. He'd been wasting away every day. He was weaker, he could barely walk. For Ron, it was a slow and certain, painful death." She was talking down into her coffee and tears were welling into her eyes as she spoke. "It was so hard for him. We talked about it every day. He was still mentally sharp as ever. He remembered things better than I do. That made it worse. I think it would've been better if he hadn't known how he would eventually die. Older people aren't afraid of death usually. We just want to die in a reasonable way. There is nothing about ALS that's reasonable. Nothing!" She spilled her coffee when she slammed the cup down on the table. Then, she ruefully wiped the spill of the table with her napkin.

"Do you know what killed Ron?" George asked her.

"No. I guess I thought it was a heart attack. Most ALS patients die from respiratory failure, is what the doctors told us. But Ron was a long way from that. I just figured his bad heart got him. He should have had bypass surgery a couple of years ago. He was on nitroglycerine several times a day. He wasn't a good surgical candidate. And he wanted to die of a heart attack. He always said it would be better to die quickly." Her chin quivered at this, fresh tears glassing her eyes.

Larry Davis came in just at the tail end of her answer. He bent down to give Margaret a kiss on the cheek. "Good morning everyone. Willa, George. Is there somewhere I can talk privately with my client?"

"Sure, Larry, but I'd like to talk to you when you're finished. Would you stop by my office? And Margaret, you're welcome to stay here as long as you like. Don't feel you have to go home or come into work today," I told her.

Margaret looked grateful and nodded without response. Larry promised to call me after his client conference. He looked at me over Margaret's head in a way that I interpreted as meaning he had information to share. I showed them into the den, closed the door, and prepared to leave for my office, feeling even better with the choice of lawyer I'd made.

If anyone could defend Margaret with the kind of quiet competence and dignity she deserved, it was Larry. We have quite a few flamboyant criminal defense lawyers here in town who would have taken the case. Particularly if they knew Margaret had plenty of money to pay them with. But the best ones weren't so well known or expensive. Although a criminal defense lawyer isn't something you want to buy from a discount chain. One always needs the best money can buy. Criminal justice in this country is definitely more available to the rich than the poor. It's not a fact we're proud of, but there it is.

Tuesdays are usually a little slow in my courtroom, but Ron Wheaton's bank wouldn't open until ten o'clock and Larry would be tied up with Margaret for awhile, so I went into the office to get some things done. I don't have any regularly scheduled hearings or conferences. When there is no trial going, Tuesday is a day of catching up. Reviewing orders drafted by my clerks, planning and scheduling, meeting with my colleagues and so on. I was in no great hurry to get started, but I knew the various and sundry small tasks would grow into giant problems if left unattended.

Waiting for Larry, I started on my work. I didn't stop until one of my law clerks, who was sitting in for Margaret, buzzed me to say that Larry had arrived and had asked to see me.

Larry and I settled around my conference table so we could have a conversation between colleagues—I wanted Larry to treat me as a surrogate client in Margaret's case. Margaret had no one else to look out for her. She had no children, her husband had just died, and George and I were the only close friends who would support her. Such was my conceit at the time, anyway. Larry, who knew Margaret better than I did, soon disabused me of that notion, among others.

"So, how does it look?" I asked him.

"Not good. I'm talking to you because Margaret gave me permission to discuss her case. I need you to treat ours as privileged communications, though. You are a lawyer, after all. If you can't do that, then I'll have to censor what I tell you."

"I think that's doable. Unless you tell me something I'll be obligated to disclose. Since I'm convinced Margaret neither committed nor concealed a crime, I'm sure that won't happen. So, let's talk." I folded my hands together on the conference table.

Larry lounged back in his chair and looked at me appraisingly before he responded. "Willa, I've known you a long time, but I've known Margaret even longer. She's lived her whole life in Tampa and she's traveled very little since her marriage to Ron. She's not a worldly person."

"I know. That's why I'm so worried about her," I said.

"But, she's not naive, either," he warned me. "She's been in and around Tampa all her life. Margaret knows the score on a lot of things. She doesn't travel in the same circles you do, but she's taken care of herself for a long time."

I eyed him speculatively. "It sounds like you're warning me about something, but what?"

"Just that you, of all people, should know that things are not always what we perceive them to be. Margaret isn't the helpless little old lady you've turned her into in your mind. For one thing, she's not that old. For another, she's more feisty than you think. Don't be deceived by your own assumptions. That's all," he said.

I thought about his words briefly, but didn't have the luxury of considering them fully right then. I had my own agenda. "Ok. I'll keep that in mind. Tell me what you've learned about Ron Wheaton's and Armstrong Yeats's deaths since yesterday."

He pulled out a yellow legal pad in the fourteen-inch size--the ones I had banished from my office—and flipped through pages of notes. Most lawyers don't use the archaic long sized pads any more since most courts will no longer accept fourteen-inch paper. Knowing Larry, he probably got the last batch in Tampa at a bargain-basement price and would be the only lawyer in town using them into the next decade.

"I talked with Chief Hathaway last night after I left you. I told him I was representing Margaret and asked him what he had so far."

"What did he say?"

"He told me the toxicology screen on Ron Wheaton, and the autopsy, had revealed that Ron didn't die of natural causes."

"Yes, he told me that, too. Although Ron's symptoms would mimic a heart attack and he had prior heart problems. So, if it looks like a duck and quacks like a duck…" I allowed my voice to trail off on the thought that Chief Hathaway and the medical examiner could be wrong.

Larry was shaking his head. "Apparently not. They're treating the death as a homicide. Although they recognize it could have been suicide as well. They aren't sure it killed him, or who administered it, but they feel certain he was poisoned with insulin."

"Is it possible he killed himself?"

"Yes, it is. He could have injected himself. He was depressed, and males account for more than 75 percent of all suicides. Suicide is also on the rise among the elderly. They're alone, with failing health and terrified of what lies ahead. Hathaway is treating suicide as an active possibility."

"Where'd Ron get the insulin?"

"That's what they were looking for when they searched Margaret's house."

"And they didn't find it," I told him. "I was there and I saw what they did. There's a video tape, by the way, and you should get it." He looked at me as if to say I shouldn't tell him how to do his job.

"I did ask for the video tape. Hathaway told me I'd have to get it from the State Attorney when charges were brought against Margaret and time came for him to turn over his file. That's one of the reasons I'm talking to you, Willa. I hope you can get Hathaway to give us his file now so we can head this thing off at the pass. If that's possible." Larry didn't sound hopeful.

I wondered whether Larry knew Hathaway had done this for me before. The Florida Supreme Court had more than once held that law enforcement was not required to turn over an active investigation file before charges were formally made against a defendant. I had prevailed upon my relationship with Ben Hathaway to convince him to do me that favor once. I didn't think he'd do it again. Nor did I plan to ask him.

"Extremely unlikely, Larry, and you know it. If he wouldn't give the file to you, why would he give it to me? We'll just have to rely on my memory." I could see how disappointed he was, so I added "And the still pictures I took of Margaret's house afterward."

He was somewhat appeased. Instead of arguing with me over my decision about Hathaway's file, he asked me for the pictures, which I'd picked up at the one-hour processing place yesterday. I handed him the second set of prints. I'd already looked at them and found nothing interesting. Maybe that was because I didn't know what to look for. Or, maybe there was nothing to find.

"What else have you got?" I asked him.

"I asked a friend in the U.S. Marshall's office to search the U.S. Government files for Ron Wheaton and Armstrong Yeats," he said, looking down at his notes.

"Good. I intended to do that today, too. What did you find?"

"Even less than I feared. Ronald John Wheaton was born in Tampa in 1933, three years earlier than Margaret. He'd served in Korea, receiving an honorable discharge. His social security file showed he'd worked for Tampa schools over thirty years and retired young. There was no record that he'd ever been sued or charged with a crime. In short, there wasn't anything to help me in Ron Wheaton's official background." His voice carried the disappointment we both felt.

"What about Yeats?" I tried to keep my tone neutral.

"The same non-stuff. Armstrong Eugene Yeats. Applied for a passport in 1958. Fingerprints on file. No convictions, although there's an arrest and a criminal case pending on your docket," he read from his notes.

"I know. There's a list of cheated customers that's longer than your arm in the indictment," I told him. "Of course, the case will be dismissed now that Yeats is dead."

"Sounds like a lot of folks with a motive for murder," Larry said. "Let me take the list and I'll start running them down."

"All right, but I'll take the ones I know personally," I said as I handed him the copy of the indictment I'd had ready for his review. When he was about to object, I told him, "You'll need help, Larry."

He nodded. Larry flipped through more of his notes, obviously picking and choosing what he would share, unsure of the protection Margaret would have from me if I felt she was breaking the law in a way that I'd have to report. "Hathaway also said Margaret and Yeats were lovers. He said he had witnesses who had seen them together at the Knight Parade on the Minaret Krewe float and afterward," Larry said.

"Doing what? Having sex or something? It was a little too cold for that, I can assure you." I spoke more crossly than I had intended, but it was just this kind of idle gossip that could get Margaret in real trouble. I remembered all too well how cold it was on Saturday night, my long underwear, the freezing wind. I doubted any legitimate person saw anything resembling incriminating behavior by Margaret Wheaton. Besides that, Margaret was from the old school. If she was going to show some man her affections, she would do it in private.

"Of course not," Larry said, wounded, too. "But sitting a little too close together, holding hands, talking with their heads bowed toward each other, laughing between themselves over things others couldn't hear. The typical behavior movies tell us is reflective of those in love while they play romantic music and cover the dialogue."

"Not good," I said, in a serious bit of understatement Larry didn't bother to acknowledge. "What does Margaret say about it?"

"I'd rather not tell you that just now. But let's just leave it that she's not too happy with the facts Hathaway has uncovered so far. And it looks like Ron may have had a good reason to be concerned about someone trying to take advantage of Margaret. Have you been to Ron's bank to see what he left for you yet?"

I shook my head, "I've been waiting for you. Why does Hathaway think Yeats was murdered instead of just falling down in a drunken stupor and hitting his head? Isn't that just as likely, given the circumstances?"

Larry considered his notes again, making decisions about what to share and what not to share, shaking his head in the negative. "The autopsy isn't final yet. It's a busy time in the medical examiner's office, apparently. The cold has caused a few elderly people to die and each one has to be autopsied, I guess. But Hathaway seems to think that the wound to Yeats's skull suggests he was pushed rather hard into that piece of concrete, harder than if he had just fallen."

"Well, there were lots of people on the streets that night. Anyone could have pushed him, intentionally or by accident," I protested.

"That's true enough. Although not as many people had a motive and the opportunity to kill Yeats, according to Hathaway," Larry said.

"But that makes no sense at all. If Margaret and Yeats were lovers, why would she kill him?"

Larry looked at me appraisingly again, as if to say, "No kidding." What he said instead was, "Hathaway won't tell me and Margaret claims she has no idea. I think she was truly devastated and surprised by the news that Yeats had died. I was hoping you could help me out there, too."

I was already shaking my head before he finished the sentence. "Sorry, Larry, I'd like to help. I really would. But we'll just have to find some other way for me to do it. I won't ask Ben Hathaway to break the law."

"He wouldn't be breaking the law if he voluntarily gave you the file, Willa. He can do whatever he wants to do with it. We just can't make him hand it over," Larry cajoled.

"Besides," I ignored his plea, "my real guess is that Hathaway doesn't know what motive Margaret could possibly have for killing Yeats. Usually, whatever he knows, he's more than willing to share if it will help him arrest the right suspect and avoid public humiliation. We'll have to find another way. I'll think about it."

"Never mind. You're absolutely right. I'll just wait for the trial. It'll all come out then, anyway."

The relief in his tone was obvious, even to me. After Larry left, I dialed directory assistance for Grosse Pointe, Michigan. One of the complainants listed in the *U.S. v. Yeats* indictment was the owner of a restaurant George and I had frequented when we lived in Detroit. I had the telephone number for Jake Miller's Chop House restaurant in less than five minutes. Twenty seconds later, I was talking to Jake himself.

"It's unnecessary for you to tell me who you are, Willa. I always remember my favorite customers, even when they go into competition with me," he schmoozed, since I hadn't seen Jake in over ten years and had never known him well.

I laughed. "George isn't competition for you, Jake. He has no intention of opening a franchise in the frozen tundra."

After we chatted about the state of the restaurant business, the economy, how cold it was in Detroit and how warm here in Tampa, I could finally get to the point. "Jake, I was hoping you could tell me something about Armstrong Yeats," I started.

"Willa, I hope you're not involved with that man in any way. He's a liar and a thief. He stole over ninety million dollars from me." Jake was truly alarmed.

"That's what I wanted to talk to you about. How did that happen?"

"Pride. And stupidity. I thought I was making a good investment. I thought I'd be able to resell the merchandise for much more than I paid for it," he said. "When I started to try to resell it all, these Paulding Farnham creations he sold me were trash--nothing at all. People laughed at me. I paid ninety million dollars for a few hundred thousand dollars worth of nothing." He almost spat.

"But how did that happen? Why did you believe what he told you about these jewels?"

"A man hears what he wants to hear, Willa, and disregards the rest. Sometimes to his great loss and embarrassment. Yeats was introduced to me by a man whose name you would recognize. He was duped too, but neither one of us knew that. We thought we could trust Yeats. So we didn't do what, as good business men, we should have done--gotten the jewelry appraised before we bought it." The chagrin in his voice traveled easily over thirteen hundred miles of telephone wire.

"Did you ask Yeats for your money back?"

He snorted. "Of course, we did. The man has nothing. He owns nothing. The police say he covered up with money laundering, but who knows where it really went? If I could kill him myself, I would. It's too bad you don't use your'Old Sparky' any more." he said, referring to the Florida's infamous electric chair, or what the criminal defense attorneys snidely referred to as "our favorite bar-b-que grill," which had been retired. Now, Florida executes criminals by lethal injection. "I hope they send him straight to hell."

Miller was so bitter, so vindictive because he had truly lost much more than money. A man has nothing but his good name. The Japanese call it "saving face." It's the same here. Either he didn't know Yeats was already dead, or he'd been putting on a hell of an act. Jake Miller didn't kill Armstrong Yeats. But someone else on the long list of people Yeats had cheated did kill him. Who?

Chapter *Fourteen*

As I hung up the phone, my law clerk came in to remind me that I had been subpoenaed to testify in the CJ's ethics complaint matter in an hour. With everything else going on, I'd forgotten about it. I pulled out the subpoena and realized the hearing would be in the office of the lawyer for the Judicial Counsel downtown in the new Sam M. Gibbons Federal Court House. I could easily walk, but I didn't have much time for lunch.

As I pulled on my jacket, I regretted my choice of attire today. When I got dressed this morning, I had forgotten about the subpoena or that I'd be going over to the other courthouse, where there are many more people and more of my colleagues. I usually dress casually in my courtroom. Under my robe, no one can tell what I'm wearing. I think most judges do this. I've seen my colleagues in jeans and no socks many times. Of course, I don't for a second believe the rumor that one of my brethren on the bench goes nude under his robe so that he can masturbate at the bench during particularly boring testimony. Having heard a lot of boring testimony over the years, I can see how he'd be tempted, though.

I thought about going home to change, but then decided to hell with it. I looked okay. I had on olive dockers, a long-sleeved pink shirt that had been pressed, and a pair of topsiders. I did have on socks and I wore a tan suede blazer. I was sure the CJ wouldn't approve of my attire, but he was the one being investigated, not me. With any luck, maybe he wouldn't even be there. I'm a dreamer, so sue me.

Precisely at one-thirty, after a quick sandwich on the run, I knocked on the door at the small hearing room on the eleventh floor of the Sam M. Gibbons Federal Courthouse. I avoided going into the courtrooms of my colleagues, which I lusted after in my heart as many a middle-aged man has lusted after Playboy Playmates.

Even the magistrate judges here had better courtrooms than mine. I thought it was particularly unfair that the CJ could keep me over in the dungeon, as I had taken to calling it, long after everyone else had moved. It was a tactical mistake for him to let me be subpoenaed to testify in his case, in this building, rubbing my nose in what he wouldn't let me have. Oh, he claimed it wasn't his fault. Congress wouldn't approve his budget, he didn't have the money to relocate me, as soon as he got the money, he'd be sure I got moved. Right. And the check's in the mail.

These were the excuses he offered whenever the subject came up. Yeah, sure, I thought sourly. And in that mood, I went into the room to see a three-member panel, a court reporter, two counsel tables and the CJ sitting there next to one of the most obnoxious criminal defense lawyers in Tampa. This just kept getting better and better.

They were respectful to me, anyway, I'll give them that. They didn't ask me any unnecessary questions or keep me on the stand too long. They didn't ask me about my alleged sexual harassment, so the newspaper article that came with my subpoena was wrong, just as I had suspected. The panel didn't go into my personal and well known mini-feud with the CJ, both sides apparently understanding it would help neither to do so. Never the less, what the panel did ask me after the preliminaries was shocking.

"Judge Carson," the lawyer for the Judicial Counsel asked, "have you heard that Chief Judge Richardson has attempted to influence the clerk's office to tamper with the random assignment of judges?"

"No," I answered, truthfully. The second question followed quickly and was more outrageous than the first.

"Have you heard that Chief Richardson has improperly handled the court's funds, misplacing funds allocated for the court's business or funds paid into the court by litigants?"

"No," I said, a little more forcefully than I'd intended. What an outrageous suggestion, I thought just before the zinger. The third question.

"Have you heard that Judge Richardson has improperly tried to influence other judges by contacting them about the handling of their cases?"

They asked me these questions in rapid succession, trying to get me to answer without thinking. Okay. I was under oath here. I had to tell the truth. But the question was whether I'd *heard* about CJ's efforts to influence judges, not whether he'd actually *done* it. To me. In the *Fitzgerald House v. Armstrong Yeats* case. Just last week. But did I have any obligation to help the CJ by ducking this question? Lord knows, CJ had gone out of his way to be as unhelpful to me as he could possibly be without attracting overt criticism from all corners. He hadn't actually *ordered* me to dismiss the Fitzgerald House case against Yeats, but he'd strongly suggested it. Was that improper influence? Or just a reminder of my heavy workload and an effort to make the courthouse run more smoothly? My reaction at the time was that CJ's conduct was absolutely improper. Was I right?

Had I heard about CJ making similar calls to other judges? Yes. I'd heard about it. According to my colleagues, it was not unusual for the CJ to offer his unsolicited opinion on a variety of issues. But that's how we all took it; as a statement of his opinion. Was he trying to influence us? Probably. In the way that anyone is trying to influence someone else when they offer an opinion. CJ's "suggestions" never influenced any of us to do anything one way or the other. I really believed that. At least, he never influenced me. I usually go out of my way to do the opposite of whatever it is that CJ wants. Childish, I know. But true.

So what was this investigation about? And why was I here? Were all the judges being asked to testify? If they were, everyone already knew about the CJ's opinions and how and when he expressed them. Or, and this may have been just the tiniest bit paranoid, I'll admit, were they really investigating me? The CJ had been out to get me for years. Maybe this question was an effort to catch me lying under oath. Maybe they wanted to try to impeach me. Maybe… Oh, what the hell. I did the lawyerly thing and answered the specific question they asked me. I told the examiner that I had heard of instances where the CJ had tried to influence judges. Which had the result of keeping me on the stand for the next four hours explaining every incidence when I had heard that the CJ had called one of my colleagues to give them unsolicited advice on what to do with their cases. And a promise that I'd be called back sometime before this was all over. They never asked me about the CJ trying to get me to dismiss the *Yeats* case. But they would next time.

I left the hearing as bewildered as before I arrived, unclear as to what this investigation was about. It was the first time I'd ever been deposed, and it wasn't a pleasant experience. I vowed to have a lot more compassion for witnesses from now on as I walked back to my car in the early twilight cold. The hour was long after the bank had closed so I couldn't go to open Ron Wheaton's safe deposit box. With more unanswered questions and a heavy heart, I bundled up and headed home.

George and I had been in the Sunset Bar sharing today's experiences for about twenty minutes when the CJ walked through the door and came over to our table. He looked as wrung out as I felt. Naturally, George asked him to sit down. Sometimes, being married to a socially correct gentleman isn't all it's cracked up to be.

CJ ordered a scotch and water, pulling off his tie with a hard yank. He tossed his suit coat onto the bench beside himself, without regard for the wrinkles. He made small talk until his drink was served. I hadn't had time to tell George that I'd been subpoenaed to testify in the

CJ's hearing, so George was in the dark as to the reason for CJ's presence. I wasn't so blissfully ignorant.

"What can we do for you, Ozgood?" I asked CJ, wanting him to get it over with and leave. I spend as little time with CJ as possible at work; I certainly wasn't interested in sharing my free time with him.

"I came to talk to you about Armstrong Yeats," he surprised me by saying. CJ is, like me, a fan of the direct approach. Still, I expected him to dissemble awhile before he tried to influence me again.

George looked even more puzzled than I felt. "Whatever for?"

CJ looked at him. "Willa knows." Turning to me, he said, "I wanted to explain why I called you last week about the Yeats case. Yeats asked me to do it. He's been a friend for years. I bought several anniversary gifts for my wife from him. He's well known around town. And he knew the case would damage his reputation. So he asked me to call you and see if you could get the case settled."

George was annoyed now. "You mean, you tried to influence how Willa handled the case?"

"No, George. Not really. I just wanted to share with her that this was a case that would be better settled. As all our cases are," he took a big gulp of his scotch as he tried to make us swallow this revised version of his conversation with me. Talking to me while I was still under oath, about the subject of my testimony, might be construed as witness tampering. I said nothing. I was technically not through testifying. He was taking a big chance coming here, trying to explain himself, knowing I would eventually be asked, under oath, about this conversation, too. He was pleading with me, though, to hear him out. It didn't take a clairvoyant to see that.

"The Fitzgerald House case isn't something that should even be in federal court, we all know that. It's a minor dispute. There's insurance. The whole thing should never have gotten to this point." He looked at me then, directly. "And it's not like you don't have enough work to do.

All judges try to settle cases anyway. I wasn't suggesting how you should settle it."

But he had. He'd specifically said to dismiss the case. That isn't the same thing as settling it. Not the same thing at all.

"What did Yeats have on you to make you suggest that I should dismiss Fitzgerald House's claim?" I asked him, all too directly.

CJ's face suffused red. He turned to me with embarrassment and anger. But he knew he had to tell me before the entire situation got completely out of hand and he found himself on the front page of the paper. Not to mention out of a job and maybe in jail. Perhaps my nightmare last week was a premonition. CJ really could end up behind bars in orange prison garb.

"I did buy quite a few pieces of jewelry from Armstrong Yeats over the years, just like I told you. One year, I bought my wife a necklace that he said had belonged to Carole Lombard. He said it had been designed by Paulding Farnham. He showed me a book about Farnham and his creations, including a picture of Carole Lombard wearing the necklace at the academy awards. It was a beautiful thing. A large sapphire center surrounded by diamond baguets. Mariam loved it. Just loved it. She wore it everywhere for a couple of years and told everyone she knew that I'd bought it and what its history was." The pride in his tone was unmistakable. It must be hard to be married to an heiress of Mariam McCarthy Richardson's stature. Her family fortune was immense, her local celebrity unrivaled. How did a husband impress such a woman on a civil servant's salary?

I imagined CJ had been a "good catch" when Mariam McCarthy married him. Although his pedigree was good, it was nowhere near as good as hers. But, if the stories of Mariam's youthful indiscretions with Gil Kelley were true, when she married CJ, Mariam was already a woman with a past. If Mariam McCarthy Richardson "married down," I doubted she ever let CJ forget it. What it must have meant to him to have given her such a special gift as a piece of Paulding Farnham jewelry. And what a colossal slap in the face it was when the gift was exposed as a fraud. People had killed for less.

"So what happened to enlighten you about the jewelry's pedigree?" George asked him.

"We took the necklace with us to New York one year. Mariam wanted to take it in to Tiffany's, to show it to them because it was a Paulding Farnham design," he choked up. Really. I never thought I'd see the CJ show any honest emotion of any kind. I could almost hear the sharp tongued Mariam, lashing CJ over her humiliation, making it his.

"And it was a fake," I supplied, to help him out. He was a little pathetic, really. I wasn't used to him being so vulnerable. I thought of the CJ as a twit, but a powerful and controlling twit. At this point, he was just a pathetic victim of another con. The role fit him uncomfortably. What would he have done to restore his pride? Murder?

"Right," he said, morosely. "It was a fake. I was outraged, Mariam was mortified and Tiffany's wanted to report Yeats to the authorities right then. I probably should have let them but I thought I could handle it myself." He took another large swallow of the scotch. "Dutch courage" they call it.

"What did you do?" George was interested in keeping this story moving along.

"I swore Mariam to silence, which she was only too willing to do. We came back to Tampa and confronted Yeats. He acted surprised," CJ almost spat. "Said he thought I knew the necklace wasn't real. But he claimed it had still belonged to Carole Lombard and she'd worn it to the academy awards. That made it worth what I'd paid for it, he said. He offered to take it back and return my money. And he said if I took any action against him or told anyone, he'd sue me for defamation."

I felt the small hairs rise on the back of my neck. I'd heard this story before. Had Yeats believed he could run this scam indefinitely?

"So why not let him take it back and wash your hands of the whole matter? Except for looking foolish, which isn't a crime and has never killed anyone that I know of, you wouldn't have been any worse off for the experience." I'd been right. CJ was a twit after all. Pride before the fall and all. Such an old story.

"I should have. Of course, I know that now. At the time, all Mariam and I could think of was what other people would think. Everybody we knew was aware of that necklace. We just couldn't act like we'd never owned it. We certainly didn't want to be named in a defamation suit." CJ said Mariam wore the necklace less frequently until, in the last few years, she hadn't even had it on. People seemed to have forgotten. And CJ got a good deal from Yeats on anything else he ever bought. All of which CJ had appraised before paying, by the way.

"I think, over the years, he'd made it up to me in discounts on other pieces. And we just let it be our little secret." He finished his drink and set the glass down between us on the table.

"Why do I get the feeling we haven't heard the whole story?" I said, even though George kicked me under the table.

CJ grimaced as if he'd swallowed a sour lime. "It was the whole story. Until last week. Yeats called me at home and told me about the *Fitzgerald House* case. He said it was just like my situation," CJ sounded parched again and I shook my head at the waitress to keep her from offering him another round.

"And he suggested he'd let people know about it unless you could make the *Fitzgerald House* case go away, is that it?" I suggested as CJ nodded miserably.

"You didn't kill Yeats over this, did you?" George asked him straight out.

"No!" he blurted, then added more quietly, "But we argued about it. More than once. People might have heard us."

My heart sank, because I knew what was coming next. "When did you see him last, CJ?" I asked him.

"Saturday night. Late. In Ybor City after the Knight Parade."

"What happened?"

"We argued. I pushed him. And I left him there. Alive. I swear." CJ was trembling now, wanting another drink.

Now, I had the upper hand with the CJ and I didn't want it. It was one thing to play my little power games with him when I knew they weren't hurting anyone. But in this case, his wife's pride and his own ego got him way more than he bargained for.

"CJ, you really should tell all of this to your lawyer and see what you can work out with the Judicial Counsel. Because I won't complain, your call to me isn't something that should get you impeached. You'll get a slap on the wrist over it. That's all. You'll never be appointed to the court of appeals. But, no one needs to know. Resolve it confidentially. Do it now," I urged him as sympathetically as I could, but he remained seated, not willing to give up yet.

He still thought he could persuade me to lie for him. Given his track record with trying to control me, his confidence was sorely misplaced. "Do it before they put me back on the witness stand and ask me about this entire conversation, which you know they will do," I told him.

That seemed to galvanize him to action. He said he needed to call his lawyer. Knowing who was defending him, I hoped the CJ would offer to let the lawyer keep his retainer to resolve the case. Otherwise, the lawyer wouldn't let the matter drop. None of us needed to let this get out of hand any more than it already was.

Before he left, I had one more question. "How did the Judicial Counsel find out about this, anyway?"

CJ seemed genuinely puzzled by this. "I don't know. Anonymous tip, I was told. Neither Mariam nor I told anyone, you can be sure of that. It makes no sense that Yeats would have tipped them. But someone did."

Chapter *Fifteen*

I was waiting on the couch in the lobby at the AmSouth building at 100 North Tampa Street for the bank to open. I didn't want to make the mistake of going to my office and being delayed again so that I missed the opportunity to get into Ron Wheaton's safety deposit box.

The grey marble gothic building graced Tampa's skyline with sufficient grandeur to win an award for Building of the Year not long ago. It's interior lobby soars four stories and larger-than-life murals painted on the walls soften the stark echo of the unforgiving granite. Some days, a string quartet or a classical flamenco guitarist play here during the lunch hour. This morning, the lobby was filled with office workers traveling from the parking garage on the north side of the building to the elevator banks in each wing, beginning their work day.

The building's tenants included a more than ample supply of lawyers and bankers, so I'd had to talk to quite a few people as they arrived for work, even though I'd had my nose buried in the *Wall Street Journal*, hoping that it would keep my privacy. Instead, all it did was to give people a conversational opening.

"Morning, Judge. Anything good going on in the market?" "Hello, Judge Carson. How about that Nasdaq?" "Judge Carson, good to see you again. Hard to believe Microsoft is merging, isn't it?" In truth, I hadn't read a word in the paper. I was too preoccupied. That didn't seem to matter to my colleagues as they greeted me with enthusiasm and chattered on without regard to my minimal responses.

A few minutes after ten o'clock, a woman opened the glass door to the AmSouth branch office and I followed her inside, asking where the safety deposit boxes were kept. I provided my name and my key to the guardian, signed the register and was shown to a row of silver boxes along a narrow corridor inside a locked gate.

The guardian, a burly security guard with a gun, put his key in box number 372 and turned it. Then, he put my key in the other keyhole and turned it. This caused a small door to pop open, giving him a view of the black metal box inside. He slid the long, narrow black box from its slot and showed me to a small room, placing the box on the plain metal table in front of a metal folding chair. With a nod, he closed the door and left me alone with the box that Ron Wheaton had wanted me to have.

I pulled a regulation length, eleven-inch legal pad and a blue Flair pen, my writing instrument of choice, out of my briefcase, laid them on the table and opened the box. Inside, I saw two regular, white number-ten business envelopes. Both were sealed. One had my name written on it. The other was addressed to Margaret.

I opened the envelope addressed to me and removed three sheets of letter-sized paper. One page was a list of assets. The other two contained a hand-written letter signed by Ron Wheaton. I glanced at the list of assets and was both surprised and chagrined at the value of Ron's estate. He left more than enough money to support a motive for murder, if the multi-million dollar life insurance policy was paid out.

I was happy and concerned for Margaret at the same time. Ben Hathaway would surely feel seven million dollars was an ample motive for murder, if Margaret knew about the money, which she probably did. I shook my head at the over-protectiveness Ron demonstrated for Margaret, even in contemplation of death.

Ron Wheaton had earned a modest living, and both he and Margaret were comfortable with their chosen lifestyle. Ron had far over insured himself long before he was diagnosed with ALS. Perhaps the insurance was cheaper because he bought it through the school system where he worked. Who knows? I just never figured Ron Wheaton for a guy with a desire to be wealthy. Yet, he apparently wanted Margaret to be well-heeled after he died. He surely never believed his attempted largess might cause Margaret more harm than good.

One of my former law partners, who was on his sixth wife, once told me that men don't leave a marriage unless they have somewhere to go. Chief Hathaway's theory must be the same for women, too. He believed Margaret was having an affair with Yeats and killed her husband to be free of Ron so she and Yeats could be together. Hathaway thought Yeats had money, though. When he found out Margaret was the wealthy one, would Hathaway be more convinced Margaret had killed her husband? Or less?

I set the asset list aside for now, and read the letter addressed to me.

"*Dear Willa, Please forgive me for not discussing this with you personally,*" it began in a way that made tears well up in my eyes. This was just like something Ron Wheaton would have said to me before he died. He was always polite and kind. He thought of everyone before himself. Even in death, he was still Ron.

His letter continued, "*but I am truly hoping you will never need to know what I am about to tell you. If things change soon, I will have destroyed this letter before you've ever seen it. If not, I am dead now and you are the only one I can count on to take care of my Margaret.*" Chills ran up my spine as I read these words. Ron knew he was going to die before his ALS killed him. Would he name his killer? I read the rest of the letter.

> *Margaret is having an affair. I don't begrudge her happiness and I would give her permission to love this man, if he was worthy of her. But he isn't. Armstrong Yeats came to see*

me years ago, when he first moved to Pass-a-Grille. He knew Margaret before she married me. He wanted her back. But he had broken her heart. I found out what he'd done and I told him if he ever came around Margaret again, I'd kill him. So he waited until I was too weak to be a threat before he came back to hurt her. This is the next best thing. I've made a list of everything I have to leave to Margaret, and I've had Larry Davis create a trust for everything, including the life insurance. You are my trustee. Please look after it all. Don't give the money to Margaret, because he'll cheat her out of it and break her heart again.

Ron finished the letter simply. *Thank you, Willa, for being such a good friend to us. I know I can count on you. Sincerely, Ron Wheaton.* The letter was dated two weeks before he died.

I put the letter to Margaret back into the box along with the letter to me and the asset list. I knocked on the door and the guard came and returned the box to its place on the shelf, behind the little silver door. He gave me the key, which I put back in its envelope and returned to my purse. Then, I went on to my office, with much on my mind and no time to consider it.

I missed my journal. I needed to write down my chaotic thoughts. To set out the things I'd learned and the leaps of reasoning that came to me. But, like the CJ, I, too, am a civil servant. There was no free time in my schedule today. I took my troubled countenance into my courtroom and tried to focus on oral arguments I'd scheduled weeks before. I heard little and understood less. In my mind, Margaret and Ron Wheaton, CJ and Mariam Richardson, Gil and Sandra Kelley, and finally, Arthur Yeats, elbowed each other around, fighting for my attention.

On the way home, I stopped off at Barnes & Noble on Dale Mabry Highway in South Tampa. I wanted to learn more about Paulding Farnham. From what I'd read in the *U.S. v. Yeats* file, I felt certain there would be at least one biography of the man available in a good bookstore.

I made my way over to the information desk and spoke with Connie Brown, the community relations manager. Connie had helped me out with inquiries about other matters in the past. It only took her a few minutes to find a beautiful coffee table book full of color pictures containing a history of Farnham's work.

With a cup of Starbuck's coffee, I sat in the café and looked at the pictures in *Paulding Farnham, Tiffany's Lost Genius*. The book described Farnham as "the pantheon of American jewelry design" and "the greatest native-born jewelry designer the United States has produced."

Well, if Yeats was planning to impersonate someone's work, I supposed it made sense to choose a man of superior talent who was also surrounded by mystery. Farnham had left the public eye in 1908 and relatively little was known about him afterward. According to the legend, he left jewelry and silver for good when he left Tiffany's. But he was relatively young at the time, as well as extremely talented. It was plausible that he'd continued his work.

Yeats had done his homework well in choosing Paulding Farnham to impersonate because Farnham's work is coveted by afficionados. I was beginning to see why so many presumably wealthy people were willing to believe Yeats when he claimed the copies he sold them were originals. The famous twenty-four karat, gold-and-enamel orchid brooches, first shown at the Paris Exposition of 1889, were particularly coveted. I'd seen no evidence that Yeats had attempted to pass off copies of the orchid brooches, but he did copy and sell Farnham's insect brooches, such as a cabochon beetle and a sapphire bee pin with ruby eyes.

When I looked down at my watch, I was alarmed to see I'd gotten so wrapped up in the beautiful pictures of Farnham's creations that the time had flown by. I pitched my now empty coffee cup, bought the book, and headed home.

Chapter *Sixteen*

Saturday morning of the Gasparilla Distance Classic was cold and clear. I dressed as warmly as I dared and headed downtown. The race started at Morgan and Cumberland Streets and finished at Brorein and Tampa streets. I was running in the 15k race, and I hoped to place in the top three.

I'm not a racer normally, and I don't take care of myself well enough to compete in serious races. I eat too much rich food, drink too much gin and even the occasional smoking I do cuts down on my wind. Most good days, I run about an eight-to-nine minute mile. The Distance Classic isn't age adjusted, so I'd have to run my best times and then some to win.

Despite the odds, I was motivated to win more than the other runners. I still believed in the little engine that could, mind over matter, visualization, and all that. I've always had high aspirations and a finely honed capacity for self-delusion.

I wanted to win the full twenty-thousand dollar donation for Young Mothers' Second Chance. My mother had been a single mom for five years, from the time my biological father was killed while she was pregnant, until she'd married Jim Harper. She always told me how hard it was to take care of a baby by herself.

I'd taken on the cause of single mothers several years ago, sat on the Second Chance board of directors, and raised money for the organization whenever I could to repay Mom. Not that she would approve of my motivation. Mothers do things for their children without thought of creating an interest-bearing receivable.

Even so, not being a mother myself was somewhat justified by my volunteer efforts to support single moms. Some of the young mothers we sponsored had been able to finish college and get good jobs. I'd been working with this organization for many years and this year's race money would be the largest contribution I'd ever managed.

On the theory that we should run before the day's temperatures rose above comfortable levels, the race was scheduled to take off at eight-fifteen. This was usually good planning, but this year, it was wishful thinking. Runners wore long pants, headbands and gloves on hands that held the warm water we were drinking as we waited for the gun, dancing around in the cold to keep our muscles warm. The 5k run was scheduled to begin immediately after ours and then the wheelchair race would roll. We were holding everyone up, but many of the 12,000 runners who had planned to come hadn't arrived and the organizers wanted to wait for them until the last minute. The longer we waited, the colder I became.

Eventually, they told us to line up, and the starting gun gave us our cue to run like hell for just under ten miles. I quickly found myself in the middle of the pack, gasping heavily and watching my jerky, visible breath in the chilly air. Everyone around me was younger by ten years or more, so I guess I was doing well for my age group, which was beginning to feel like the "over 90" crowd.

There were older runners in the pack, but they were in the back and would be content just to finish. Before we started, I had had the conceit to believe I could win. Not just my class, but overall. Nothing like young bodies in top form to remind me of the mileage my body had already traveled. Now I realized I'd be lucky if I didn't die.

After about two miles, I began to get into the race and to warm up. I tried to put on a little speed and at least get nearer the front of the pack.

The problem was that younger, faster runners were getting warmed up, too, and they stayed in front of me the whole way.

When I glanced to my left, I saw Sandra Kelley on the sidelines, cheering a young man who must have been one of the Kelley children. His resemblance to Gil Kelley was unmistakable; if he was about twenty years younger, they'd be twins. Which was curious in its own way, I remember thinking, since Sandra was more than twenty years younger than Gil. They had a three-generation family. And then I had to concentrate on the rest of the run.

Maybe the old girl still has it, but not enough of it. I managed to finish in the middle of the pack. I wasn't last, but I was nowhere near first. The promoters gave me my participatory tee-shirt and congratulatory approval for the pledges I'd obtained from corporate sponsors if I finished the race. I found myself walking around near the finish line, panting hard, sweating profusely, unable to talk and breathe at the same time.

Why did I do all that training if it wasn't going to make a bit of difference? Running alone and running in a race are not the same. Maybe it helps to think you can, but I'm here to tell you, positive thoughts alone cannot make you a fast runner.

Walking around with my head down, looking at the ground, trying to catch my breath and keep my legs from cramping, I didn't see Sandra Kelley until I ran right into her and spilled most of the bottle of water I had in my hand all over her. "I'm sorry, Sandra," I said as I tried ineffectually to brush the water off of the bulky fur coat she wore. I snagged my hand on the sharp edge of the large, elaborate pin she had on the lapel. I stuck my hand in my mouth, trying to make it feel better, without success, thinking it more than a little ridiculous for her to be wearing a mink coat. It wasn't that cold. Only about forty-five degrees, not minus forty-five. She wore the coat just like she did everything else--to show off who she was and what she had. If your husband owns the bank, you damn well better look the part, seemed to be her motto.

"Don't worry about it, Willa. It's not the only thing you've ruined lately," she said, sourly, as she tried to move past me, wiping my blood off her jewelry. But the crowd of runners, well wishers and fund raisers was too thick to let her go through. She was stuck next to me, unable to get away.

"I have (puff puff) no idea (puff puff) what you're (puff puff) talking about," I huffed and puffed and mumbled in her general direction, around the hand in my mouth. Really, I couldn't believe how out of breath I was. I had been running fifteen to sixteen miles a day for weeks. Could it possibly be just the cold? The stress? Too much food at dinner last night? What?

"Your kind never does," she snarled. "You go through life thinking you can just do whatever you want and damn the consequences." She turned her back to me.

This was just too much. I took her arm and pulled her around. Mustering all of my wind, I said in one complete sentence, "Exactly what the hell are you trying to say?"

She looked down at my bleeding hand clutching a big hunk of the fur on her coat along with her arm. The look could have dropped a flying quail at fifty yards. She made me feel even colder than I already was. People aren't often downright nasty to me. I'm not used to it.

"Do you think exposing thefts at Gil's bank is going to be a good thing for his depositors? For the city? Did you think for one minute that just the scandal of the investigation itself wouldn't harm us?" I dropped her arm like it had singed my fingers. Why had I thought she looked anything like Margaret Wheaton? Margaret would never, ever say anything so vicious. Sandra looked feral. She frightened me. I'd never thought of Sandra as dangerous, but I'd underestimated her.

"I'm not investigating Gil or his bank, Sandra. I don't think anything about it."

"Did you think we'd just *take* that? From *you?*" Was she threatening me?

"What are you saying?"

"Watch yourself, Willa Carson. You're not untouchable. I'd have thought you'd learned that by now." She moved off and the crowd quickly filled in the void behind her. I was cold, sweating, tired, my hand was stinging and I was more than a little shocked. I needed to go home, have a hot bath, a pot of hot tea and get out my journal. Now was definitely the time for some serious thinking. It seemed to me that all of South Tampa had completely taken leave of its senses.

Home alone, in the den, in my favorite chair with my feet up, in front of a fire with hot café con leche and my journal, the dogs laying at my feet, I felt calmer and more able to think through the events of the last few days. I picked up journaling where I left off. I started to record everything that happened in chronological order as I knew it.

There were holes, things I wasn't aware of, things I was sure I was forgetting. But all in all, it took me about two hours to write everything down, with the bandage on the outside of my right hand protecting the cut and, I hoped, keeping me from needing stitches. When I'd finished, I had a clearer picture of some things and more questions than answers.

I made a plan, as I always do. I could hear my mother saying, "If you fail to plan, you plan to fail." Why do these old tapes play in my head when I need guidance? I used to so rebel against this piece of advice when Mom was alive. It was unfair of her to haunt me with it now.

In any event, I refilled my coffee cup and turned to a new page in my journal where I spent another hour. I wrote out my plan for helping Margaret Wheaton avoid being arrested; Ben Hathaway see that Ron Wheaton had either died by natural causes or Yeats had killed him; Larry Davis prove that Armstrong Yeats either died accidently or was killed by someone currently unknown to me; Dad wrap up his investigation of Gil Kelley's bank and either file charges or go back to New York.

I paid little attention to the CJ, my continued testimony or his problems; George's concern over Aunt Minnie's jewelry or mine; Suzanne; or my work load. All of these issues dealt with my personal life. I rarely spent any time being concerned about my own problems. Which was a mistake, of course.

Kate tells me I spend too little time inside my circle of control and too much out there tilting at windmills on issues over which I have no influence. The problem with her advice, I thought with a smile, is that she doesn't realize just how influential I can be. For if there's anything my experience has taught me, it's how much one person with good will, positive effort, and the right attitude can do. Never mind that this approach doesn't help win races.

I closed my journal and put it aside. My stomach was rumbling to remind me that it was three o'clock and I hadn't eaten today. We had nothing edible in the kitchen and I didn't want microwave popcorn, so I did a quick once-over of my appearance and went downstairs for lunch. The dining room was closed between lunch and dinner, but the Sunset Bar was always open and would serve me a sandwich or a salad or something.

Expecting the Sunset Bar to be near empty, I was surprised to see Dad was there. Deep in conversation with, of all people, Sandra Kelley. They seemed to be arguing and at first, even though I thought the curiosity might kill me, I wasn't going to join them. But Dad saw me come in and motioned me over, without interrupting whatever Sandra was saying.

I stopped off at the bar, ordered a tuna salad sandwich on white, picked up an iced tea and took it over to Dad's table. Sandra sat on the bench across from him with a cup of hot tea.

"Sit down, Willa," Dad invited. "You know Sandra Kelley, of course, don't you?"

"Yes, of course. Hello, Sandra," I smiled weakly at the woman who would have killed me with her venom this morning. I was still considering a tetanus shot. Sandra gave me a curt and distinctly unfriendly nod.

"Sandra and I were talking about Tampa Bay Bank. She was telling me the unfortunate history of her deceased father-in-law, weren't you, Sandra?" Dad said, putting her on the spot and me into the conversation, despite Sandra's obvious wishes to the contrary. She said nothing, so he went on. "It turns out, Willa, that the late Mr. Gilbert Kelley, Senior, was a thief. Isn't that right, Sandra?"

Sandra looked decidedly uncomfortable discussing this with me. She had a string of pearls around her neck that was in danger of becoming a noose if she twisted them any tighter. Her left hand was gripping the table as if she would fall down without the support, even though she was seated.

"That's not what I said, Mr. Harper," she hissed.

"Call me Jim," he said, with all the concern of a Las Vegas Black Jack dealer watching a gambler bet the farm. "What did you say, then? I thought you were asking me not to investigate thefts from your husband's bank. Because, you said, it was really his father who had stolen millions of dollars from the other shareholders, the depositors and ultimately, the federal government when we had to pay those insured accounts back. Depositors like Willa and George, here. Isn't that what you said?"

This was a side of Jim Harper I hadn't seen before. He was completely without compassion for her, even though Sandra Kelley was obviously in acute distress. She was dressed in a lavender wool St. John suit with a long-sleeved jacket. The temperatures had not warmed up outside, but Sandra was perspiring and fidgety. If she broke those pearls before they broke her neck, they'd scatter all over the floor, she was twisting them so ferociously now. Dad remained unmoved.

"No," she whispered, "that's not what I said. What I said was that Senior, as everyone called him, treated the bank's money as if it was his own because for many years, it was his. His wife inherited the bank, but he became president when he married her. Senior ran the bank from then until he died. I said if there were any, um, improprieties, then, um, they must have happened when he was still, um, in charge." She seemed to stumble a little on this last part, when she'd been reasonably articulate before she tried to slander Senior.

"Let's just say I believed you, Mrs. Kelley," Dad started.

"Sandra," she said, automatically.

"Let's just say I believed you, Sandra," he began again. "How does that change anything? You and your husband are both officers of the bank. You're both responsible for what happens there. You didn't come to me and offer to pay the money back. You're only here because you're worried that I'll be able to prove that your husband is an embezzler and send him off to jail. Isn't that true?" He said this with a frightening calm. If she was trying to make Dad feel sorry for her, dressed to the nines in an outfit that, including jewelry, would set him back more than two month's salary, she'd come to the wrong place. Dad didn't begrudge the Kelleys of the world their silver spoons. He had accumulated a nice portfolio himself over the years. But he did begrudge them the theft of cheap stainless from the rest of the "little people," particularly little *old* people.

Sandra was so incensed, she actually sprayed spittle all the way over to Dad's face in the process of hissing her answer in four distinct words as if they were separated by exclamation points. "You Are A Horrid Man."

Dad said nothing while she gathered up her dignity and stalked out. "So much for Tampans never telling anyone exactly what they think of you," he said, bringing his iced tea up to his mouth.

"Yes," I smiled at him and we both laughed out loud. Not at Sandra's distress, but at the irony of Dad's wit. We talked a little while longer, and

I became engrossed in Dad's day and his investigation of Tampa Bay Bank. He brought me up to date as we ate lunch.

"Are you planning to look into the father-in-law's culpability?" I asked him. "Sandra seemed pretty certain about it."

"I did a lot more than look at bank records in Miami," he said.

"What sent you down there in the first place?"

"It was that story your friend Marilee Aymes told you about Gil Kelley being banished to Miami in the fifties. It seemed like the money problems with the bank began about the time she said Gil Kelley was working in Miami. The story could have supported Sandra Kelley's version, which I'd already heard before today, of course."

"What do you mean?"

"Well, if the embezzlement started then, it could have been Senior who did it from Tampa or it could have been Gil from Miami. I couldn't just walk into the Tampa office and ask, without tipping my hand, so I went to the Miami branch and looked at the books myself."

"They let you do that?"

"There's a clause in their insurance policy that requires them to let me look at their books whenever I want to," he said, a little wounded. "The bank has no choice but to let me investigate. I just wanted a little freedom from Kelley's personal oversight while I did it."

"I'd think Gil Kelley would have learned about your snooping pretty quickly either way. But what did you find out?"

"That over three-hundred thousand dollars disappeared from the Miami branch office over a two-year period back in the late fifties—coinciding with Gil Kelley's period of expulsion from the family nest."

"But you knew that before you went there, based on Marilee's story."

"Ahh, but what I didn't know before I went there was what happened to the money and how it got paid back." He savored his own tuna sandwich as if he were dining on the finest smoked sturgeon, taking his time, forcing me to ask him the next question.

"Ok. What happened to the money and how did it get paid back?" I can be stubborn myself, but this wasn't one of those times. I was curious, and didn't mind showing my curiosity.

"Well, that's quite an interesting story. The money disappeared in dribs and drabs. Just a few hundred at first, every couple of weeks. Then a few thousand. Then larger amounts. I was hoping to be able to pin that on Kelley, but it turned out to be a dead end. Literally."

I'd finished eating and we were now talking over freshened glasses of iced tea. "The thief was a low level auditor named David Martin. Guess what happened to him?" Dad asked me.

"I give up."

"He died. Killed himself. And that's not all." At this point, Dad looked a little like the remaining smile on the Cheshire cat. He waited for me to ask, but I didn't this time. So he said, "It was the bonding company that paid off the debts after the guy died."

"So those early thefts didn't have anything to do with Gil Kelley?" I asked.

Dad sounded deeply disappointed. "Apparently not, unfortunately. It was a good lead. I'm just sorry it didn't pan out. If I could have tied those early thefts to Gil Kelley it would have been a lot easier to tie the later ones to him, too."

"What a coincidence that there was a bonding company to pay. In those days, three hundred thousand dollars was a lot of money."

Chapter *Seventeen*

I needed a change of pace, somewhere else to go to think. I didn't tell anyone where I was going. When I left home Monday morning, instead of driving Greta toward downtown, I took Gandy to Westshore. Turning north, I reached Tampa International Airport in plenty of time for the nine o'clock flight to Miami.

Everything about this case seemed to point to Miami. Gil Kelley, Margaret Wheaton and David Martin were in Miami from 1955 to 1957. What happened there? And how did it relate to what had gone on in Tampa the past few weeks? Was there a relationship between the three of them?

The commuter flight was just under an hour and I was on the ground, in my rental car, by ten-fifteen. Studying the map Hertz provided, I found my way to Coconut Grove. I drove to the Tampa Bay Bank branch where Gil Kelley and David Martin had worked.

The bank manager was a portly man, about sixty-five or so, who looked as if he'd never had a good hair day. I introduced myself, telling him I was the executor of Ron Wheaton's estate and I had come to look into some accounts Ron had held at the bank. It only took a little flirting and I had him in my pocket.

Once we had struck up a friendship, I said, "Mr. Wheaton asked me to look up a friend of his who works here. I think he left the man a little something in his will. I wonder if you could point me in the right direction to find him?" I broke my self-imposed rule against lying, but rationalized it as for a good cause. I promised myself a strong penance afterward.

"I'll surely try. What's his name?"

"David Martin," I told him and watched his friendliness dry up like a slug exposed to salt.

"Mr. Martin died, quite some time ago. I'm afraid you won't be able to talk to him," he said curtly.

"Did he leave any family? I could give the gift to his wife," I coaxed.

"No. He had a young girlfriend, but when he died she left here. I don't know her name." His easy manner was completely gone now, replaced by fidgeting with the papers on his desk to let me know he was ready to terminate this conversation. Now.

"Well, where did he live? I can see you're busy. Maybe I can trace the girlfriend through his last address."

"I'll get that for you, ma'am, if you'll wait just a minute," he said, decidedly cool in his tone, making it clear that I'd be dismissed after this last courtesy.

When he came back with the address, I asked him straight up, "Is something wrong? You seem like you're not too happy that I'm asking about Mr. Martin."

"Not at all, ma'am," he said, not convincing me or himself, but offering nothing further. I put his reaction down to Martin's thefts from the bank. Men from the old school would have taken a dim view of bank theft, just as most of us do today. But a forty- year-old theft, paid back through a surety bond when the thief died, shouldn't engender such a long-held animosity. At least, I couldn't hold a grudge that long.

I stayed a while longer, talking to a couple of other employees who looked old enough to have been working at the bank while David Martin was there. Then I had to hustle to finish my investigation in time to catch my plane.

When I left the bank branch, I drove through McDonald's for a hamburger and fries on the run. I made my way over to the local library, gobbling the food out of the bag on the way and rolling down the windows to get the smell out of the car. Once settled at the library machine with the microfilm of the local newspapers from 1956, I began to flip through the pages looking for references to David Martin. It didn't take me long to find the story of Martin's suicide by drowning in early 1957. Checking my watch and knowing I had one more stop to make, I copied the articles without reading them and paid for my copies at the desk. I jogged out to the rental car, remembering my vows after the distance classic to get in better shape. Of course, I should have remembered that before I ate a thousand calorie, junk-food lunch.

I traced Martin's address to a dreary rooming house close to the bank branch where Martin had worked as an internal auditor. I parked the car at the curb, walked up to the house, and leaned on the button for the door bell.

A woman as unkempt and unattractive as the house answered the door. She identified herself as "Joan." Then she smiled, showing what was left of her teeth: cavities and broken pieces. Bad teeth are usually a sign of someone who fears dentists and, in my experience, has other irrational fears as well.

"Hi, I'm Willa Carson. I'm looking for a man who used to live here. His name is David Martin. Did you know him?" Joan had started to nod before I finished the sentence.

"Yep. I did know him, before he died. My momma used to own this place then. David was pretty quiet. Good lookin', too. I was only about ten years old when he killed himself." She pronounced it "kilt hisself," lisping through the "esses."

"Did he kill himself here? in your house?" I tried to sound properly horrified.

"God, no!" It sounded like "Gawd, nah." The accent was music to my ears. Amazingly, I'd found the only redneck left in Miami. "He went out fishin' and never came back. Curious thing was that he'd only taken up fishin' a few weeks earlier. But the night he died, he went out on the ocean by hisself. Everybody here found that odd at the time." The heavy Southern accent and the missing teeth made her difficult to understand. It gave me the feeling that my mind was processing the speech just a second or two behind, like the delay between dialogue and subtitles on a foreign film. Joan was speaking English, of sorts, even if I couldn't translate it in real time.

"Did Mr. Martin leave anything here that you might still have?" I asked her.

She was already shaking her head of lank dirty brown hair before I got the question out. "Nope. That friend of his that he was always hanging around with took his car and everything after they found the body."

"Well, who was that? Maybe I can ask him."

"He was that big banker David worked for. What a flirt! I thought he was real handsome at the time though," she laughed, showing her bad teeth to full effect.

Back at the airport just in time to catch my plane by running to the gate, I found myself cursing my junk food lunch and vowing to give up french fries forever. Once I was seated on the plane, I pulled out my journal and wrote down the day's conversations as well as a few thoughts for investigation.

Joan said David Martin owned an old car, so he must have had a driver's license. I planned to contact the state to check it, maybe get a picture that I could then run through the Florida Department of Law Enforcement's facial recognition software. Martin had been fingerprinted for the bonding company, which filed his prints with the FBI. I would contact the FBI to run the prints to see if he had any kind of a criminal record. "Maybe all the leads won't be dead ends," I wrote, smiling at my own bad pun.

When I got home, I searched until I found Dad in our den alone with the television tuned to a college basketball game. But work is always a more interesting topic to him. It was easy to convince him to compare notes on our respective trips to Miami.

"The newspaper accounts of his suicide describe Martin as an internal auditor who stole money from the bank and then committed suicide when the bank examiners found out. He had been there for about two years before Gil Kelley arrived, but the money didn't start disappearing until Kelley got there," I told Dad.

He took a swallow of his iced tea. "That sounds promising."

"I thought so, too. Martin lived a quiet lifestyle until about the time Kelley arrived, though. I didn't see anything that would suggest he lived large."

"Did you find anyone still at the bank in Miami who remembered Martin?" I was already nodding my head before he finished the question. "What did they tell you?" he asked.

"I talked to a couple of old timers while I was there. They remembered Martin because of the theft. But not much else. They said he was a loaner, kept to himself, and then struck up a friendship with Kelley because they were about the same age. They said Martin and Kelley got into some pretty wild living and there was even the idea that they'd gotten on the wrong side of the Mafia somehow, until Martin killed himself. Then, that idea went by the wayside. Other than that, they knew nothing."

Dad thought for a few minutes and then volunteered "I can check the employment files, but it's probably too long ago. They've more than likely been destroyed. I already tried to pull up Martin's old IRS files, but even those have been archived somewhere. The IRS might find the files, but I'm not holding my breath until they do."

Dad had access to information not easily available to me. I asked him,"What about running the Social Security number?"

"I did that when I checked all this stuff before. David Martin is listed as deceased in 1957. I could contact the bonding company for you, if you want me to. I didn't look back that far when I called them originally. Since we're both in the insurance business, they would probably share their files with me," he said.

"I already asked them, actually. Since the investigation was so old, they didn't have much on it. But they faxed me what they had. I have their file here somewhere." I started rifling through the papers piled all over the table and onto the seat next to me. Then, in my briefcase on the floor. Finally, I came up with a thin green folder which, when I opened it, had a few sheets of photocopied microfilm. The pages were dark and blurry. "There's not much here. The complete file was destroyed long ago."

I showed him the bottom of the third page which said "Disposition: Paid." The first two pages were the rest of the claim form and the comments by the investigator at the time. The claimant was listed as Tampa Bay Bank and the contact was Gilbert Kelley, Senior, now deceased. The description of the claim was "embezzled funds." The investigator's comments were equally terse. "Accounting irregularities beginning in 1955 and ending in 1957 equal to a loss of $300,000. Attributable to internal auditor, now deceased."

"What about the bond company investigator, can we interview him?" Dad was getting as frustrated about this as I was. Now I was shaking my head. "Let me guess," he said. "Deceased?"

"Yes. About ten years ago. Heart attack."

"So what you're saying is that you know the money began to disappear at the time Gil Kelley came to the Miami branch. You also know that he and Martin were friends. Then, the bank examiners found the money missing. Martin committed suicide and the bonding company paid off the debt. Case closed. Unless your other inquiries turn up something else."

"Except for one thing," I said.

"What's that?"

"The money kept disappearing from the bank. For years afterwards."

We both thought about the facts some more, trying to fit the pieces together to create a complete picture. But critical pieces of the puzzle were still missing and we couldn't even organize all the pieces of one section of the puzzle board on what we knew now. It was like those jigsaw puzzles where the finished picture is solid black. Only the shapes were important. There were no vivid pictures to match up.

"Did Martin have a wife? Kids? Other family?" Dad asked.

"Apparently not. He lived alone at the rooming house and as far as the old-timers at the bank knew, he had no family."

"Well, everyone has parents. What about that?" He raked a frustrated hand through his still thick head of salt and pepper hair.

"When I get the reports back I'm looking for, I think I may be able to trace him. At this point, it's a brick wall. I don't know where he came from, don't even have a place and date of birth."

Dad looked at me quizzically. "I don't understand that, Willa. I checked his Social Security number. He had one. Didn't he have to provide a birth certificate to get the number in the first place?"

I shook my head again. "Now. Not back when Martin applied. I'm hoping the finger prints will check out and compare to some others somewhere. But in those days, people didn't get fingerprinted in the hospital or for most jobs. If Martin wasn't arrested somewhere or in some type of law enforcement, the finger prints are likely to be a dead end, too." I ran my hands through my hair in frustration now, too. "Can a man just disappear without a trace in this country?"

Dad laughed out loud at this, got up and collected a couple of beers from the small fridge in the bar in our den. "Well, that's not exactly the question. We're not talking about him disappearing here."

"Sure we are. He's got no history. He just showed up at the Tampa Bay Bank in 1954 and they hired him, the bonding company accepted him, he embezzled money from the bank and then killed himself. That's it? That's the whole story?"

I hadn't wanted a beer, I was about to say as Dad twisted the caps off both bottles, clinked the neck of my bottle with his, handed me one and resumed his seat. Oh, what the hell, I thought, and took a big swig out of the long neck bottle. I just love Labatt Blue Ribbon beer. We started drinking it when we lived in Detroit. Now, George orders it in relatively small quantities because Canadian beer is not a big seller here. But, it's my beer of choice, when I drink beer. And it's best fresh, too. I was looking at the bottle, admiring the taste, when an idea occurred to me. "What about Canada?"

"For beer? Can't beat it." Dad gave me his biggest grin.

"No. I mean, what about Canada for tracing this guy? Could he have come from Canada? Florida gets thousands of tourists a year from Canada, if not millions. Miami must get them, too. Could he have come to the U.S. from Toronto or Windsor or something?"

"Maybe. But don't let yourself get distracted. It's probably unimportant where he came from. Once David Martin died, the link between Gil Kelley and the missing money was severed. And to answer your question, it's pretty easy to disappear in this country. Even today. Hundreds of people do it every year. All you do is to cut all your ties to your old self by telling no one about your plans, fabricate a new name and history and pay for everything with cash. It's fairly easy if you just take on the identity of a dead person. What's hard is to stay away from your old life. Most people can't manage it. Even Mafia witnesses who have been granted witness protection and given new identities can't do it. And those guys are highly motivated." Dad and I both laughed at the image of highly motivated Mafia witnesses.

"So, he came from somewhere. I think it's important to find out where that was," I insisted. "And why he left there. And how."

"I'll humor you on this one, Willa. I'll see what I can find out. But I honestly think it has nothing to do with what you're investigating. Which is, who killed Ron Wheaton and Armstrong Yeats."

Chapter *Eighteen*

George and I were dressed and waiting for Dad and Suzanne to join us for the Minaret Krewe Coronation Ball at the Tampa Convention Center, where next year's King and Queen would be crowned at the end of the night. I hadn't invited them to join us, but apparently, George had. He didn't tell me because he expected fireworks. I gave him none. It doesn't pay to become too predictable, Kate always says. Takes the mystery out of marriage.

The ten-minute drive was spent with pleasantries, the only conversation besides work Dad ever has with anyone. We pulled up in front of the Tampa Convention Center to use the valet service Minaret Krewe had hired for the night. I was busy getting my wrap around the bare-shouldered silver gown I had foolishly decided to wear to this event about six weeks ago, when it was still warm enough for it. I'd chosen the dress because I planned to wear Aunt Minnie's jewelry. A spectacular emerald necklace set in platinum, with matching earrings. As I often did when using Aunt Minnie's things, I wondered what admirer had given her emeralds at a time when emeralds were not "manufactured," as most of them are now. Aunt Minnie had lived a colorful life, and I was reaping all of her life's benefits while paying none of its costs. This was especially true in the case of her jewelry. George had had Aunt Minnie's pieces appraised. Thankfully, we learned they had not been stolen by Armstrong Yeats when George had taken the pieces in for cleaning.

I turned around to speak to Suzanne, just as she shook her head, revealing diamond drop earrings that were hanging from her lobes. They must have been five carats each. I couldn't imagine how strong her ears must have been to hold them up. Is it possible to do earlobe exercises?

"What beautiful earrings, Suzanne. They look positively fabulous on you." And they did. Suzanne was a beautiful woman. She looked so much like my mother I almost cried.

Suzanne beamed at Dad, who by now had made his way around the car. As she took his arm, she cooed, "Jimmy bought them for me from that Mr. Yeats you introduced us to. Aren't they just perfect?"

Just perfect, I thought. Probably, just perfect fakes. But why spoil her night? With Yeats dead, it wasn't likely Dad would get his money back. He must know now that the earrings weren't real. I gave George a meaningful look as he took my hand. We all walked over to the outdoor escalator and rode to the second floor where Minaret Krewe had rented one of the larger rooms for its grande finale of the season.

A few of the other Krewes were having their balls here at the Convention Center, too. For tonight, the Krewe members left their pirate costumes at home. All the rooms were filled with women in gowns and fine jewelry and men in tuxedos. Almost everyone we knew in Tampa would be here somewhere.

It was the longest night of the year for me, but the one I most looked forward to. Each of the Krewes would crown its Kings and Queens and then announce the results of its fund raising for the year. Except for the Gasparilla Festival of the Arts, which was thankfully not related to the Krewes in any way, this would be our last big night of the Gasparilla season.

Next week, we could enjoy the art festival like the rest of the more than 200,000 people who would be there. More importantly, as far as I was concerned, our lives would return to normal beginning tomorrow morning. I almost sighed, I was so happy with anticipation.

Suzanne and Dad were both mesmerized by the splendor of the whole thing. There was more jewelry here than you'd find at all the Tiffany stores in the country. More taffeta, silk, strappy sandals, fine cigars and expensive perfume. Tonight, there seemed to be an equally large number of furs, something the center had hurriedly set up a coat check room to accommodate. Usually, there's no need to wear coats in Florida so there's no need to check them. Houses don't even have coat closets here. But tonight, the mercury promised to dip below the freezing point, and the Tampa ladies took the opportunity to show off what they had.

By midnight, I had been standing for five exhausting hours on four-inch spike heels. We had dinner, but it was heavy hors d'oeuvres passed around by waiters in black tie and tails. We didn't sit, even when the King and Queen were crowned. I felt like I might soon collapse.

George was talking in a group that included Gilbert Kelley, which I found surprising since he knew as much about Dad's investigation as I did. I suppose George had no choice. Gil Kelley was the past Minaret Krewe king and George was the Krewe's main sponsor. They'd have to speak to each other occasionally. It might as well be in a public place.

I was standing there thinking about Gil Kelley when Ben Hathaway came up behind me and touched my elbow. "I know where there are a couple of seats out in the lobby. Are you interested?"

"Chief, you do know how to turn a girl's head," I told him, mocking the coquet, batting my eyelashes and lowering my gaze. I followed Ben out into the lobby and into a blissfully comfortable upholstered chair. Ben handed me a cup of coffee he'd snagged from the last of the circulating trays.

"You look mighty handsome in that tuxedo, Chief," I continued with the drawl.

"Thank 'ye, Ma'am." If he'd had on a hat, he'd have tipped it. He smiled back at me as I drank the best coffee I'd had in weeks and actually groaned with pleasure. I was way too old to stand up all night in four-inch heels. What was I thinking?

"It was a good thing you hired Larry Davis for Margaret, Willa," Ben said seriously now. "She's going to need a good lawyer and Larry's one of the best."

"What do you mean?"

"I'm going to arrest her tomorrow. For the murders of Ron Wheaton and Armstrong Yeats."

I nearly spit out my coffee, which now tasted like old grounds in my mouth. He'd picked this time and this place to tell me about Margaret's arrest so I couldn't protest about it as much as I would have anywhere else.

"I gather you think you've got a good reason to do that," I said in a quiet but mean-spirited tone.

He had the grace to look troubled. "It isn't what I want to do, believe me. The evidence has left me no other choice."

"What evidence? What possible evidence could you have against a little old woman as sweet and gentle as Margaret? What?" I wasn't letting him off the hook. I set the coffee down and turned my full attention to him. I didn't want to be overheard any more than he did, but I wanted to know what Margaret was facing.

"I found a disinterested witness who saw Margaret push Armstrong Yeats down in a quarrel at the Knight Parade. And, as you know, I got the autopsy and the full tox report back on Ron Wheaton. He died of an overdose of insulin. Margaret's an insulin-dependent diabetic. I'm sorry, Willa. I didn't want it to be Margaret, either." He looked so much like a basset hound after a bad meal that I believed him. I didn't like it, but I did believe him. I was a little relieved. Dad had admitted to pushing Yeats down, too. In front of witnesses. If Hathaway focused on Margaret, he must have discounted Dad as a suspect. It seemed Yeats had a knack for inspiring people to violence that ultimately got him killed. If Margaret pushed Yeats down, which I doubted, it was because he asked for it. That didn't mean I'd let Hathaway arrest Margaret. Because she didn't kill anyone. I knew it, even if he didn't.

I thought back to the evening of the Knight Parade. I, too, had seen Margaret on the float with Armstrong Yeats. But they were so far toward the back that I never got around there to speak to them. Gil and Sandra Kelley were on the right side of the front of the float, opposite George and me. They could easily have gone back there and pushed Yeats off. He could have hit his head then. But that's not when he died. It was later, on a dark street, off Seventh Avenue.

I remembered sweating and still being freezing cold while I waited for the shuttle bus to take us back to Minaret after the parade. We were standing at the end of the parade route, on 22nd Street. I didn't see Margaret and Yeats there then. In fact, I'd seen Yeats without Margaret. Then, I never saw either of them again. Nor did I see the Kelleys after that until we were all back at Minaret, later in the evening.

Someone must have argued with Yeats, pushed him harder than intended, and Yeats, being drunk, fell and hit his head. That's not really murder. But, leaving Yeats alone on the street to die was at least negligence, if not depraved indifference to human life. He wouldn't have died right away. It took a while for the bleeding inside his skull to kill him. If the pusher had called for help, Yeats might be alive today. Could Margaret have pushed Yeats in anger, stalking off and leaving him there to die, not knowing the full extent of his injury? I now had to acknowledge that she could have done that. Anyone could have done that. It wasn't murder without an intent to kill. But, Yeats was dead just the same.

I continued to replay the scenes of that Saturday evening in my mind. Until I remembered the random thought I'd had when I first went down the stairs from our flat into George's restaurant lobby. When I saw Margaret standing next to Sandra Kelley. They had been made up by the same artist, their black eyebrows, brightly rouged cheeks, and strong red mouths, applied with the same heavy hand. Their costumes had been the same colors and they both wore black wigs. Maybe the "disinterested witness" Hathaway had interviewed didn't know both Margaret and Sandra. If not, and eye witness could easily have confused them that night. Had Margaret pushed Armstrong Yeats down to the sidewalk in anger? Or was it Sandra Kelley?

I finally got home and was able to change into jeans, leaving George sleeping in the flat. The drive to Margaret's house at two in the morning took only a few minutes. When I got there, the house was dark and not one small light was burning. I rang the bell several times, each ring longer and more insistent. Margaret never came to answer it. In freezing frustration, I jogged quickly around to the back of the house where I'd found the door unlocked once before. It was unlocked again and I resolved to tell Margaret that she absolutely had to be more careful.

I opened the door quietly and went into the mud room off the kitchen, just as I had the last time. I didn't want to startle Margaret, but I didn't want to kill myself walking around in the dark either. I felt around the doorway for a light switch and found one, but it turned on the outside light over the door I'd just come through.

The porch light provided dim illumination as I walked into the kitchen and continued feeling around for another light switch. I found it on the opposite side of the door way from the last one. When I flipped it, the hanging lamp over the kitchen table came on and illuminated the entire kitchen. A good thing, because the light kept me from tripping over the body in the middle of the floor.

Chapter *Nineteen*

It took me about two seconds to recognize Margaret laying there. She was fully dressed. I stooped down to check and found her breathing normally. Trying to wake her up took a few minutes, but eventually she did. I helped her to the living room couch. After giving her some water and finding her eye glasses under the kitchen table, she righted herself and was coherent enough to talk to me, but barely.

I spoke to her gently. "Honey, what happened? Why were you on the floor? Did you fall?" Elderly people were always falling down and breaking their hips. I feared this had happened to Margaret, although she didn't seem to be in any pain. She seemed bewildered and disoriented, but she knew who I was and where she was. As the doctors say, she was oriented to time and place.

After a little while Margaret was able to speak coherently. "I don't know what happened. I came out into the kitchen to get something and the next thing I remember is sitting here with you." As she exhaled, I got the slightly sweet smell of processed alcohol on her breath. I never thought of Margaret as a closet drinker. Maybe she'd gotten drunk and passed out. People have been driven to drink by lesser things than she had been dealing with lately.

"Well, come on, we're going to get you over to Tampa General and have them take a look at you." I started trying to get her up, but she was surprisingly resistant. She refused to budge.

"I'm not going to the hospital. I think I must have fainted or something. Nothing's broken. I don't hurt anywhere. I'll be fine in a few minutes." She started feeling her hands, her arms, her feet and her legs. She turned her head this way and that, feeling it with her hands as she did so. She straightened her shoulders and flexed them. Finally, she stood up, bent over at the waist, then stooped down by bending her knees and standing back up. All while I watched in silence. Her flexibility was remarkable. But then, I was learning how remarkable Margaret really was in many respects.

"You could have had a stroke or something, Margaret. Be reasonable. We should check it out, at least," I pleaded with her.

"I'm fine. Nothing's broken. I'll be okay," she told me with firmness that meant I'd never get her to the hospital unless I called an ambulance and they sedated her, which I wasn't going to do. She patted me on the hand sitting in my lap. "Don't worry so much, Willa. I've been taking care of myself and Ron for a long time. I know when I need a doctor. I don't need one now."

We sat there in silence while she let me decide for myself that she wasn't going to any hospital with me voluntarily. Then she got up and went into the kitchen to put on the kettle for tea. I had no choice but to go after her.

"Why are you here, Willa?" she asked, her back to me while she worked at getting the tea put together.

"I came to tell you that Ben Hathaway is planning to arrest you tomorrow for the murders of Ron and Armstrong Yeats. Unless we can figure out a way to do something about that, he should be here bright and early."

Her hands were shaking slightly as she got the china cups and saucers out of the cabinet, but she said nothing.

"I need you to talk to me, Margaret. I can't help you if I don't know what's going on here. I tried asking Larry Davis, but he rightly feels he can't disclose your confidences to me." I got up from the table and walked up behind her, giving her a hug. She was so tiny, especially next to me. She felt so frail in my embrace. "Let me help you, Margaret. I really want to." And then she crumpled in my arms and started to cry. I held her for a while as the tears fell. When the tea kettle began whistling insistently, I helped her over to the table and handed her the tissue box. I finished up the tea while she composed herself. Then I sat down across the table from her and asked my question again.

"Tell me what's going on here. I have some influence with Ben Hathaway, but I don't know what to tell him. I need something to work with." She nodded her head, not trusting herself to speak yet, lest tears begin afresh. I continued in her silence. "Ok. Here's what I've been told. I know that Ron was dying of ALS. I also know his death wasn't by natural causes. Hathaway believes you were having an affair with Armstrong Yeats and that you killed Ron to be free of him so you could be with Yeats. Then, he thinks you killed Yeats in a quarrel, unintentionally. He says he has a witness who saw you two arguing and saw you push Yeats after the parade Saturday night. I don't know what other evidence he thinks he has, but this is a big piece to start with." As I recited these facts, tears began to fall from her eyes again, but she was composed. Just sad. "Tell me about this, Margaret. Did you kill Ron?"

Her voice was quiet, but I could hear her. "No."

"Well, that's a relief. Do you know who did?"

"Yes."

"Tell me, Margaret. If you want to stay out of jail, I need to know."

"My first husband killed Ron."

"You were married before Ron? I had no idea. When was this?"

"Years ago. I was young. So was he. I thought he'd died, but he didn't," tears continued to pour out of her eyes and down her cheeks. "I'd never have done it if I'd known he was alive. Never."

I was confused. She told me she hadn't killed Ron. "Done what? What wouldn't you have done if you'd known your husband was alive?"

"I'd never have given our baby away" And she began to sob in loud gulps. She put her head down on the table and cried with deep grief, for her lost child, her lost husband and her lost life. There was nothing I could do but wait it out, feeling such sadness for her that tears appeared on my own cheeks.

By the time she stopped sobbing, Margaret was so exhausted she couldn't keep talking. It was after four o'clock in the morning. If I put her to bed, she'd sleep until Chief Hathaway came to arrest her in the morning. No matter what else happened, it would do no good to put Margaret Wheaton in jail. I couldn't call Hathaway at this hour and ask him to put off the arrest another day, although I believed he would do so if I told him why. If I called the police station and left a message, it would be recorded. I didn't want that. Besides, why did Hathaway tell me he was going to arrest Margaret tomorrow if he didn't expect me to do something about it? So, what I did next wasn't obstruction of justice. Not exactly.

I found Margaret's coat and helped her into it. I packed her a small bag, carried it out to the car, and then helped her into the car. As I drove back to Minaret in the deep darkness of early morning, I tried to plan how I would explain this to George, who would definitely understand. And how I would explain it to Hathaway, who might not. I avoided thinking about how I might have to explain my behavior the next time I was testifying under oath in the CJ's hearing.

It was too late, or too early, to go to bed after I had Margaret safely stowed in our guest room again. I made coffee and settled in the den with my journal. It was still quite cold, so I started another fire. While George, the dogs, Dad, Suzanne and Margaret all slept, I picked up my journaling where I had left off, adding Margaret's revelations to what I knew already.

"Find Margaret's first husband and you'll find Ron Wheaton's murderer," I wrote.

Margaret had given me few clues before she'd completely broken down in her kitchen. But she said she'd been married a long time ago, for a very short time, and had a child. There must have been a record of the marriage somewhere. I logged onto my computer and entered the programs available to me through the contract the courts have with a public records search service.

If I wanted more information, I'd have to call one of my friends in the U.S. Marshall's office, and for now I wanted to avoid the questions that would raise. I found Margaret Rodriguez Wheaton's Social Security number and ran a check on it. I found the calculation of her benefits when she turned sixty-five next month and her work history reflected in the list of deposits to her account through the years.

Margaret had been employed by the U.S. Government as long as I had. We'd started at the courthouse the same month and the same year, because I hired her right after my appointment was confirmed. Before that, she'd worked in law offices around Tampa. Her last law firm secretarial position was with my old firm. I knew she'd been married to Ron Wheaton for over thirty years, so her earlier marriage must have been when she was less than thirty years old.

I scrolled back to the early deposit records, checking from her first employment in high school at the Colonnade, which was then a drive-in restaurant on Bayshore popular with the kids. Probably, she'd been a waitress. Her earnings were reported at less than a dollar an hour.

There were a few more entries in what looked like a series of waitress jobs in her teens and then a curious entry by an employer listed as "Mrs. Robert Prieto." The contributions continued each year for three years. There was a gap in the history then for about six months and the next entry was another waitress job in Tampa. After that, all the entries were from Tampa law practices until she became employed as my secretary.

In the 1950s, a pregnant widow of very modest means with no family would have had a hard time taking care of herself and her child. My own mother was in the same situation, and she had told me many times how hard it was for her. She said it was so difficult for her to manage even when Kate Austin had helped her by taking us in. We lived with the Austin family while Mom finished nursing school and got a job. If Margaret didn't have a Kate to help her, and I knew she had no family, being a young woman with a child and without a husband would have seemed impossible.

I looked at the records a little more closely. My eyes were so tired and the screen print was small. Even with my bifocals, I was having a hard time reading the tiny print. Now, though, I was focused on that six-month gap in Margaret's employment history. I calculated that in 1957, Margaret would have been twenty-one years old. Her work with Mrs. Prieto must have put her in a position to meet her husband. I looked closer at Mrs. Prieto's contribution history. The address listed was Coconut Grove, the same suburb of Miami that housed the branch of Tampa Bay Bank where Gil Kelley had worked.

So Margaret had left Tampa when she was eighteen, probably right after high school. She began living in Miami with Mrs. Prieto, doing some kind of domestic work, I imagined. She'd met and married, gotten pregnant and then her husband had died. Margaret gave the baby up for adoption and then returned to Tampa, where no one would know she'd been married or pregnant. A few years later, she met and married Ron Wheaton.

Only Margaret's husband hadn't really died. Margaret must have found out at some point. How did she know? When did she know? Where was her husband now? And where was the child? I finished off my journaling with the questions that were puzzling me now. Maybe, my sleep-deprived brain said to my still-awake and coffee-wired self, the answers would come to me if I could just close my eyes for a little cat nap. My head fell back against the chair and the next thing I knew, Harry and Bess had two feet each in my lap, licking my face with the vigor only well-trained Labradors can manage.

Chapter *Twenty*

Judging from the way I felt, Margaret must have been at least as tired, so I let her sleep. It was seven o'clock Sunday morning, but I called Hathaway at home anyway. The last thing I wanted was for him to go to Margaret's to arrest her and find her gone. Then, I'd have hell to pay. It was going to be only slightly better when I told him myself that she wasn't at her home before he got there.

I held the cordless phone to my ear as I walked around the kitchen collecting coffee making materials. I heard the telephone ring several times and then Hathaway's machine pick up. At least it was his home answering machine and not the office. Still, I was careful with my message.

"Ben, this is Willa Carson. Please call me first thing this morning. I have something important to tell you." That was urgent enough, I hoped, to keep him from making a fool of himself at Margaret's and then doing something equally stupid to save face. After that, I argued with myself for a while over whether to call Larry Davis, going back and forth, with excellent arguments on both sides. A good lawyer can always argue both sides of any issue. Before I decided, George walked into the kitchen, gave me a hug and a morning-breath kiss. I held onto him much too long. I was lucky to have him and feeling worse about Margaret's situation by the minute. She'd lost not one husband she loved, but two. Not to mention her child. How far would Margaret go when pushed beyond what a woman should be forced to endure? Was she capable of murder? We forget, sometimes, how fragile humans are. Maybe Margaret snapped. It's happened before, under far less onerous circumstances.

"Hey," George said as he gently pushed me away so he could look into my face. "Let a guy get a cup of Joe before you go mauling him in the morning so he can at least be awake enough to enjoy it, hmmmm?" He gave me a kiss on the top of my head and then turned to pour himself some liquid fortification.

"The coffee's a good idea. I have a lot to tell you and not a lot of time to do it in." I poured a cup for me and placed the cordless phone back in its cradle. I moved both of us into the den where we could close the door and talk undisturbed. I told him about my evening's adventure.

George is used to my nocturnal wanderings around the house and Plant Key, but he doesn't like it when I leave our island in the wee hours. Before he could get his protective bluster up, I gave him the short version. George is a quick study. It didn't take him long to grasp the implications of Margaret being in our guest room, both to Margaret and to me. But we've been married a long time. He knows better than to try to scold me into changing my mind. Especially over something I've already done.

"So, where are we?" he asked when I'd finished.

"I'm not sure. Margaret said she didn't kill Ron and I believe her. She said her first husband did it. I still don't know why or how. I need to find that out."

"Aren't you a little confused here? Isn't that Ben Hathaway's job? Finding killers?"

When I started to say, "But, George," he cut me off at the B. "It's one thing to rescue people you know and care about, Willa. I've accepted that I can't keep you from doing that. But you don't know anything about this character except that he's a killer. You've helped Margaret. Hearing the piece of news that we know who killed Ron Wheaton will be enough to get Ben Hathaway not to arrest Margaret until he checks it out, at least. Why not stop while you're ahead? Think about that while I refill my cup," he said as he patted my knee and walked out of the room.

Before George came back for my answer, the telephone rang. It was Ben Hathaway returning my call. I could tell he was up and dressed and ready to get to work, even if it was Sunday. He was wary of my tale, but knew me well enough to trust my word. At a minimum, he knew I believed Margaret's story. That was enough to make him want to investigate it.

Ben Hathaway has arrested the wrong person more than once when I told him not to. The State Attorney was getting a little sore about looking like a fool in public because Hathaway had done the wrong thing. Ben must have been "talked to," as they say downtown. He was a little more cautious than he's been in the past.

Ben agreed to meet here with Larry Davis, Margaret, George and me in three hours when I convinced him Margaret needed to sleep and I hadn't called Larry yet. At least now I knew I was going to do so. That was progress, of a sort.

Larry was home and answered the phone on the first ring. If you despise telephone tag and answering machines, early Sunday morning is a good time to call people in Tampa. Larry wasn't too keen on my interference with his client last night, but he agreed to come right over to Minaret and discuss it with me. "Then, I'll decide whether and what we tell Ben Hathaway, Willa. It's my job to represent Margaret. I'm not sure what it is you think you're doing."

A half hour later, I'd showered and changed into clean jeans and a long-sleeved tee-shirt. As an accommodation to the temperature, I'd put on socks with my topsiders. I was forced to put some concealer on the dark circles under my eyes to keep from looking like a racoon. Otherwise, I wore no makeup and no jewelry, the same as any other Sunday when I expected to stay home alone.

Larry Davis arrived on time. He and George and I repaired to the den and I told him everything I'd told George. Again, the short version, although he'd want more of the details later.

"So," Larry summarized at the end of my narrative, "what we need to do is to get Margaret to identify her first husband, to tell us how she knows he killed Ron Wheaton, and to give that information to Hathaway in exchange for his agreement not to further harass Margaret. Do you think he'll go for that?"

"I think he'll investigate it. If he confirms Margaret's story, no one need ever know that he was planning to arrest her today. Then the question is whether she can testify against the killer," I said.

Both men looked surprised at that. "Why couldn't she testify?" George was first to ask, which gave Larry a minute to think about it and reach his own conclusion.

Larry said, "Because Margaret was married. She never divorced him. We don't know whether he was ever declared legally dead. If he wasn't, the spousal privilege could keep her from testifying against him. On the other hand, she'll have to disclose whatever Ron Wheaton told her about wanting to die, because he wasn't really her husband."

I finished up, "And two marriages may also make Margaret a polygamist, technically. She could be prosecuted for that, although I doubt anyone would press charges, especially since she didn't intend to marry twice. But if she's not technically his wife, it may mean that Margaret won't collect Ron's life insurance or the rest of his estate. If anyone protests her claim to be Ron's sole beneficiary, it would be one unholy mess, that's for sure."

Larry said, "Trusts and estates are something I know about. It's highly unlikely that Margaret's first husband wasn't declared dead. Given that she believed he had died, surely there was a body, a death certificate and a funeral."

George seemed perplexed by all of this. "But, if he wasn't really dead, isn't all of that null and void?"

"Actually, no," Larry explained. "Once you've been declared dead, in the eyes of the law, you're dead. To change that, there's yet another legal procedure to go through."

"That figures," George said, with a wry smile. "You can't even be alive in this country without government intervention."

Larry laughed. "At least, not if you've been dead, first."

"Just one more thing I need to bring up," I said, finally deciding that now, if ever, was the time. They looked at me expectantly. "I have a piece of physical evidence to give Hathaway. I think it will help Margaret, but I'm not sure."

Larry was the first to jump in, "What kind of physical evidence?"

"I found a syringe in the bushes outside the verandah where Ron died. I suspect the syringe is the murder weapon. And that it'll have the killer's finger prints on it. I want to give it to Hathaway."

As I thought, this piece of news didn't make George or Larry very happy. Before they had time to jump all over my frame about it, though, Dad showed Ben Hathaway into the room, saying, "I found this guy ringing the doorbell downstairs when I returned from my run. He says you're expecting him."

Another hour later, Larry and I had filled Ben in and secured his promise to investigate Margaret's claims that her first husband had killed Ron Wheaton. But to do that, he needed more information. By now, it was going on eleven o'clock, so I thought I could awaken Margaret and have her come in to help us with this piece of the puzzle. I went down the hall to the guest room to find her while the others drank even more coffee.

I knocked on the guest room door, calling Margaret's name several times. When she didn't answer, I pushed the door open and looked into the room. Margaret's bed was empty. I saw the door to the bathroom was closed, so I went over and knocked there several times. Again, no response. When I opened the bathroom door, it was empty, too.

Margaret had left sometime this morning, but when? Where did she go? And how did she get there?

The four of us discussed what to do about finding Margaret and investigating her claims about the mysterious husband, divided up the job and went our separate ways. Larry fought with me over who got to go to Margaret's house, but in the end, agreed it was a job I could do best while he went to his office and began preparing to defend Margaret's arrest, if it came to that.

I gave Hathaway the syringe I'd been keeping in Greta's glove box. After sputtering at me about chain of custody and obstruction of justice for a relatively short time, he went off to investigate Margaret's claims. He had some ideas as to where he could look, and access to law enforcement files, he said. George, who was feeling a little left out, although he tried to describe it differently, came with me.

George drove us over to Margaret's house, which looked empty from the outside. I had him pull up in the driveway and we went to the back door, which had been unlocked the last two times I'd come here. It was unlocked again. George protested at just walking in without ringing the bell, but I was fairly sure Margaret wouldn't be here anyway, so I wasn't worried about catching her *in flagrante dilecto* or anything.

George walked into the house calling Margaret's name. After we'd made a thorough check of all five small rooms, even he was convinced that Margaret wasn't here. I'd expected as much. The reason I arm-wrestled Larry Davis for the right to come here was so that I could look around for evidence about the mysterious first husband, not because I really thought Margaret had gotten up this morning and taken a cab back home. By now, I knew her agenda was something more complicated than that. There was more to Margaret Wheaton than I had initially suspected.

Hathaway was checking with the cab companies to see who picked Margaret up at Minaret this morning and where they took her. He had the manpower for that. I needed to investigate more cleverly.

After facing down George's protests, I began a systematic search of the places in Margaret's house where I thought she might have hidden something related to an earlier marriage and birth of a child that she'd wanted to keep from her husband for thirty years. It was pure assumption on my part that Ron Wheaton hadn't known about Margaret's first marriage, but it was based on knowing Ron as I had. I believed that when they couldn't have children of their own, Ron would have suggested that they find and attempt to reclaim Margaret's first child, if he'd known about the child. Ron loved children and it had been a source of great sorrow to him that he and Margaret never had any. They'd tried to adopt, I think, years ago. Ron would definitely have taken Margaret's child, if not when he first met her, certainly in later years. I felt sure of it.

"I don't know, Willa. It's not right to snoop through Margaret's things. And, I have no idea what Ron would have done," George was getting in his usual mode of trying to do the "right thing," which I didn't have a lot of time for. I let him keep talking, but I continued to search. I tried under the bed, behind all the pictures, in her lingerie drawer. What I was looking for would have been overlooked by Hathaway and his men when they searched because they weren't looking for old documents and pictures.

George kept up a steady stream of objections until I finally turned to him and said, "Just look in plain sight, then. Don't touch anything. Or wait out in the car. I'm going to finish here, one way or the other."

Giving me the "I know that voice" look, which is the way he deals with my stubborn refusals to listen to his good counsel, George left me to go back into the living room and wait. I kept looking through drawers, books, and other likely hiding places in Margaret's room.

The Wheaton house doesn't have a basement. Most houses in South Tampa don't. The water table is too high. But the small ranch style house does have an attic that I could reach by pulling down the stairs in the hallway between the two bedrooms. Despite the cold outside, the tiny crawl space was stifling. No air had circulated here for a long time.

The attic was filled primarily with dust, bugs, cob webs and stale air. Ron Wheaton had probably never been up here. He was as tall as I am, if not taller, and quite a bit heavier before he got sick. Ron couldn't have maneuvered around the ceiling joists and the electrical wiring on his stomach. There wasn't enough room for him to walk around on his knees, if he'd been so inclined, even before he developed ALS. After ALS, such a maneuver would have been impossible.

No, this attic was Margaret's exclusive domain. She was so small, she could have stored things here that no one else would ever find. There was no lighting except for what came in through the vents on the side of the house.

Between sneezes caused by the dust, I cursed my lack of planning in not bringing a flashlight. I waited for my eyes to adjust to the dimness. After a while, I was able to make out boxes. They were just out of arms' reach from the opening where I stood, trying to figure out how to get to them.

I hoisted myself onto the floor and slithered out toward the boxes off to the left side. The dust continued to make me sneeze and I felt a couple of crawly things on my bare midriff when my tee-shirt bunched up. Was I out of my mind? Probably. George says I'm stubborn, but I like to think of it as tenacity. Whatever you call it, I thought as I sneezed again, it's not always a positive trait.

Slithering a few more inches, I was able to touch the boxes, grab their flaps with my fingers and pull them toward me. There were five in all. I couldn't raise up enough to move them quickly. Eventually, I inched them all toward the pull-down stairs and lowered myself back out through the opening. I took all five boxes down the stairs and sat them on the floor. When George came around the corner, he burst out laughing.

"What?"

"You look like a fly caught in a giant spider's trap," he said, when he could contain his mirth.

"Thanks a lot. I sure appreciate your help," I said, with more than a little annoyance, as I started to brush the dust and dirt off my black jeans and black tee-shirt. My hands and face felt positively grimy, so I didn't dare wipe one with the other. I folded the stairs back up and went into the bathroom to survey the damage and wash up. George was right.

I saw my ridiculously filthy visage in the mirror and did the best I could to repair myself. When I got back into the hallway, I found George had taken the boxes and put them on the kitchen table. He'd apparently decided that he'd speed up the process by helping out. He'd already opened the first box.

I surveyed the boxes first. This was where Margaret's organizational skills, so important in a legal secretary, had spilled over into her home life. Each box was clearly marked. As I suspected, all pre-dated Margaret's life with Ron Wheaton. Maybe, she'd put them up in the attic crawl space and forgotten them. In any event, they were labeled "High School," "Taxes 1952-1965," "Mother," "Miami," and "School." All the boxes were the same size and color, suggesting they had been bought and organized around the same time. They were also about the same weight.

"George, let's take these home and look through them. I want to finish up here while Margaret's not home." To his credit, he'd given up arguing with me. He re-closed the box he'd opened and began carrying them all out to the trunk of the Bentley. I went back to Ron Wheaton's bedroom for a last look.

Ron's room had been thoroughly searched by the police and I had watched them do it. I didn't really think there would be anything here that would help me solve Margaret's life riddles. But I looked anyway. I checked the drawers of the night stands, looked in the dresser drawers, under the bed and in the closet. I felt inside the pockets of all the jackets and shirts. I used to hide things in clothes I hadn't worn in a long time. Indeed, I'd once lost a pair of diamond earrings for over five years because I'd hidden them in a pair of snow boots left in our attic. I didn't know what I was looking for, but apparently Margaret and Ron Wheaton either never had anything to hide or had better hiding places than I'd been able to find. There was nothing in any of Ron's pockets and I was about to give up. Then, I decided to go ahead and check all the pockets in all the closets. There were only three closets, so it wouldn't take long.

Glancing down at my watch, I saw we'd been here over an hour and a half and I was worried that Margaret would get home and keep me from taking the boxes from the attic. Yet, I felt pulled to try the pockets before I left.

In the guest bedroom, all of the clothes were packed in hanging garment bags. I started with the first bag and checked Margaret's clothes. Judging from the number of outfits she had, she and Ron must have once been avid square dancers and party goers. The closet was filled with petticoats and western wear, evening clothes and party outfits, all from an earlier time. The closet was small, like the other two, and I found nothing remarkable in any of the clothes; a few tissues, a pen, some coins and one or two matchbooks. Remembering how I'd lost my earrings, I bent down and opened the large plastic boxes on the floor that contained western boots and dress shoes, one for Ron's and one for Margaret's. In Margaret's box there was a pair of red cowboy boots. I smiled at the younger, more vibrant Margaret that I imagined must have worn them. But I found nothing hidden in their depths.

A similarly thorough search of Margaret's closet revealed nothing but the matronly dresses and sturdy shoes she now wore to work. I dutifully, and with much less enthusiasm, felt each of the pockets in her sweaters and dresses. Then I bent down to check the shoes. The only thing I found was a great deal of sand on the bottom of her sneakers. I'd wasted over thirty minutes on this project and I could feel time was running out. I closed the closet door, took one last look around the bedroom, living room and kitchen, and let myself out. I left the back door unlocked, the way I'd found it.

Chapter *Twenty-One*

George and I had Margaret's boxes on our kitchen table. We both knew what we were looking for. I was tempted to start with the box labeled "Miami," but I thought it would reflect more general information about Margaret's work for Mrs. Prieto. Instead, I selected the box labeled "Mother" on the theory that what I was interested in happened long after "High School," and the "Mother" box might contain clues about Margaret's child. George had taken the "Taxes" box. I felt I already knew what it would contain, since I'd seen Margaret's Social Security records. Dad walked in just as we got started and for sheer speed, we gave him the box marked "High School."

"Mother" turned out to relate not to Margaret as a mother, but to Margaret's mother. She had died in 1954, the year Margaret graduated from Plant High School. There were neatly labeled manilla folders with Margaret's mother's birth certificate, death certificate, and life insurance policies that had paid just enough to bury her. The death certificate listed her as "widowed" and said she'd died of "heart failure." I recalled Margaret telling me her father had been killed in World War II and her mother had never remarried. The death certificate gave the age at death as forty-three, significantly younger than Margaret was now. There were a few pictures of Margaret's parents and Margaret with her mother, who was a much larger woman than Margaret, although still small.

The rest of this box contained memorabilia and letters between Margaret's parents when her father was stationed overseas during the war. Although the letters probably would have told me a lot about their marriage and the young Margaret's life, reading them felt too intrusive, somehow. I might read them later, I thought, but not right now. I set the letters back in the box, put the dusty lid back on and set the box aside.

I stretched my back and got a glass of water before attacking the box labeled "School," thinking I could get through it quickly. I noticed that Dad was completely immersed in the box labeled "High School." He'd only removed about half its contents, and he'd made little progress with what he'd taken out. I could see yellowed newspapers poking out from more labeled manila folders. Whatever he'd found, it was certainly capturing his imagination.

George was just as immersed in the "Taxes" box, which from my vantage point looked like old tax returns and back-up receipts. Of course, George is a numbers man. Just looking at the prices of goods and salaries from 1954 to 1965 would interest him. I shook my head and smiled at the differences between us, stretching my arms above my head getting the kinks out, on my way to the bathroom to get rid of some of the gallons of coffee I'd drunk today.

When I came back, both Dad and George were still engrossed in their boxes, so I pulled the "School" box toward me and opened the top. Again, the folders, labeled in Margaret's neat block printing, faded from years in the attic, filled the box. This one was about Margaret's career at business school where she'd learned to be a legal secretary. I flipped through the folders containing transcripts, resumes, letters seeking employment, a few pieces of written work that had earned her top marks, and some old class notes. I guessed that Margaret had simply put this box in the attic when she moved to the little house on Coachman Street and never thought about it again. I moved through the box quickly because there was nothing in it I needed.

Not too hopefully, I opened the remaining box, the one labeled "Miami." I expected materials related to Margaret's job with Mrs. Prieto, and I wasn't too far off. Again, the neatly labeled folders. This box contained more folders than the other two boxes I'd already looked through. One folder contained a death certificate for Margaret's employer, Mrs. Prieto, which explained why Margaret stopped working for her. It gave Mrs. Prieto's date of death as 1957, and said she died of cancer. There was a letter and resume from Margaret to Mrs. Prieto dated three years earlier, when Margaret was still in high school, applying for the job as "companion."

I was piecing together Margaret's early life. Just she and her mother had lived together after her father died in the war. When her mother died the year Margaret graduated from high school, she must have been interested in getting away and seeing a little more of the world. She'd applied for the job with Mrs. Prieto and gotten it, moving to Miami. It must have been fun to be in Miami in those days, even if one was stuck being a companion to an elderly invalid. Still, Tampa was a pretty sleepy town in 1954. There would have been relatively little here for the young Margaret. Miami was a fairly sleepy town then, too, but it would have seemed ever so much more exciting.

The "Miami" box contained several old newspaper articles about Mrs. Prieto, who must have been something of a socialite at the time. The house where Margaret's employer had lived was shown in several pictures. It was a mansion of magnificent proportions. Eighteen year-old Margaret the orphan must have felt she was in the middle of a real adventure when she arrived to take a job with the obviously wealthy Mrs. Prieto.

I marveled again at the fortunes that were amassed in this country. Even in 1956 Miami, the gap between the poor and the wealthy was a vast chasm. The folders held stories from the society pages of parties at Mrs. Prieto's house and even a few pictures of her. She was a childless widow, the same as Margaret is now. I wondered whether Margaret ever thought about that. About how our lives progress in repetitious patterns.

One of the stories, dated 1956, had Margaret's name in it. Someone had underlined her name with a blue pen, which was now faded and faint. I read the short piece. It said Margaret was Mrs. Prieto's constant companion on frequent trips to Nassau, Bahamas, where Mrs. Prieto also had a home. It was somewhat surprising to me that travel between Nassau and Miami appeared to be easy in 1956. A short boat ride from Miami, Nassau was a paradise, complete with casinos, at a time when legalized gambling didn't exist in Florida.

Another article mentioning Margaret described her gown as "chic" and her dancing as "superb." A picture of Margaret, in a gown that Jackie Onassis might have worn at about the same time, showed her dancing with a middle-aged man. Clearly, the orphan girl from Tampa had landed in a posh environment and seemed to be thriving there. If Mrs. Prieto had lived, I wondered whether Margaret would have ever returned to Tampa.

There were several other articles of this sort and I started to move through them more quickly until another faded blue underline caught my eye. The names caused me to read the small article completely. It said:

> *Gilbert Kelley, Jr., son of the president of Tampa Bay Bank, and his friend, David Martin, of Coconut Grove, were among the many young professionals at Mrs. Prieto's Gasparilla Bash, given in honor of her guests from Tampa, to coincide with Tampa's annual Gasparilla Pirate Parade. More than one hundred members of Miami society attended the gala event, which was a charity ball held to support Young Mothers' Second Chance, a national organization providing financial support to the young widows of the Korean conflict.*

Why did it never occur to me that Margaret might have been in contact with Gil Kelley in Miami? Just because they travel in different social circles now didn't mean they always had. I looked over at Dad, who had the "High School" box.

"Dad, do you have high school yearbooks there?"

He pointed inside the box and I looked to find four high-school yearbooks for the years 1950 through 1954. I didn't know how old Gil Kelley was, exactly, but he was older than Margaret. I picked up the 1950 year book first and turned to the index. Bingo, on the first try.

Gilbert Allen Kelley, Junior, was listed several times. The first few pictures were group shots: Gil on the football team, the basketball team, the tennis team, the golf team. Gil on the homecoming court and being crowned "King," just as I'd seen him crowned as Minaret Krewe King last night. Gil had been a senior that year, so he was four years older than Margaret. His senior class picture carried the title: *Most Likely to Succeed.*

Gil Kelley was attractive, athletic and popular. Maybe his father's owning the bank had something to do with his popularity, but he must have had some athletic skill too. Margaret could easily have fallen in love with him. Probably every girl in her freshman class would have been swooning over the "dreamy" Gil Kelley, as he was described in one of the yearbook pictures.

"Dad, when did Gil Kelley work at the bank in Miami?"

He was still distracted by something he was reading from the "High School" box. "1955, why?" I didn't answer him because I was looking for a piece of paper and a pen so that I could sketch out the dates.

If Gil Kelley was a senior in high school in 1950, that meant he would have finished college in 1954, at the same time Margaret was graduating from high school. Gil would have returned to Tampa that summer to sow his wild oats, as Marilee Aymes had put it to us when she told the story. Margaret could have been one of those "wild oats," or she could just have known Kelley or some of the girls he dated. Margaret could have known him, although he would have been ahead of her in school.

It would have been only natural for them to hook up again in 1956 when they were both in Miami. Kelley could have been drafted into the armed services, but for some reason, he wasn't. I considered that Gil Kelley could have been her first husband, but Margaret said she'd believed her first husband died. Kelley had been living right here in Tampa for years and Margaret had to know it. Tampa Bay Bank was highly visible, as was its current and former president. So, Kelley must not have been the one.

But this other guy mentioned in the faded newspaper article, David Martin, it could have been him. I looked through the four high school yearbooks just in case the first husband had been a high school sweetheart. I found no evidence of the young Margaret even having a social life at the time. There was one picture of her in each yearbook, the one taken with her class, and her senior picture in the 1954 book. Margaret was voted, *The Sweetest Girl.* Maybe we never surpass where we were in high school. I wrinkled my nose at the thought.

On my list, my doodles said something like this: 1950 Gil Kelley graduates h.s.; 1954 college; 1955 moves to Miami. 1954 Margaret graduates h.s.; 1956 moves to Miami. Coincidence? I don't believe in coincidences, but I didn't know what it meant, either. Then I wrote: David Martin, 1953 Miami. Margaret married, 1956? Husband died? Margaret's baby born 1957?

I turned my attention back to the "Miami" box and now felt I knew what I was looking for. I pulled out the folder labeled "Young Mothers' Second Chance." And there it was. The birth certificate. The adoption papers. The father's name and "deceased" following it. Baby's sex was listed as female.

And at the very bottom of the folder was an obituary. For David Martin, who died in 1957 by accidental drowning.

The obituary had a picture of Martin on the top. The picture was over forty years old, yellowed and grainy. The hair was darker and the eyes more vibrant. But I recognized him, and Margaret must have, too. The first time she laid eyes on him. The man who held the key to all her dreams and heartaches. David Martin, a/k/a Armstrong Yeats.

I'd taken the final folder, my coffee and my cryptic notes back to the den to work it all through in my journal. An hour later, George and Dad both wandered in, with their most interesting pieces of the puzzle from Margaret's boxes. I'd switched to gin half-way through my scribbles. George poured himself and Dad a scotch. We sat and watched the fire for a while. "You were pretty engrossed in that 'high school' box. What did you find?" I asked Dad first.

"What you'd think might interest me. Quite a bit about Tampa during Margaret's high school years. She's kept some old newspaper accounts of events going on here in the early fifties, including some stories about Gil Kelley, Senior, and the hijinks of Gil Kelley, Junior."

"Anything you can use in your bank fraud case?" George asked him.

"Maybe. Nothing conclusive, but it did seem the Kelleys lived pretty far above what I would think a 1950 banker's means would be."

"Meaning?" I asked.

"Meaning Sandra Kelley may have been telling the truth. Maybe Senior did embezzle from the bank. And maybe that's where Gil, Junior, learned it. Doesn't excuse the thefts. Just gives me an explanation for them. One story was interesting, though. It was about Gil, Junior, being caught at an illegal poker game over in Ybor City on a Saturday night during his senior year. Charges were dropped because of who his parents were."

"I'd heard Kelley had a gambling problem. Being in Miami all those years must have made that worse," George offered.

"How so?" Dad asked.

"Well, Miami is a short hop over to Nassau, where gambling has always been legal. Of course, the casinos are all owned by the Mafia, or they were then. A young fellow with ready cash could easily and quickly get himself into a lot of trouble. Especially if he had a wild streak already," George told Dad as another little piece of the puzzle clicked into place for me.

"I wonder," Dad said aloud, letting his voice trail off as he stared into space.

"What?" I asked him.

"George, when you were in banking, did you have any dealings with Caribbean offshore banks?" Dad said, turning his attention to us.

"A little. Mostly, we were leery of the whole process, so we kept away from it."

"What are you two talking about?" I asked.

"Well," George explained, "when a large and reputable American bank like ours was queried about accepting millions of dollars from what amounted to little more than a laptop computer on a Caribbean island, we were more than just a little curious about the origin of the money. So we wouldn't take it."

"Not all of your competitors are so conscientious, though," Dad replied. "Some bankers are just so happy to have the deposits that they don't question those accounts. They end up abetting money launderers. It's been going on for years, but recently the feds are poking into the practice. The off-shore banking process is under investigation right now in the Senate investigations subcommittee. It seems American banks have facilitated quite a bit of money laundering through their so-called correspondent accounts for high-risk foreign banks."

"How much money are we talking about here?" I asked.

"Well, I got an executive summary of the hearings the other day. The summary claimed a dozen off-shore banks have moved billions of dollars through certain American banks in the last few years."

George whistled. "That's a lot of motivation."

"What are you thinking?" My brain was just too mushy at the moment to grasp Dad's idea.

"He's suggesting that Gil Kelley may be embezzling even more than we first thought," George responded.

"That's right," Dad picked up the thread. "If Gil was laundering money from a Nassau rogue bank, he could have been taking even more money out of the bank than appeared on the legitimate books I've looked at. He could be taking a cut off the top before the money is ever deposited."

"Which would give Kelley more than enough to share with Armstrong Yeats. So why kill him?" I voiced my own conclusions.

"True." Dad admitted. "And the deals typically pay a finder's fee on the front end, too. That kind of a fee would usually be paid off the books. There would be no way to trace it. But, if they've been dealing in off-shore banking, the Kelleys should be extraordinarily wealthy by now."

The Kelleys should be "wealthier than God," as the kids say. But they aren't. Or at least, not obviously so. I filed away this piece of the puzzle in my weary brain. It fit somewhere.

George was standing at the fireplace, trying to warm up, if the chill I was feeling was any indication. I asked him to throw another log on the blaze. We were all lost in our individual thoughts for a while. Later, I looked down at my watch and noticed the rapidly fleeting time. "How about you, George, what did you learn? You looked pretty involved in your files, too."

"Like Jim, it was clever of you to give me the box that you knew fit my own interests. Margaret's tax returns from 1952, before she graduated from high school, until 1965, when she married Ron Wheaton, were full of the names of old Tampa locations. People whose names I've read and heard, but never met. Or friends of ours long before we met them."

"Like what?"

"Well, Margaret worked at several law offices from the time she came back from that Miami business school. One of them was the CJ's office, did you know that?" As I shook my head, he continued, "She's also been on the board of Young Mothers' Second Chance since 1958. She's given them a bundle of money over the years." And I knew why, if they didn't yet. "There's also a gap in her work history for about six months. Even when she was in business school, she held down a few part-time jobs. But for six months in 1957, she had no income at all. I wonder how she lived? And why she didn't work?" Of course, I already knew the answer to that one, too.

We continued comparing notes and working out the back story, but I was convinced that Margaret had met, fallen in love with and married David Martin in 1955 or 1956. She'd become pregnant, which I doubt that he or anyone else knew. Martin and Gil Kelley were embezzling from the bank. They must have been having a wonderful time over at the Nassau casinos, where they had no doubt met Margaret while she was working as Mrs. Prieto's companion there. I made a note to check the Miami marriage licenses, but I suspected we'd find the license, if at all, recorded in a Nassau, Bahamas, clerk's office.

When the bank examiners got close to uncovering Gil Kelley and David Martin's early embezzlement, they must have come up with the suicide scheme to get the bonding company to pay back their debts. When David Martin "died," Margaret gave birth to her daughter and gave her up for adoption. She had no support to raise a child. Margaret returned to Tampa heartbroken and didn't marry again for nine years. Then, she married Ron Wheaton.

Did Ron know? The whole story? It would have been like Margaret to tell him before she married him. And it would have been like Ron to have married her anyway. On the last day I saw him, Ron was as in love with Margaret as ever. I believed he would have done anything for her, always.

How Kelley convinced Martin to go along with the suicide scheme, I still didn't know. Whose body did they bury? There was only one person left alive to tell me that now, and I intended to ask him. I didn't have the strength to do it tonight. I needed sleep. To work out a few of the loose ends first in my office in the morning.

Chapter *Twenty-Two*

The *U.S. v. Aielo* case was begging for my attention. My clerks had read the briefs and prepared a three-page order for my review. I read it through quickly. I was about to sign the order transferring the case to Philadelphia for trial, when the short statement of relevant facts at the beginning caught my eye.

> *Mr. Aielo reinvented himself in Miami. He opened a club in 1992 that was destroyed by fire, providing the insurance money to start his more trendy and lucrative clubs believed to be money-laundering operations.*

Something about the statement tickled my brain. I chased it around in my head for a while, but couldn't catch it. I re-read the passage several times and finally put it aside, knowing that I'd remember if I thought about something else and let the thought peek around the corner like a kitten. Only in this case, it was a lion. About thirty minutes later, it fairly pounced on my thinking with claws fully extended and a deafening roar.

I checked the computer once again. In just a few minutes, I found the death certificate I was looking for. Death records for Miami going back fifty years had recently been updated in the Dade County database, but not integrated into the search service database. Which explained why I didn't find it when I looked the first time.

I pulled out the tattered article George had given me from the *Tribune* the Sunday after Gasparilla and read it one more time. The article related the story of a former IRS agent who had made a living in much the same way as Dad, by pursuing white-collar criminals. The agent compiled the more legal methods of changing your life and wrote a book about it. The article reflected the agent's advice about how to hide your assets and disappear.

The most difficult aspects of changing one's identity were not the initial strategies, such as acquiring foreign passports under assumed names. Instead, the hardest thing to do, the agent said, was to cut all ties to your old self. Most people can't manage it and eventually return to their old lives in some fashion. The article talked about well known, admitted former Mafia criminals who became government informants, but have abandoned the federal Witness Protection Program. The fear of Mafia retribution has disappeared and was probably over-stated anyway, the agent claimed. But the big problem is that once one creates a certain lifestyle, it's nearly impossible to abandon all of the past. Friends, family and co-workers are our firmly tethered human anchors. They drag us back when we float too far away.

Some secrets never leave us alone. Eastern mystics say that no karmic debt ever remains unpaid. Scientists claim the human body replaces itself once every seven years. The problem is, the new body is exactly like the old one. It's got the same scars, the same colors and a few more aches and pains. We think the past is past, but it's the foundation for all that comes after. The past seeps into our very sinews and remains in our cells, just like the genes we're born with. It doesn't mean that humans can't change. But it does mean we don't change much at the fundamental level. Those cells just keep reproducing themselves, over and over and over.

Americans attempt to reinvent themselves all the time, without hiding their assets and disappearing. How ironic that the *Fitzgerald House* case had found its way to my docket, obscuring my first clue to Yeats's identity. After all, F. Scott Fitzgerald's myth of reinvention when James Gatz became Jay Gatsby, was the very reason for Fitzgerald House's existence as a charitable organization. Like many clues, this one was right in front of me all the time, and I didn't see it. Without Gatsby, Fitzgerald House would have had no historical significance. Without Fitzgerald House, Martin's becoming Yeats might never have been discovered.

Yet, James Gatz did no more than get a fresh start by attempting to leave his past in the past. I thought of everyone I know who has done the same thing. Jim Harper has become a good husband and father. Suzanne Harper has become a wife and soon-to-be mother. Mariam Richardson became a well-respected matron and wife of the Chief Judge. Sandra Kelley, an abandoned and adopted child, was now a wealthy socialite. Even George and I changed our lives from a staid banker and Detroit attorney to a Tampa restauranteur and judge.

To David Martin and Gilbert Kelley, young men who were looking for fun and fortune gambling in Nassau and wound up on the wrong side of the Mafia-owned casinos, re-inventing the obscure David Martin must have seemed the logical answer. The readily accessible money from Kelley's bank was an overwhelming temptation to solve their problems. They met the young, unchaperoned Margaret, another American, and added her to their youthful exuberance.

In 1956, when the bank examiners arrived, Martin and Kelley must have panicked to learn that their actions had serious potential consequences. The suicide plot they concocted had the added benefits of stopping the investigation and forcing the bonding company to pay off their debt to the bank. They must have also found a source of living money for Martin "after death." Exactly how they managed that, I couldn't guess. Maybe that was when they got hooked up with the offshore banks. The entire scheme would only have worked if Martin had no ties to anyone. Either Kelley didn't know Martin and Margaret had married, or he didn't care. Or maybe they just saw no way out. It was the kind of youthful solution that didn't plan for all the consequences. Like maybe there was a child on the way.

I had no way of knowing how long Martin had managed to stay away from Kelley. But, at some point, whatever money they had managed to get Martin for his fresh start must have run out. Martin/Yeats seemed to have an insatiable appetite for spending that could only have been a problem from the very beginning. So Martin resurfaced as Armstrong Yeats, and Kelley had been helping to feed Yeats' voracious demands for cash from the vaults of the Tampa Bay Bank, via off-shore banking deposits.

When did Ron Wheaton find out that Margaret's one true love was not dead? That he was, instead, alive and well and living just over the bay in Pass-a-Grille? It was likely a long while ago. The Wheatons didn't socialize with the Kelleys and their set, but it was unlikely that Martin/Yeats would have been able to stay away from Margaret. Or maybe he saw Margaret by accident. In any event, Ron definitely knew about Yeats and planned to protect Margaret in death as he always had in life.

There were just a few loose ends yet for me to tie up, and I would have it all resolved. I picked up the phone and called the CJ's chambers, dialing the number for his secretary instead of Himself. I confirmed that CJ was in his office, grabbed my purse and walked the short block between my building and his. It took me only about ten minutes from the time I'd made the call.

When I arrived, unannounced, CJ consented to see me. He wasn't in a position to antagonize me today, since I still hadn't completed my testimony in his ethics hearing. I tried to keep the envy from putting an unnecessary edge in my tone as I sat in his palatial chambers, admiring the rich mahogany and beautiful upholstery.

He offered me coffee. I declined. I didn't want to get too comfortable--with him or in these surroundings. "I came to ask you some questions about Armstrong Yeats."

CJ looked down at his desk, then back up at me, with resignation. "I was afraid that was why you're here."

I came right out with it. No point in dissembling. "Why was Yeats asking you for money outside Minaret the Friday night before the Knight Parade?"

He jerked back, startled. "How do you know about that?"

"I was the one who walked past the two of you. Didn't you recognize me?"

Shaking his head, he said, "I didn't want to recognize you. I was hoping you were a misplaced tourist."

"But, I wasn't. Tell me what you were arguing about."

For a few seconds, he looked like he would refuse. Or, at least, come up with an excuse not to answer the question. He spent some time rearranging the pens on his desk, fidgeting in his chair. He looked past me to the Picasso on his wall that his wife gave him when he was elected Chief Judge. Then, he sighed with resignation, and told me what I'd come to find out.

"Yeats had been in trouble for a long time, but I didn't know about it. I swear, I didn't. I didn't even know that he was involved in a criminal case until after I'd tried to get you to dismiss *Fitzgerald House*." CJ sounded insistent, because he was. He needed me to believe he hadn't known that Yeats was being prosecuted for a massive fraud that could have put Yeats in prison for much longer than the rest of his life. The curious thing was that I believed CJ hadn't known. Because I hadn't known. Just because we're judges, doesn't mean we're any better informed than most other citizens on a lot of issues. There's no way I could know all the cases pending on my docket. There were just too many of them to keep track, except on the computers.

I nodded my understanding and he continued, "Well, in the past, Yeats resolved complaints against him by offering restitution of some kind, counting on people like me and Mariam to keep quiet because of shame and pride. Or, if that didn't work, he'd deny the validity of the complaint and threaten to counter-sue. He told me later that the complaints that got the U.S. Attorney's attention were started by that restaurant guy in Michigan. Yeats said the guy had bought millions of dollars worth of gems, intending to re-sell them for billions. When the guy wasn't able to make the profit he wanted, he collected a bunch of other claims and filed a criminal complaint."

Yeats's version of the facts wasn't too far from the allegations made by the U.S. Attorney. It was easy to believe that Yeats would probably have been convicted. There didn't seem to be much of a defense building there.

"How does that relate to Yeats trying to get money from you?"

"He was shaking down everyone he knew. He thought if he could get enough money together to pay off the restaurant guy, he could get the criminal complaint dismissed and then avoid going to jail."

"Sounds like a plan," I said, with some sarcasm. "At least, it would have been better than getting himself killed to stay out of prison."

CJ gave me a grimace. "I'm sure Yeats didn't plan on his arm-twisting scheme getting him killed. He'd had good luck with it in the past."

Yes, I thought, he certainly had. For years, he'd been collecting money from every available source. I was sure now that Yeats had killed Ron Wheaton because he'd found out that Ron had life insurance and other assets worth over $7 million. That was probably why he'd contacted Margaret again after all the years he lived in the Bay area, too. He could have found her at any time. His buddy, Gil Kelley, would certainly have told Yeats where to find Margaret.

And Yeats's desire to stay out of prison explained, to a certain extent, Gil Kelley's continued embezzlement from Tampa Bay Bank. Yeats was probably using their past crimes to support his ongoing ones. I didn't doubt that Kelley also had a gambling problem. That's one addiction that can easily take over your life. Gambling, plus Yeats's voracious and insatiable appetite for luxurious living, gave Kelley a powerful motive for murder, too. Yeats had been bleeding Kelley for decades. And who knows? If they were both involved in Mafia money laundering, they might have wanted to stop. The Mafia has a low tolerance for quitters. The sky was literally the limit to their need for money.

But as I sat there working it through, I knew Gilbert Kelley wasn't Yeats' only source of cash. Yeats would never have thought Kelley could give him enough to satisfy all of the creditors listed in the *U.S. v. Yeats* criminal indictment. "One last thing, CJ," I said. "Did you give Yeats any money?"

His defeat was now complete. He shrunk before my very eyes. The man who had seen fit to lecture me on appropriate judicial conduct had let himself down. He couldn't meet his own high standards, to say nothing of the lower standards set by the law for the behavior of judges. Paying a blackmailer was more than the appearance of impropriety. There was no way his behavior, and the reason for it, wouldn't become public. "What else could I do? Mariam couldn't be humiliated again."

So, I added two more names to the list of possible suspects in Yeats's death, although I continued to believe whoever had killed him hadn't intended to do so. That would keep the killer off death row, anyway. I had to make one phone call and then I could do the final interview.

Chapter *Twenty-Three*

Gilbert and Sandra Kelley lived in a new house in the gated community at the foot of Gandy Boulevard. Technically they had a Bayshore address, although their house was on a cul-de-sac that served six homes. All were three-storied, peach-colored structures built to have a waterfront address without Bayshore Boulevard running between them and the water.

The Kelleys had moved here from their home near the Tampa Yacht Club a couple of years ago. We attended the housewarming party, but we hadn't been back since. Even though Gil Kelley is a charter member of Minaret Krewe, the Kelleys are not in our social circle. Avoiding the Kelleys was mostly my doing, but George didn't protest.

The gate wasn't guarded, but it did have a system that required a numerical code to open. I knew another couple with a home in this development, so I rang them on the intercom and asked their maid to let me in. Like many communities in Tampa, if you know the staff, you can expect quite a bit better treatment than if you don't. I make it a point to cultivate the domestic help of my friends and acquaintances, just as I cultivate my friends' office staffs. You never know when you might need a favor.

I'd had enough experience confronting killers to know that I needed backup. I'd called Chief Hathaway from my car and asked him to meet me here in half an hour. He wouldn't be able to wait that long. I expected him sooner. I only had about fifteen minutes to speak to Gil Kelley alone. What surprised me when the maid let me into the front hall were the loud, angry voices from the sitting room on the right. One of those voices belonged to Margaret Wheaton.

The maid tried to keep me waiting, but I pushed past her and went into the room where Gil Kelley and Margaret were arguing. I caught the tail end of Margaret's accusation. "You didn't have to kill him!"

"No, Gil," I said as I entered the fray, "You didn't. So why did you?" They were both startled into silence when I appeared. Margaret had been crying. Kelley seemed as cool and collected as ever. It was an act to keep Margaret from going completely wild.

"Why did I what?"

"Why did you kill David Martin?" Again, both were shocked by my statement. Margaret jerked her head over in my direction.

"How did you know about him?"

"You told me, Margaret. Don't you remember? You said you had married and you believed your husband had died. But he didn't. It didn't take a lot for me to connect him to Armstrong Yeats."

That was true, but some people would call breaking, entering and burglarizing Margaret's home of her most personal possessions quite a lot. I tried not to add up the list of my own crimes. I was fairly sure Margaret would never file a complaint against me and my intentions were good. I wish I had remembered the saying about "good intentions" and the road to hell.

"Has he told you why he and David Martin faked Martin's death?" I looked over at Gil Kelley and could see he was getting a little rattled now. He felt he could subdue and control Margaret Wheaton, but he knew dealing with me was another matter altogether.

"They did it to cover up Kelley's crimes. They'd been embezzling from the bank to cover those trips to Nassau where you met them." I heard Margaret draw a sharp breath. "When the time came to pay the piper, they needed the money from the bonding company to cover the debt. Killing David Martin was an easy way to get it, wasn't it Gil? You didn't care about Margaret or her husband, did you? You gave no thought to the child."

When I mentioned the child, out of the corner of my eye I saw Margaret lift her right arm. Watching Kelley, I didn't turn fast enough to catch Margaret before she pulled the trigger. The sound was deafening. Gil slumped against the wall, holding his chest while Margaret crumpled to the floor at the same time. I didn't know who to help first, but the noise brought Sandra Kelley and the maid running into the room. I left them to attend to Gil while I checked on Margaret.

She was in shock, holding tight to the gun, which was still radiating heat where she held it out to her right side. I left it in her hand. I heard the siren of Chief Hathaway's car as it pulled into the driveway, followed by his loud pounding on the front door. He was just in time to arrest Sandra Kelley for the death of Armstrong Yeats.

The Gasparilla Festival of the Arts began on Saturday, the first weekend in March. For the first time during Gasparilla month, daylight brought a bright, warm Tampa morning. I looked forward to spending the entire day at the festival.

George and I planned to walk around downtown on Ashley Drive and in Curtis Hixon Park with Dad and Suzanne, enjoying the many fine art pieces on display for the two-day festival. The live entertainment promised groups from schools in both Hillsborough and Pinellas counties during the daytime. Jazz vocalists and Latin bands would round out the music in the evening. All of us were interested in the jewelry exhibits and the fate of Armstrong Yeats's "*Gasparilla Gold*" pin. We were looking forward to a day of relaxation, beauty and music.

Margaret was going to the festival with us. I went to collect her while everyone else was still getting ready. When I pulled into the driveway of her small home, I saw that she already had a "for sale" sign on the front lawn. I parked in the driveway and went to the front door. Fully intending to put my breaking and entering days behind me, I rang the bell.

Margaret came to the door and ushered me inside to wait while she collected her fanny pack. She sat on the sofa across from my chair and tied on her red walking shoes. Today, she was dressed in a snazzy red silk slacks outfit that would have been more suitable for Suzanne. If I'd ever thought of Margaret as "grand motherly," she was so only in the thoroughly current sense that grandmothers can be so young and vibrant too.

I watched Margaret with recognition that, once again, life is often not what it appears. I had thought Margaret was an elderly, happily married woman, utterly content with the quiet life. Nothing could have been further from the truth. Instead, she was a lively woman with a life and a mind of her own. I would miss the Margaret I had created in my mind, but I felt more confident that this Margaret would get the most out of the rest of her life.

"Margaret, it's time for you to tell me some things, now that Chief Hathaway has decided not to prosecute you for shooting Gil."

Gil Kelley didn't die. Margaret wounded him in the shoulder and he spent time at Tampa General Hospital before being arrested for theft and fraud. He's hired a well-known defense attorney to try to get him off, and he probably will. Maybe Gil Kelley had some kind of conscience, after all. He couldn't be held to account for ruining Margaret's life. Perhaps he accepted that pressing criminal charges against her would be more than he should, in all decency, do.

"Like what?" she asked me, bent over at the waist, tying the red shoelaces.

"Several unanswered questions have been bothering me. For instance, why did you faint when you saw Armstrong Yeats in our courtroom on the day of the *Fitzgerald House* motions?"

She could have told me to mind my own business, I guess. But as much as I had underestimated Margaret, she wouldn't be rude to me. I might not have given her enough credit for having a full life, but she had spent every day with me for years. I did understand some things about her character.

Margaret dusted off her hands, reached into her pocket and pulled out a lace handkerchief, the kind my grandmother once carried. I hadn't seen a woman with a lace handkerchief in years. Somehow, it didn't seem odd.

Margaret shrugged and smiled slightly as she answered my question. "My life hasn't turned out like I thought it would. When I graduated from Plant High School, I was the first person in my family to have gone that far in school. My mother was so proud of me. I felt I had the world by the tail. I was going to go great places, do great things." She sounded as excited as that long-ago school girl.

"Like what?"

"Oh, I don't know that I knew exactly what I would do, even then. But I didn't expect to wind up a sixty-five-year-old adulteress. I suppose, if I had grandchildren they'd be appalled," she smiled with a little wickedness and no regret.

"So you were having an affair with Armstrong Yeats?"

"I wasn't having an affair with Armstrong Yeats. At least, I didn't know that I was. I'd never met Armstrong Yeats in my life before that day in the courtroom."

"I don't understand," I said.

"No, I don't suppose you do. Your life has been so different from mine, Willa. You've never been on your own. You've never been completely free, with no one to answer to and only your whims to guide you. You wouldn't know what it's like to fall madly in love with a dashing young man who loved you back, and have no chaperone to tell you 'No.' You have no idea how quickly and completely a young girl with a little spirit can lose her heart. And her head."

As much as I hated to admit it, even to myself, Margaret was right. I had never been so footloose, so free with myself. I've always felt a keen sense of responsibility, a need to work hard, to keep my nose to the grindstone. I didn't know what a carefree life would be like, but I was more than a little envious of those who had lived one. "So you were in love with Yeats?"

"Not exactly. I fell in love with David Martin in Nassau. He was friends with Gil Kelley, a boy from home. Although Gil and I certainly were never social equals. David was handsome, kind, fun. I ran into the two of them one day in the straw market and we started doing things together. Exciting things. Like drinking and gambling and riding in fast cars. Things I'd never done before. I loved it. And pretty soon I loved David too. It was a short step from there to an affair and a secret marriage a few months later." She shook her head at her own folly.

"You must have been thrilled, then?" I imagined a younger, care-free Margaret, in love and happy with the man of her dreams.

"For a short while, I was. Exceedingly happy. Happier than I'd ever been before or have ever been since. But then David died and I was devastated. We'd kept our marriage a secret, so I couldn't tell anyone I was a widow," she said. Margaret went to the funeral, where they had a closed casket. No one came except Martin's co-workers from the bank. She never saw his body or knew who identified it.

"For a long time, I though David really hadn't died," she told me. "The kind of wishful thinking young girls engage in when they want to avoid the truth."

"But you were right. He hadn't died," I reminded her.

"Yes, but I didn't know that. I didn't know it for forty years," she said. "Right after David died, I found out I was pregnant. There was no way I could have raised a child alone in those days. So I gave the baby up for adoption, came back to Tampa. Eventually, I met and married Ron Wheaton and started a new life. I thought Ron would be my life forever. Until I saw David Martin again, quite by accident. I was over at St. Pete Beach, just thinking, one day. I went into the Hurricane restaurant for lunch. Ron was dying, my life was changing before my eyes. The man I had always loved more than any other was truly alive. I had no choice but to keep loving him. I counted on Ron to understand that." She blinked back tears at the memory.

Another piece of the puzzle fit into place. Margaret's reaction to Yeats when she saw him in the courtroom had bothered me. What had caused her to faint? There was nothing particularly shocking about his appearance as far as I could tell. Yeats was dressed a little better for court, but otherwise, looked much the same as I had seen him the day Ron Wheaton died.

But Margaret hadn't known "David Martin" was "Armstrong Yeats." It was hearing her lover called by the name of a man she knew to be accused of countless crimes in *U.S. v. Yeats*, the case on my docket that she was familiar with, that crushed her. Margaret's dreams of a return to an idyllic life were extinguished by one chance encounter.

"How did you know Yeats had killed Ron?" My gut had been right on this one. Chief Hathaway had confirmed the syringe I'd found in Minaret's azalea bushes was Ron Wheaton's murder weapon. And, he'd confirmed Yeats' finger prints on it. Yeats had easily overpowered Ron and injected him in the stomach. The medical examiner found the puncture.

Margaret shrugged. "Just a feeling. Ron and I had been arguing about Yeats, who I still thought was David Martin at the time. Ron knew all about my marriage to Martin and our daughter, of course. But he also knew about Yeats living in Pass-A-Grille. Ron wanted Yeats to stop seeing me. They quarreled the day of the Parade of Pirates at Minaret. At first, I really thought Ron had had a heart attack. But when the suggestion was made that he'd been murdered, I just felt Yeats had killed him. It made sense. No one else would want to hurt Ron."

"Now, let me ask you something," she said to me. I nodded. "How did you know it was Sandra who had killed Yeats?" She managed to say the name clearly, without choking up, which I saw as another sign she was healing.

What should I tell her, though? I didn't *know* Sandra had killed Yeats. Not for sure. But when Hathaway told me he'd found a witness who saw Margaret push Yeats to the ground on Eighteenth Street and leave him there, I remembered how much alike Sandra and Margaret had looked that night. I suspected her, but couldn't figure her motive. Until Dad told me about the off-shore bank deals.

Sandra was an officer of Tampa Bay Bank, too. She could easily have set up the off-shore deals and taken the finder's fee. I figured Gil didn't know Sandra was taking the finder's fee. Nor did she know Gil was embezzling funds from the bank after the deposits were made. Somehow, Yeats had found out and was bleeding them both. I made the connection when I remembered cutting my hand on the sharp sword point of Sandra's lapel pin on the day of the Distance Classic. The pin that was a perfect copy of Yeats' *Gasparilla Gold*.

As nasty as Sandra had been to me and to Dad, it was no small bet that she was as vicious as a female tiger when protecting her children and her way of life. Yeats must have threatened to expose her thefts when he tried to squeeze her for more money. Sandra probably hadn't meant to kill him when she shoved him down. But we'd never know.

"Just a lucky guess," I said in response to Margaret's question. "Let's go."

I pulled Margaret up off the couch, helped her lock the door and we fairly sauntered out to Greta, who already had her top down, basking in the Florida sunshine. Today, Margaret and Willa would have a carefree, frivolous adventure. And, I vowed, more such days to come. It was time for me to lighten up.

Epilogue

Using what we learned from Margaret's old boxes and what she told us afterward, Dad filed a federal complaint against Gil and Sandra Kelley. Dad hopes the Kelleys will be convicted and go to prison. The insurance company will pay off some of the money they embezzled. On Dad's recommendation, the company sued Gil and Sandra for restitution. The legal wrangling will go on for years, but at least Dad stopped the bleeding from Tampa Bay Bank.

Margaret has retired. She was eligible to retire anyway and she wants to spend time looking for her daughter. Adoption laws in Florida have changed in the last forty years. With the help of a good investigator, Margaret should be able to find her only child.

Ron Wheaton's estate went to Margaret. He had no other heirs and since no one objected, the life insurance company paid the death benefits to Margaret. She was lucky, but she was also helped along by a certain United States District Court judge. Not me. The CJ. He had not only employed Margaret at one time, but he thought very highly of her work at the court. CJ made a couple of telephone calls and actually did influence someone to do the right thing. Not that he thought of it all on his own.

The CJ's investigation was settled quietly when he admitted guilt. He was able to arrange a confidential agreement allowing him to remain on the bench in an administrative capacity until retirement. His opportunities for advancement to the Eleventh Circuit Court of Appeals are ruined now. This is unfortunate for me, since the only hope I had of getting rid of him was the Peter Principle--to have him kicked upstairs to Atlanta. I thought maybe this experience might make him more humble. But, of course, it did nothing of the kind.

Dad and Suzanne returned to New York after the Gasparilla Festival of the Arts. Dad was tempted to buy a few more of Yeats' "Jewels of the World." Since Yeats had died, Dad thought they'd increase in value because of the notoriety of the case. We talked him out of it for the time being. We can only hope that he forgets about the gems until after Yeats' estate is settled.

Yeats left Margaret everything in his will, except that his debts so far exceeded his assets that she'll be unlikely to inherit anything. Margaret did want the *Gasparilla Gold* pin Yeats entered in the Festival of the Arts. She had to pay fair value for it, which was considerably higher because it won the Raymond James Financial Best of Show award. What she inherited from Ron Wheaton's estate, after I gave it all over to her, made Margaret a wealthy woman. She hopes to spend the money spoiling her grandchildren.

Early in March, after all the Gasparilla hoopla had finally ended and everyone had left, George and I were sitting at our favorite booth in the Sunset Bar, enjoying the quiet. My soul-mother, Kate Austin, walked in unannounced, two days early from her month-long trip to Italy. I jumped up from the booth and hugged her like I hadn't seen her in thirty years, not just thirty days.

I was telling her how much I missed her and how happy I was to have her home when I noticed, finally, that she wasn't alone. There was a young man standing behind her. He looked to be very Italian and about twenty-five years old. He had dark, curly hair and fabulously blue eyes that reminded me of the Aegean.

Kate was always bringing someone by the restaurant asking George to give them work. Oh, no, I thought. Not another chef. The last one she'd offered us was Japanese. I could see George preparing to tell the young fellow that George's Restaurant didn't need any more chefs at the moment when Kate pulled back from me a little and gave George a hug, too.

Then, holding both our hands, she said, "Willa, George, darlings, I'd like you to meet Leonardo Columbo. My husband."

0-595-21271-9